WE FIT: WE THREE TOGETHER
a bisexual FFM polyamorous erotic romance

Lara Zielinsky

Supposed Crimes LLC • Matthews, North Carolina

This book is a work of fiction. Names, characters, places, and incidents are products of the author's imagination or are used fictitiously. Any resemblance to actual events or locales or persons, living or dead, is entirely coincidental.

All Rights Reserved
Copyright © 2022 Lara Zielinsky

Published in the United States.

ISBN: 978-1-952150-38-8

www.supposedcrimes.com

This book is typeset in Goudy Old Style.

For my community partners and friends

CHAPTER ONE

JESS LADLED some home fries and hash from the two warming bins set out on the pool deck. It was a Tuesday. Wearing t-shirt and shorts because it was Miami in January was a new experience. There was only a light chill in the air, and the forecast was for 75 by two o'clock. She took her paper plate and plastic utensils to a white plastic chaise by the steps and started scooping her breakfast.

Only three actual guests milled around the hotel in the middle of any week, so Tuesdays until around four in the afternoon had become an unofficial employee day off at the Caliente Club and Hotel. After kitchen staff made a breakfast buffet and put cold cut sandwiches and fruit trays in cold storage for grab'n'go lunches, they went home. Staff living on-site could use the hotel facilities–as long as they cleaned up after themselves. Hector and Maya, the swing club's owners, kept to themselves.

Jess paused with her fork halfway to her mouth when a shadow fell across her feet. She looked up to see Gus. The older man, her supervisor in the bar, had a head of sparse gray hair and, though stoop-shouldered, stood over six feet tall. He wore tan cargo shorts, gray boat shoes, and a gray polo shirt with a Miami Dolphins logo. When she gestured toward the deck chair beside her, he sat down with a similar plateful of food.

"Hi," she greeted.

He finished chewing his bite, then lifted a red plastic cup to his lips. Watching him reminded Jess she'd skipped the juice bar in her rush to eat. But she waited for him to speak first.

"Mornin'," he said. "What're your plans?"

Jess smiled. Since they worked shoulder to shoulder most nights, the "How are you?' that might start most polite conversations was unnecessary. "Haul my stuff to the laundromat and read a book," she replied. "You?"

"Got some stupid thing with my government checks to iron out, so I'm standing in lines all morning. Wan' a lift to the laundromat?"

"Are you heading out right after you eat?" She stood up.

"Yeah."

"I'd appreciate ~" Her phone beeped. After retrieving it from her pocket and reading the screen, she sighed.

"Something wrong?"

"It's... no–Well..." She sat back down. Could she talk about this with him? He'd been helpful other times. She asked, "Could I talk to you about something?"

He pursed his lips, then shrugged his shoulders. "Shoot."

"It's about swinging." She dropped her voice a bit. For all that they were in a swingers club, it still felt like a weird thing to be discussing out loud.

"You and that couple?" She nodded. He shrugged again. "Haven't seen 'em 'round. Something changed?"

"That's...well, that's...I think I changed it." She hugged her hands between her knees, which rounded her shoulders.

"You broke up?" He sounded surprised. "I thought it was just the holiday busy-ness that you'd hadn't seen them?"

"No. Well, maybe? I don't know. We had a really, really great date just before Christmas. I mean it was this incredible...really.... Dinner, dancing, and everything...sex," she finished. "At the end of it they asked me to move in."

"Wow." His eyebrows went up.

Jess frowned and exhaled before replying, "I said no." His expression turned almost comical–a mix of disbelief and amusement. She rushed to defend her thoughts, her words stumbling out. "I mean, of course I said no. It's crazy, right? That's insane. We were close, yeah, but... it's all playtime. They're married and I'm just...not. It's not... Was I wrong? Oh, god, I was wrong, wasn't I? What's the right answer? We were getting together a lot, yeah, and it was fun, sexy. I really lo-liked all the things we did. I had fun even when we weren't, but...It's...moving in, that's like...bigger. Calling it a relationship. They can't... that's not supposed to happen, right?"

"It can," he replied so calmly she was stunned into just staring at him as she caught her breath. He added, "There's seldom sex with no feelings at all, y'know."

"There aren't supposed to be those kinds of feelings, right?"

"Are you sure that's why they asked?"

Jess hesitated. Elena and Eric had shown they cared about her in a lot of different ways. But was the proposal to move in because they wanted more? She shook her head. "I don't know."

"Did *you* ask?"

She opened her mouth to reply when she felt her phone buzz again. She exhaled. Reading the screen, she hesitated with her fingers poised, but then pulled it up to show the screen to Gus. "Elena," she said. The message was simple: *Can you talk?*

Gus asked her, "So, can you?"

Tossing the phone aside on her chair, Jess asked, "What am I going to say?"

"Maybe start with why you said no."

She gestured around herself and then gestured outward from her face with both hands. "You mean that word vomit that just came out? I'll sound like an idiot."

Gus leaned back and set his plate aside, looking up at her with his hands calmly on his knees. "Jess, you'll sound like what it is... processing. Talk it out. It certainly appears like they want to listen," he finished, pointing at her phone.

Reaching for the device again, Jess's mind flashed through all the fun times she, Elena, and Eric, had since September. As she stared at the words, her memories sifted through everything, from the sex to the conversations. It had been good, really good. Then Christmas came and she'd gotten so much work–when she did see them, it was together. *"They're the couple that's gonna last,"* some drunk guy at the Diligent Air company party had said. And she'd been hit with.. Jealousy?

No, not jealousy, but she'd felt miserable all the same, sensing it was something she wasn't meant to be part of. Her melancholy had been followed up by the intense attention from both Elena and Eric on that amazing dinner date. She'd felt she belonged. She'd felt...cherished.

"Can I sit here?"

Jess froze at the sound of the oh-so-familiar voice. She then turned so quickly that her deck chair started to tilt. Brunette hair was suddenly so close–too close–as Elena Tanner crouched, reached out and grabbed the far side, pulling it back to level.

"Shit!" Jess cursed and put her hand to her heart in an attempt to slow its sudden attempt to gallop from her chest.

"I'm sorry." Elena stepped back and straightened. Her gaze went briefly to Gus before returning to Jess. "I'm sorry," she repeated.

"What are you doing here?" Jess asked, her voice high from her scare and panic as she wondered if the woman had overheard Gus and her talking.

It was hard not to simply gape at Elena, whom she hadn't seen in nearly a month. She looked incredible. Her brown eyes seemed even lighter than Jess remembered. Was it a trick of the sunlight? So often she'd looked into those eyes in dark rooms lit only by small lamps. No, Jess realized after a moment more of searching the woman's features, Elena wasn't wearing makeup.

The usually throaty voice was hesitant when she disrupted Jess's silent appraisal. "Eric and I...we thought...can we talk?"

Elena wore a simple wrap dress, with dark and light blue pattern of flowers. The length was even modest, past her knees. It looked more like a housewife's dress than an effort to look sexy. Even for Netflix and chill nights at her home, Elena had always dressed up.

Burning with curiosity at this different look, Jess asked, "Where'd you come from?"

"Home, well..." Elena's hands moved in front of her, drawing Jess's gaze momentarily to the lightly twisting fingers. Then the woman continued to speak and Jess looked back to her face. "By way of the airport. I dropped Eric off to work." Elena paused and looked toward Gus again. Turning back to Jess, she asked, "Can we talk?" From the way her eyes again slid sideways to Gus before returning to Jess, it wasn't hard to guess that the unspoken request included speaking alone.

Jess said nothing for a moment while she considered Gus's advice, her own turmoil, and what she saw now as evidence of Elena's troubled thoughts.

A muscle ticked in Elena's cheek as their gazes continued to hold. Then Jess saw her swallow. She sensed a subtle shift in the woman's balance and realized she was turning away. "Wait!" Jess stood.

Elena backed up a step, again lifting her chin to meet Jess's gaze.

"I'm...messed up," Jess started.

"You are not messed–" Elena cut herself off even as she jumped forward. She exhaled then and straightened. "Look, Jess, I...I don't want–should we do this here?"

Gus stood. Jess saw him shake his head. "I gotta go," he said. His plate was only half eaten, but Jess saw he meant for her to deal with this.

"I still need to do laundry," Jess said. "Please wait." She turned back to Elena. "I–"

Elena held a hand toward Jess, looked from Gus then back to her. "I could drive you to the laundromat? If you...well, if it's OK?"

"Talk," Gus said, his staid gruff voice punctuating the silence. He grabbed up his plate and cup and walked away.

Wincing at Gus's clear disappointment. Jess turned back to Elena, studying her and willing her mind to stop racing. Finally, she said quietly, "OK."

"Lead the way."

Despite wanting to kiss Jess or just take her hand, Elena took a step back and gestured for the other woman to move ahead of her. She already knew the way to Jess's room here at the hotel, but she was trying to follow Eric's advice and give Jess space. Even though she really wanted to talk about what had clearly gone wrong between them. Jess hadn't been answering her texts or voicemails for almost two weeks. The uncertainty had been eating away at her.

While the younger woman walked ahead of her, Elena longingly drank in the vision. Jess had longer curls than Elena recalled. The honey blonde lay unruly across her shoulders. Her body was outlined in a tight white t-shirt. Jess's waist was thin, and the jeans, clearly cut to be tight fitting, gaped a bit at the waist. Too easily she recalled the wonderful beauty she had repeatedly uncovered. Seeing the woman's plateful of food, she wondered if Jess might be underfed.

Jess hesitated before going through a doorway Elena had opened. "Why are you here?"

Elena swallowed and spoke as directly as Eric had advised. "I wanted to see you. You haven't answered any of my texts. I wanted to find out how you were doing," she added earnestly.

Jess frowned. "The holiday season only just finished. I've been swamped with work."

"I know, that's why I haven't ... Yesterday was Three Kings Day. I thought, maybe, the busy season might finally be over?"

"I have today off, yeah."

As Jess turned to put the key in her door, Elena exhaled and smiled. "I was hoping that."

The key turned in the lock and then the door went in a few inches. It stopped and, when she followed the arm upward, Elena was suddenly pinned in Jess's direct green gaze.

When those green eyes continued to study her but Jess remained silent, Elena inhaled and nodded at the door. "I thought we were going to get your laundry?"

Jess pulled her room key from her pocket. "You really want to watch me do laundry?"

"I don't mind." Taking a gamble, Elena reached out, placing her hand on Jess's on the knob. "I just want to talk." She released Jess's hand before it could be pulled away.

"I don't know if that's a good idea."

Elena inhaled in recognition that Jess had guessed her first thought. But Eric had advised against it. Jess had turned down their invitation to move in and she needed to understand why—*understand Jess*—before she offered again what she still felt was a great idea. Instead of revealing any of that though, she said, "I thought you were just busy with the holiday rush and bartending gigs."

Jess didn't speak while moving around her room. Elena stood back, leaning against the wall with her hands behind her back to hold herself in check as she drank in every movement Jess made. First Jess straightened the bed, pulling up the white sheets then the cream cover, and smoothed everything as she went. The tightness of her jeans as she bent and lifted, and twisted, caused Elena to lick her lips. She jumped when Jess popped and fluffed the pillows and set them back against the headboard. Finally Jess crouched and collected clothing items from the floor beside the bed.

A moment after disappearing into the bathroom, Jess emerged with a damp bra and several panties. The sight made Elena's stomach do a quivery flip. All the clothes were tossed into a bag hung inside a frame in the corner by the three-drawer chest. When that was done, Jess pulled the bag out then tugged and tied off the drawstrings.

Turning to Elena with the bag slung Santa-like over her left shoulder, she said, "That's it."

Still drunk on the whirlwind of Jess's efficient movements and simultaneously holding herself back, Elena was slow stepping off the wall where she had been leaning. That hadn't taken long. The contents of the bag seemed like a single load. "Take your sheets? Fill out a second load?" she suggested, hoping to increase their time together.

"The sheets belong to the hotel. They do them in the industrial laundry. Mine go in once a week on Mondays. Yesterday. So they're still clean."

"Oh." Elena nodded. "All right. The car's out front. Anything else you need?"

Jess went to the dresser and opened the top drawer. Shoving her hand inside, she came up with a couple rolls of quarters. "Can't forget these."

Seeing the green eyes light up in her direction, Elena nevertheless bit her tongue to keep from offering her home's washer and dryer. One load would take no time at all and then Jess would be requesting to be dropped off again. If they went to the house, at least they could do something else together, maybe visit a little longer. She stomped on her premature disappointment. They'd at least get to talk. She brightly returned Jess's smile. "Let me just visit the bathroom."

Stepping away from the sink, Elena reached for a hand towel. Her bag from the counter fell to the floor. Bending to retrieve it, she caught sight of a box in the trash can, a distinctive logo at the top. She frowned and was reaching for it before she fully registered what it was. *A pregnancy test?*

"Jess?" She stood with the box in hand. "Are you all right?"

"What?" Jess met her gaze from her seat on the bed. "Oh."

"Yours?"

"Yes."

She walked to the bed and sat down next to her. "Something you want to tell me?"

"No. I'm not pregnant." Elena frowned. Jess insisted, "I'm not. I'm late."

"When were you due?"

"Last week."

"It's only been a few weeks since our dinner date."

"The test was negative."

"Maybe it's too early."

"El–"

She laid her hand across Jess's knee, cutting her off. "No. I haven't been a very responsible partner. That changes now, OK. C'mon. I'll take you to a clinic to get checked out."

CHAPTER TWO

ELENA'S MIND and body vibrated each time she was able to step close to Jess. Despite knowing Jess's reluctance, she was excited to be in the young woman's presence again. Standing next to her to unlock the trunk, she said, "You can put the bag in here."

The way Jess hugged the dirty laundry as she took it off her shoulder, it looked like she wanted to keep the bag with her. After a moment of looking from Elena to the open trunk and back again, Jess finally tossed it into the space. Elena backed up and reached out a hand to encourage Jess back a step, then closed the trunk.

Walking to the passenger side, she unlocked the door. "Here you go." She smiled at Jess and pulled the door wide, standing behind it while Jess walked up to get in. Her hands on the frame trembled.

Jess's gaze briefly met hers then she nodded. "Thank you."

"You're welcome." So many other words, questions really, clamored behind the easy polite words she knew. Elena hoped they'd get to share those other words and she'd understand Jess better by the time they parted today. After checking that Jess had hands and feet safely tucked inside, Elena closed the passenger door and hurried around to the driver side.

Noticing Jess still regarded her warily, shoulders tight and hands gripping her knees, Elena reconsidered her priorities. Going through the startup of the car, she kept her voice light and asked, "Where's the laundromat you use?"

"Next to the high school. There's a library branch in the plaza." Jess pulled out a business card. "Here's the address. It's just a few miles."

"That's fine." Elena tapped the address into the car's dash GPS and pressed "GO." The computerized female voice directed them out to the roadway. When the GPS spoke, the radio, playing a Latin jazz station, fell briefly silent. She let the music seep into her and do what it did best, relax her. Hopefully it was relaxing to Jess too. The young woman didn't move and only looked forward out the front windshield as Elena drove.

She spotted the high school first with its two-story adobe facade, a relic of the Spanish-styled building boom of the 1970s. The plaza was the next turn, past the school's bus circle. The directory sign stated blandly "library" and "laundromat," one under the other, along with the names of a Cuban diner and a check cashing chain. She found a parking space close to the library. By the time she had the engine turned off, Jess was out of the car. She retrieved her clothes bag as soon as Elena popped the trunk lid.

Again, Elena let Jess take the lead when entering the laundromat. Of the dozen industrial washers, four were occupied. A stoop-shouldered Black woman looked up from behind reading glasses to take them in and dismissed them in the same glance. The opposite wall held an equal number of dryers, two of which were currently running. Jess moved to an open washer at the front of the line and started pulling clothes from her bag resting on the floor.

Elena commented as she looked around. "It's been a while since I've been in one of these."

Jess looked up then around as well before she replied, "This is weird, right? You really don't have to stay. I can deal from here."

"I think maybe we should hit up the free clinic while we're in the area." Elena put her purse down on the top of the front-loading washing machine Jess had commandeered and leaned in close so she could look directly into Jess's green eyes.

A worried furrow formed in Jess's brow at Elena's words. "But I'm not pregnant."

"I know. But we can also both test for STDs," Elena said. She grasped Jess's hand, stalling the toss of clothes. "It's important to me that you take care of yourself."

Jess swallowed. "I got scared." The admission was accompanied by a hard swallow.

"I know you did. If you'd really been pregnant, would you have called us?"

"I didn't think it was your responsibility." Jess rolled backward on her heels until she sat on a chair with the ball of clothes in her lap. Elena noticed it had put some space between them, so she took a step back and sat down in another chair. Jess's gaze had turned a turbulent hazel-green.

Elena thought before responding. But really there was only one thing to say: the truth. "If the baby was Eric's he'd want to take responsibility."

"Would you?" Jess stood to finish loading her laundry into the machine.

Staying seated in the chair Elena looked up at Jess's profile. Would she have wanted to know if Eric had fathered a child with Jess? "Yes."

"What would you have done?"

"I don't know, but we would have talked about it."

Jess pulled back and finished loading the washer, added quarters, pushed the button for detergent and cycle, and hit start. As the machine rumbled to life, the noise almost drowned out her words. "It would have changed everything. You've said you're not parent material."

Elena realized Jess may have hoped that she didn't hear. She frowned, both hurt that Jess would think that, and disappointed in herself that they hadn't addressed this topic before. She had been selfish, she guessed. She risked reaching out and touching Jess's leg. The other woman jumped.

"I don't right now know what we would have done, but Jess, we would not have left you to deal with it alone."

"We were just having sex." Jess rightfully sounded anxious.

"You can't have thought our relationship was 'just sex' since the first weeks," Elena said honestly. "Jess, Eric and I *care* about you. Why else would I be here, trying to find out why you wouldn't answer my texts?"

Green eyes shined with tears. "I was so scared, Elena. Eric...you two are a package deal."

"We can work that out *if* you talk with him."

Jess straightened slowly. "You want me to tell him what? There's no baby."

"He deserves to know that's what made you pull away."

"And if I don't want to have sex with him again?"

"But you do with me?" Elena asked hopefully.

"It's not like you can get me pregnant." Jess sounded rueful.

Elena nodded. "True. But let's go to the clinic, look at some other options. Eric and I haven't talked about pregnancy for years because I'm on the pill and we all use condoms. We could at least get that for you."

"And if sex with Eric stays off the table until I'm sure?" Jess asked. "How's he going to feel about me sleeping with his wife?"

"But we also had movie nights, dinners, and breakfast wake ups." Elena smiled and was gratified to see Jess smile back. "Are you up for dates that go beyond sex?"

"No more talk of moving in?"

"I'll hold my tongue," Elena agreed. "On that subject," she added. "But I reserve the right to use my tongue in other ways."

The lighthearted tease caused a blush in Jess's cheeks, accompanying as it did Elena's study of Jess's body from head to toe. Jess appeared to be thinking hard about the question. Her gaze was up and down and all around as she processed. Elena wanted to reach across the space and take Jess's hand, hold her, and tell her it wasn't going to be terrible. But she tangled her own fingers and resisted trying to push Jess's thinking in any particular direction.

Finally, Jess said, "I can agree to that."

"Good."

The silence between them grew thick and Elena felt herself starting to get anxious again. The rattling washing machine made Elena's head ache. In addition, she would love to get a moment to really touch Jess again. Could she convince Jess to go for a walk? Maybe hold hands around the plaza? Reminded of her own advice to Jess to speak up with concerns, she swallowed and asked, "When you're done here, can we go to the clinic?"

Jess bit her lip. Finally she nodded. Elena let out the breath she was holding.

Jess knew hanging out at the laundromat was boring. Still processing their conversation, she watched Elena shift and huff, apparently trying to read something on her phone. Giving her an out, not sure if she wanted the other woman to take it or not, Jess said, "You don't have to hang out here."

Elena shook her head and stopped shifting. "I'm hanging out

with you. Here or anywhere else is good with me." Her smile made Jess's heart beat faster. Someone sticking around for her, for any reason, felt so unreal.

When she looked up again, Elena was looking at her expectantly.

"Well, I guess we could...go to the library, get a book to read?"

"That sounds like a great idea." Elena stood and grabbed her purse.

Jess followed her to the door.

Elena's voice was bubbly and eager, and Jess found herself hanging on every word. "I used to snap up the abandoned books on planes when we were cleaning the cabin. Read some wild stuff over the years."

Walking next to Elena, Jess smiled as Elena kept turning backward as they walked along the storefronts.

"Here." She stopped at the library entrance. Fingers brushing against Elena, Jess felt a warm tingling in her chest.

"What sort of books do you like?" Elena asked.

Taking her hand away quickly, Jess pulled the door open and gestured for Elena to enter first. "It's silly," she hedged.

"No, no, share! I'd love to know."

"Oh, um, well..." Jess looked around. The library had a few patrons but none within earshot. That gave her confidence. "I, um, like fantasy. Stories about quests, magic, dragons. Not so much princesses but adventure, stuff like that."

Elena smiled wider and didn't look judgmental at all. Jess relaxed a bit.

"All right." Elena looked at the signage and led the way over to the fiction section. "So let's see what we can find."

Jess's finished laundry was safely stowed in Elena's trunk, and some new reading material sat in a bag at Jess's feet. She couldn't believe the woman had allowed her to check out books on her card. She'd fobbed it off, but Jess knew there were fines for overdue or lost books. It was why she only read the books on her laundry trips, and simply hunted the most interesting ones back up each week instead of checking them out. But Elena had simply put Jess's book with her own two titles in a newly purchased cloth bag with the library system's logo and scanned all three after inserting her card in the self-checkout kiosk.

"Here we are," Elena said. Jess looked up from the floor as she felt the car jolt slightly and the radio fell silent.

Looking up, she swallowed. She'd hoped Elena had forgotten this idea as the time passed. "Are you sure?"

"Yep."

The clinic was a nondescript gray building, box-like, and looked to be under a thousand square feet. It was mostly hidden from the street by thick bushes and large, old overhanging trees. The only thing that identified it was a sign by the door which wasn't clear until they were up close. It read "community clinic."

Jess followed Elena up the cracked sidewalk and inside. "How'd you know about this place?" Elena hadn't used the GPS to navigate.

"Didn't have a regular doctor the first time I needed one," Elena replied. The direct words reminded Jess that Elena hadn't always lived the middle-class lifestyle she did now. She walked to a small window in the wall and Jess followed. "We sign in here." Elena then Jess signed the clipboard. Jess checked under 'testing' just as Elena had.

A few magazines lay neatly stacked on a small table in the center of about half a dozen thinly padded metal chairs. Other than the two of them, and the woman behind the window who'd said nothing nor looked up as they signed in, no one was there.

"They don't get a lot of traffic here."

Jess tried to think how far they were from the Caliente. "No appointments needed."

"But most do come in by prior arrangement," Elena replied. She sat down.

"From other clinics?"

Elena nodded.

The solid door next to the small window opened up. The woman who hadn't spoken to them from behind the desk, looked up from the clipboard. "Miss...Tanner? Have either of you been here before?"

"I have." Elena stood up. "Suarez," she said. "I got married."

The woman, who Jess realized must be a nurse as well as a receptionist, didn't change her expression. She said, "All right. Come in."

"Can she come in with me?" Elena asked, nodding toward Jess.

"Privacy?"

"We're both here for the same tests."

"Miss?" The woman looked at the sign in sheet. "Davies?"

Jess stood. "Jess. Yes."

"Do you want to come back?"

"I guess." She looked at Elena and stood. "Yeah, sure." She stuck her hands in the back pockets of her jeans.

Once behind the door, Jess could see an alcove that led to the front desk window and a hallway that had four visible doors. The first, immediately to her left, was closed. The next two, also on the left, were open. One at the end of the corridor was also open and looked to be a bathroom.

As they walked forward, another alcove appeared to their right, behind the reception one, and it had school desks, the ones with the attached writing surfaces, and a metal cabinet on wheels. Three canisters labeled gauze, alcohol, and bandages sat atop the cabinet. "Have a seat," the nurse said.

"What sort of testing do you do here?" Jess asked, taking a seat in one of the desks. Elena sat next to her.

"Drugs, STDs, pregnancy. We process those right on site," the woman answered. "We also do collections for a few other tests, but send those to other labs for analysis." She looked from Jess to Elena and then back. "What are we doing today?"

"STDs," Jess said. "Also, is there anyone I can talk to about the pill?"

"I'm the only one here at the moment. The pill? I presume you mean to prevent pregnancy?"

"I'm not pregnant. I just figured I should protect myself, y'know?"

She looked again from Jess to Elena and then back. "Are you married?"

"No. We're in a relationship."

Elena added, "We've also both had sex with my husband."

Jess bit her lip. The woman's face was still expressionless, but Jess couldn't help curling in on herself a bit as the silence lengthened. But finally the nurse just nodded and Jess felt her stomach unknot.

"I've got some pamphlets then. You both read those while I assemble the tests."

"That wasn't too bad." Jess massaged her inner elbow after she pulled off the gauze and tape. She and Elena were walking down the employee corridor at the Caliente. Elena held Jess's finished laundry.

"I'm glad we did it," Elena said. Handing back the laundry

basket, she hugged Jess's arm, leaned in and kissed Jess's cheek.

"I am too." It was the truth, even though being open and honest about this stuff still felt all kinds of weird. She'd never had this level of connection with anyone else. She turned her head and met Elena's lips with her own.

A door opened ahead and Jess looked away from Elena to notice a hotel maid coming out of her room. No cleaning cart stood in the corridor. The linens had been changed out the day before during the weekly cleaning. She wondered what the woman was doing there then saw she had a small bag of what was probably trash. She wracked her brain for the maid's name.

"Hey!" she said simply, loudly, when she couldn't.

The maid looked over toward them. "Miss Maya said your trash needed emptying." The maid looked from Jess to Elena and nodded. "I gotta go."

"Thanks." Jess turned to see Elena already walking into her room. She shut the door behind her and tossed the bag of clothes to the bed. "Weird."

Elena leaned back on the pillows. It was surprisingly comfortable to talk about what they'd read in the pamphlets as Jess put away her laundry.

"You want to go to the bar and get a soda?" Jess asked.

"No. Thanks." Standing from the bed, Elena hugged her. "Actually I should probably go."

"OK."

"Next week?" Elena asked.

"I'd like that."

CHAPTER THREE

THE FOLLOWING Tuesday, Elena texted Jess again. "Can you hold off errand day?"

Having just put her laundry together and tied off the bag, Jess sat on her bed and typed quickly. "Something wrong?"

"Just inconvenient," Elena replied. "I just arranged some workmen to come today. Forgot it was Tuesday. But I do want to see you before another week goes by. Can I get a raincheck til Thursday?"

The words warmed Jess. The visit to the clinic and getting tested together, even though it had only come up because of Jess's negative pregnancy test, had led her to remembering all week how wonderful all the time spent with the other woman had been back in the fall. Not just the sex. She sighed at the memory of sitting together on her bed just a week ago talking.

"OK," she typed back. Elena responded with a thumbs up emoji. Jess set her laundry aside and set her alarm for an early wakeup on Thursday. After her breakfast, she went to the hotel's weight room and did a circuit to battle the holiday roll that had her breasts puffing out around her bra.

On Thursday morning when Elena's car pulled into the lot, Jess was already waiting, her bag of laundry on the ground next to her feet. Elena smiled at her then the trunk lid popped open. Jess dropped her bag in the back and closed the lid before sliding into the passenger seat.

"Hi," Elena said.

"Hey," Jess said.

"You got everything?" Jess nodded. "After we do laundry, you want to help me shop?"

"I'm not on shift until four, so I guess I could, yeah."

"I have to do the grocery shopping before Eric gets home."

Jess swallowed. The clinic had said she was a good candidate for the pill. Her prescription had been filled and mailed to her in a plain paperwrapped package. But crossing paths with Eric meant telling him what had happened. Elena's mentioning it clearly meant she still wanted them to talk. "What's Eric's schedule these days?"

"Monday through Thursday. You may remember he started right before the holidays," Elena said. "He'll be in from Houston by noon. You can say hi before you leave for work."

"Maybe." Jess remembered when he'd go to Toronto and tell her about his sightseeing; she inhaled as the reality hit her: *I do miss him.*

"Whatever you want. So we'll do the shopping and then you can hang out at the house? I've got a washer, you know."

Jess studied Elena and accepted that she wanted to figure this out. Seeing her but not seeing Eric, or seeing him just as a friend. It was, in a word, weird. But she found herself willing to try because Elena made her believe, yes, she would be in charge of anything that happened. "OK. I guess I could. Yeah."

Still not quite believing her luck, Elena led the way into her home; Jess had insisted on being useful and carried several of the grocery bags, leaving Elena with only one to carry, so she still had a hand free to unlock the front door.

"Just put the bags on the counter." Turning aside, she put her keys on a small table beside the door. When Elena entered the kitchen, Jess was already unpacking and putting the groceries away.

Jess moved surprisingly efficiently. Granted, all cold things needed to find their way into either the refrigerator or freezer. That was all completely logical. But she was startled all the same. The young woman really didn't know how to just be a guest.

Her mind cast back over the other times Jess had been at the house. She had sometimes washed dishes after a meal, or made them all sandwiches and cold drinks after a vigorous evening in the playroom.

When she saw dry goods stacking up on the counter next to the stove, Elena realized she still had more knowledge of her kitchen and moved forward to get those items put away. Jess glanced at her several times and Elena was sure she was memorizing the kitchen layout as she went.

The last of the items put away, Elena said, "Thanks." She turned around and rested her hips back against the cabinets. Crossing then uncrossing her arms, she finally braced her hands against the butcher block countertop. "So, I offered you lunch. Do you have an idea what you'd like?"

"I can make sandwiches," Jess said.

"How about we *both* make sandwiches?" she suggested. Jess nodded. "Grab the deli meats and cheeses, I'll get the bread."

"Condiments, too," Jess said as she opened the refrigerator and started withdrawing the various items.

"Yes. Oh, and I'll grab the new jar of pickles." She went to the narrow pantry and pulled out the just-purchased jar of garlic dill spears. Looking at the label again, Elena remembered asking Jess to select "something, anything is fine," when they were in the store. A fan of both dill and garlic, she couldn't recall having ever tried the mix. She found she was looking forward to it.

The cutting boards were easy to find, but the bread Elena pulled from a drawer in the refrigerator. "It's too humid in Miami to leave bread out for long," she explained when Jess looked at her with an odd questioning tilt to her head.

Shoulder to shoulder they assembled two sandwiches, preparing both plates with sides of a small pile of potato chips and a dill pickle spear. Elena filled two glasses with ice from the refrigerator door then poured lemon-lime diet soda in each. So pleased, Elena absently turned from her task and pressed her lips briefly to Jess's cheek when they shifted past one another.

When she pulled back, Jess stood in profile, still and silent. Her head turned slowly, revealing a turbulent sea of green that Elena immediately fell into. Pale pink soft lips slotted over hers and arms went around her back, pulling at her hips.

Their first full kiss in several weeks did not disappoint. Jess's heart pounded under Elena's palm on her chest, and the way she clutched at Elena's ass communicated intense craving.

A pleased moan escaped her lips, but she silenced the cheer bubbling up. Lifting her hand from Jess's chest, she instead cupped the young woman's cheek, raised slightly on her toes, and extended the kiss.

After lunch, Elena showed Jess the laundry room. She suggested Jess could do two loads, separating at least her underthings from her other clothes and running them on a delicate cycle. When the load was running and the sound of water rushing into the wash basin filled the room, Elena said, "We can change it over in half an hour. You wanna watch something?"

"Yeah, sure." When they entered the house, Jess held back and followed Elena to the living room.

Elena pointed her to the roomy white couch. As she sat, Jess's arms spread out across the top of the cushions before she pulled them back into her lap. A memory vividly struck: spreading Jess's naked body open on the couch's cushions, kneeling between her knees, and tasting her.

Swallowing down her arousal, Elena fought the heat gathering in her face. They'd kissed; it was a step in the direction she wanted to go, but Jess was clearly still figuring out if they would resume having sex.

"So"—she cleared her throat—"movie?"

"Something shorter?"

"OK. Do you have a sitcom you like?" Elena asked, swiping up the remote and turning on the streaming service as she sat down next to Jess, though they were not touching.

"You pick."

Elena nodded. She selected a program she had herself just been getting into, *One Day at a Time*, a reboot of some 1970s show. The title was not lost on her as being very, very applicable to her situation with Jess. They were taking everything about this one careful step at a time.

After a couple episodes, Elena was glad to see Jess smiling. She had laughed in quite a few places and that pleased Elena. They moved Jess's laundry to the dryer and put on the second load.

"The mom is great," Jess said as they came back into the house.

"She's a famous actress," Elena said. "Been around forever on stage, movies, and television."

"I can see why."

Elena smiled. When they sat down together on the couch, she leaned close and put her hand over Jess's on her lap, breathing into her ear. "Another one?"

Jess shivered and her fingers squeezed around Elena's. "Yes."

Nothing ventured, nothing gained. Elena decided just to go for it. "Or...would you rather do something else?" She stroked her thumb along the ridge of Jess's knuckles.

Again, Jess shivered. When her gaze met Elena's, she licked her lips. "What did you have in mind?"

"This," she said, looking down at their hands. "I'm enjoying touching you again."

"My hands aren't as soft as yours," Jess observed. She sounded a bit frustrated by that.

"We don't have to just touch hands," Elena replied. "Though"—she leaned forward, slowly, scanning Jess's gaze for any sign of reticence—"I love your hands." She pressed her lips to Jess's and sighed as Jess's mouth softened immediately, welcoming the kiss.

When they parted, Jess lifted Elena's hands and kissed the knuckles. "Would you like some lotion?" Elena suggested.

"Would you let me touch you first?" Jess asked when the kiss ended.

"I would enjoy that."

CHAPTER FOUR

ERIC HAD no idea what to expect as he walked up the steps to the house. He'd taken an Uber from the airport when Elena didn't answer a text about where she was. She'd said on Monday she would pick him up at the airport today. He also knew she'd been hoping she and Jess would work out what they needed to, and resume some form of intimacy.

Elena had told him a bit about her first visit with Jess, saying they'd talked, and Jess had felt certain that they wouldn't want to see her again after she had said no to moving in. He'd been careful not to tell Elena, "I told you so," but he had realized the young woman's doubts about commitment almost from the beginning.

Pushing open the front door, he looked around. He cocked his head to listen more closely when he heard Elena's voice from the living room. She sounded like she was having a conversation, but he couldn't hear the other half. Maybe she was on the phone. She had been trying to schedule some meetings for her travel business.

Turning toward the bedroom where he could finally get out of his work clothes, he stopped when he heard another voice interrupt his wife. "Mm, right there."

Immediately he recognized Jess and smiled. It sounded like Elena had been successful in getting Jess to come around again. He had missed Jess, too. Leaning his travel case up against the wall he walked out to the living room.

Jess lay on the floor with Elena on her knees by her side. Elena was naked from the waist up, skin shining. Eric guessed Jess had given Elena a massage and was now getting the favor returned.

Jess's back was bare under Elena's hands, her arms crossed up under her head which was turned facing the faux fireplace. Her shoulders were already shiny with oil. She wore only a small pair of shorts and was using a gray t-shirt as a pillow.

The pair had spread out a sheet on the living room rug. The coffee table normally in the middle of the floor had been moved to the side. A small box of trial size massage oils rested next to Elena's hip. He recalled the assortment had been one of his Christmas presents to her. His wife was currently massaging the muscles in Jess's back from shoulder to waist as Jess moaned with the appreciation of someone who spent their workdays (or nights in this case) on their feet. He smiled and inhaled the scent of lavender.

Ambient music barely registered through the room's sound system. Not wanting to startle anyone, Eric stepped forward until he was certain he caught Elena's peripheral vision. She registered him with a dip of her lashes, but quickly returned her attention to the muscles under her hands. She leaned forward over Jess's back, keeping up the massage, and spoke quietly. "Jess, hey." She paused and Eric saw Jess's shoulders roll. "Eric's home."

Jess rolled her shoulders just once more before lifting up to turn her face toward him. He guessed it was a testament to his wife's skilled hands as a masseuse. When Jess's green gaze found him, he smiled and said, "It's good to see you."

"Yeah," Jess replied. She sounded very hesitant.

Thinking he should keep it simple and direct, he asked, "You wanna put a top back on, stay for dinner?"

"Can't. Gotta work," Jess replied, her voice remained quiet, sounding almost sleepy. Elena was very good at massages. Jess continued to study him though he stood mostly behind the couch, before lifting her eyes back to meet his. "Sorry?"

He shook his head quickly. "No problem at all. I'm home for a few days before my next run."

Elena suddenly got to her feet; crossing the room, she patted his shoulder. "I'll start dinner. I think you two should talk." To Jess she nodded. "It'll be OK."

While Elena disappeared into the kitchen, Jess gathered her

clothes. She held them in front of herself; she hadn't moved away, but she also hadn't moved toward him.

Eric frowned. "What was that all about?"

Jess bit her lip and pursed her lips, then her brow furrowed before she shook her shoulders loose. "I-Eric, there's...something I need to tell you."

He didn't like the sound of that very much. "Um. Should I sit down? Or..."

"It's your house." She pulled the t-shirt on over her head.

"Will you sit?"

She looked at the couch, then at him again. Finally she settled to the far end. She still held her jeans on her lap, fists around the denim. "OK."

Recognizing the silent request for distance, Eric sat down on the cushion at the near end. "So what is it?"

"You know I said no to your offer to move in here."

"Yes, of course. It was busy. We'd sprung it on you." He had not been anywhere near as upset as Elena when Jess said no. While they'd all enjoyed their time together, it was always clear to him that Elena and Jess had grown to be more intimate.

"I have been busy," she said. "Too busy. The holidays were stressful. That's why..." She trailed off and looked down. "I—my period was late."

Eric inhaled. He began to see a very different issue. "How late?" he asked tightly.

"Almost two full weeks."

"But you have had your period?"

"Yeah. Like I said it was stress."

"And if you hadn't?"

Jess was quiet for a long moment. She squared her shoulders and lifted her gaze to his. "I don't know."

Eric felt himself get tense. "Would you have called?"

"I don't know. I didn't thin—"

"I would want to know." He realized his voice was sharp when Jess pressed back into the couch arm and dropped her head. He lifted his hand out toward her in concern, but stopped when he saw her eyes widen. Instead he pushed his hands through his hair and put them back in his lap. "Jess, I would've helped you."

"We used condoms. It wouldn't have been your fault."

"Or yours," he pointed out.

"But it would have ruined everything."

"No. We would have talked about what to do. Made the decisions together."

She was quiet for a moment, then asked, "What would you have wanted?"

He didn't have to think about it. Becoming a parent wasn't his ideal, but he knew he would never have told her what she should do. "I would support your choice."

Jess exhaled and he heard a watery edge to the sound. "I— didn—" She shook her head. "I'm—God..." She started to her feet. "Well, look, it's not a thing. There wasn't, and I'm not. It's good."

That didn't sound to him like it was good. Eric got to his feet. "Jess?"

She backed away from him. "I—I gotta go."

Elena returned to the living room. "If we're going to go forward from here, we should all discuss it."

"I really don—" Jess started. Eric watched her gaze meet Elena's. Then Jess's shoulders rounded and she sat back down.

"Call the club. Surely Gus can handle the early crowd for a few minutes?" Elena asked. "This is important."

Jess pulled out her phone and scrolled with her thumb before tapping. A moment after putting it to her ear, she said, "Hey, Gus. I got held up for a bit. Give me an hour?"

Eric faintly heard the gruff older man answer through the line, "Sure." He wondered how much Gus knew of what happened. After all, he lived in a room right across the hall from Jess.

After Jess hung up, Elena said, "Come to the table. We can eat and talk."

At the table, Eric held the chair for Jess; she looked at him then dropped her head and sat down. She looked chastised. Elena put a salad in front of each of them.

He picked up his fork. "So, what do we do about this?"

Picking at her salad, Jess said, "I was having a good time." She looked up, hunching her shoulders. "But I...didn't want you to be angry."

"So you decided it would be better if you didn't see either of us again?" He nodded to Elena. "She was worried. Texted you several times."

Jess swallowed. "I'm sorry," she said looking at Elena. "But if I told you—"

Elena's hands were on the table, gripping the edge. "I would have helped you. We asked you to move in because we want help you."

"But if I am here and don't sleep with Eric, that's not the deal."

Eric tried to think if they'd ever said something like that, but couldn't recall anything. Perhaps she'd assumed. Hell, maybe they'd all assumed things. But...Elena and Jess had time alone without him, right? Then he recalled that he and Jess hadn't had time alone. He decided to be clear. "I've always known you were more into Elena." He held up his hand when Jess started to speak. "Really. It's OK. Look, that's what it means to be open. I have sex with some women Elena doesn't. She's got the same right to separate partners."

"But that wasn't how it was before."

"It's been just the two of us a few times, right?" Elena said. "We've never put that limitation on each other, or you."

"No, you never said it, but...that's what...I understood." She sounded uncertain now.

"And we both enjoyed spending time with you, sex or not," he clarified. "Sometimes we all watched movies, ate dinner." He pointed at the table now. "And just talked."

"That's what Elena said." Jess looked over at Elena then back at him. "So you'd really be OK?"

"Yes."

"I...What are the rules?"

"What do you want them to be?" he countered.

"Elena took me to get on the pill."

"And we use condoms," Eric said. "Do you want something more?"

"Like what?"

"Do you need a promise of no penetration?" he asked.

"That's not—"

"I'll do it," he interjected. "There's always choices," he added when he realized he'd interrupted Jess. "I don't want to be a stranger to you, but...maybe you and I just talk for a while? Go on some actual dates? Just me and you. Take in a movie. Sit here and watch some games. Get ice cream?"

Elena said, "We can use spermicide, too."

"That would affect oral sex," Jess said.

The mention of it admittedly recalled for him just how talented Jess was with her mouth. He swallowed but said, "True."

"So what else do we do?" Elena asked.

Eric offered, "You two shouldn't be the only ones making adjustments."

Jess wondered, "What else can you do?"

"I'll ask around," Eric said. "So...you OK?"

"I-I guess," Jess said.

"No guesses," Elena asked. "Be certain. Talk to us."

"You may know how to do this, but I don't," Jess said. "I need time to think about it."

"Please don't disappear?" Eric asked.

Elena couldn't hide her hopeful expression. Jess nodded. "I'll call you." She headed for the door.

"Let me drive you to the club," Elena said, starting to her feet.

"No, I'll find the bus."

"Jess," Eric said.

She paused at the door. "Yeah?"

"Keep in touch, OK?"

She nodded and disappeared through the door, shutting it behind her.

Eric resettled in his chair. "That could have gone better. Did she tell you about the pregnancy?"

Elena shook her head. "Saw the discarded test in her trash."

"So she'd gotten spooked very recently."

"She and I worked past that." Elena gestured toward the living room. "You saw me giving her a massage. She'd already given me one."

He nodded. "So she wants to resume things with you, but not me." Eric turned the idea over in his mind as he chewed on a bite of salad greens.

"I did say at one point I thought you were wooing her."

"So that's what I'll focus on."

The two of them ate in silence for several bites.

Elena asked, "What would you have done if she was pregnant?"

"I told her truthfully whatever she decided to do, I'd support her."

"Her own parents gave her up. She spent years in foster care."

"Yeah, I know. I don't know if she'd put a child up for adoption, if it came to that."

"Abortion?" Elena's voice held a note of alarm.

"Maybe."

Elena inhaled and exhaled slowly. "We would help her keep it then."

"She was right about one thing, everything would change."

"You'd become a father."

"I'd try my best," Eric said.

"You would," Elena agreed. After a moment she added, "You are more considerate than your father ever was. More loving, too."

He thought about the chain-smoking, hard-drinking man who had... Well, "raised him" was not quite the right phrase. Thankfully, the man had been dead for almost six years now. Eric pursed his lips. "I like to think so."

CHAPTER FIVE

THE SIGN read "Pilot exams." In the appointment it said he was here for his annual flight readiness physical, but Eric was not thinking about his eyesight, blood pressure, reflexes, or any of the other status checks he needed in order to keep his job. He wasn't sure how to bring up contraception, or family planning, other than to just come right out with it. He'd done a little reading and a little research over the last week. After he'd learned of Jess's scare, he had scheduled the appointment with his physician.

In his mind's eye he was remembering Jess and her scared eyes. Scared of him. What he was capable of doing.

"So," the doctor said as he finished filling out the online form. "Looks like you'll keep flying."

When Eric didn't move, the doctor looked over the top of his half-lens reading glasses and asked, "Is there something else you'd like to discuss today?"

"Yeah, um, can we talk about my plumbing? If it's not your thing, can I get a referral?"

"You having incontinence or something?" The doctor started looking through his tests again.

"No, not that plumbing."

"You don't have erectile dysfunction."

"No. I want to discuss a vasectomy. I've read doing that will prevent pregnancy."

"Well, yes, it will. It cuts the sperm supply from reaching the urethra."

"It's pretty simple?"

"You're only forty-what-two?"

"Yeah."

"Married?"

"Yes."

"Got any kids?"

"No."

"Your wife?"

"We don't have any children."

"So whatever you've been doing has been working so far." The man sat back. "Seems to me a vasectomy would be overkill."

"I just want to be sure. Condoms break."

"Mm hmm. Yeah." He crossed his arms over his chest. "Has she gotten her tubes tied? Have you discussed this with your wife?"

Elena wasn't the only person he wanted to do this for, but the doctor didn't need to know that. "No. Not yet."

"Talk to her about it." He stepped out. Eric felt his heart rate tick up while he waited alone. When the doctor returned he gave Eric a pamphlet. "It may not be as hard as a tubal ligation for your wife, but it's still surgery."

"I understand." Eric rolled the pamphlet into his back pocket. "Thanks."

"You're welcome."

After they had dropped Eric at the doctor with a reminder to call when he was done, Elena drove with Jess to the mall. She maneuvered the car into a space outside one of the anchor stores and turned off the engine. Putting her hand back on Jess's leg, she waited until Jess looked at her.

It was Friday. This time Jess had called, saying she wanted to put off her laundry and just spend some time with Elena. And Eric. When he'd said he had an appointment, they'd all piled in the car.

Elena looked directly into the uncertain green eyes and said, "I am glad you called. I told you I wanted to spend time together. If errand day once a week is the only day we get, I'm all for it." She caressed the muscle under her palm. Her smile widened as her enthusiasm grew. "Besides, I love shopping. C'mon."

She gave Jess's leg a squeeze before releasing her and exiting out of the driver side door. With a quick tap to the fob in her hand, she locked up.

"How about a coffee first?"

"OK."

From Jess's tone, Elena guessed she'd have a bit of a discussion of who was paying for the drinks, but she was so damn happy to be out once again with Jess that she shook her head.

She surveyed Jess walking around the back of the car and met her next to the trunk. The blue jeans were well-worn with faded patches in the knees and rear. She wore a white baseball jersey with three-quarter length sleeves in cardinal red without a logo. The white had a few gray stains from things that had obviously not come clean with the laundromat detergents. The white athletic shoes on her feet were scuffed and the leather was cracked throughout the blue piping.

Lifting her head, she smiled again at green eyes that silently questioned her. "Let's go." Brushing Jess's hand she turned shoulder to shoulder with her.

Jess looked around them as they started walking toward a mall entrance. After several emotions crossed Jess's features, Elena felt Jess lightly entangle their fingers.

Once inside the mall, Jess walked up to a board listing all the stores under a neon-lighted map.

Elena asked, "Looking for someplace in particular?"

Ducking her head close to Elena's, Jess murmured, "I need a new bra. And some underwear."

Knowing Jess's figure intimately meant the words filled Elena's mind with very clear pictures of the other woman nude. Her arousal hit her, making her take a sharp breath.

"I would've just gone to Target," Jess added, "but there's not one listed here."

"There's other department stores," Elena said helpfully, "with changing rooms," she felt necessary to add.

She looked at the map herself and her gaze briefly caught on Victoria's Secret, Frederick's of Hollywood, and Lane Bryant. She knew immediately that Jess would decline the pricier places. She thought about Jess's style. "Are you looking for something sexy?" she asked.

Jess hesitated. "Let's just go to one of the department stores."

"Macy's?" Elena suggested. They would pass a couple of the

lingerie stores on the list while walking to the anchor store at the farther end. Maybe she could entice Jess into a little window shopping.

"All right."

They walked down the wide corridor. Just a few stores down, they stopped at a window service Starbuck's. In the end, there wasn't any argument over who would pay. Elena asked Jess what she wanted to drink; Jess chose a Blonde Roast with cream. Elena hemmed and hawed so long, Jess's simple drink was readied first and she had to step away to the far window to retrieve it. So Elena ordered her Caramel Macchiato and paid for both.

As they walked further through the mall, Elena was pleased when Jess's head turned at a few store displays. They stopped in a few and laughed over quirky and suggestive novelty items. She'd have to let Eric know the other woman had been attracted to quite a few things in Spencer's. Jess had also lingered in the comics shop looking at several fantasy figurines. Jess might not be one for buying things for herself, but maybe Elena and Eric could gift her with a few just to see her smile.

Thinking of possible gift-giving occasions, Elena asked, "When's your birthday?"

"October," Jess replied absently, studying the clearance Christmas ornaments in the window of a Hallmark store.

"Oh, we missed it." Elena frowned.

Jess blushed. "Um, actually we had some pretty fun sex that night. I was good."

"What night?" Now Elena was curious.

Leaning in close, Jess whispered, "Do you remember the night we had sex in your hotel room at Caliente?"

"When Eric arranged for us to meet up after you and I got our signals crossed?" She wasn't going to forget that anytime soon; she'd had an amazing time.

Jess nodded. "That's the one."

"That night was your birthday?" She resolved to look back through the credit card statements and find the exact date.

"Mm hmm."

Walking on, they paused again in front of Victoria's Secret. Jess turned her head but then quickly turned back, cheeks reddening. Elena couldn't resist asking, "See something you like?"

"All that lace," Jess said. "Sometimes I feel like it might be nice, a little more feminine. But it's so impractical."

It's only impractical if you aren't showing it off to someone. Thinking quickly, Elena said, "I think that's the first time you've really said you like feminine things. I do like the way you look, but you in lacy lingerie would be very, very sexy." She walked a couple steps then turned back. "Why don't we go in? Especially if we're going to repeat that birthday for you with intent this time."

"October is a long way off."

Elena's heart tightened, worried she might have presumed too much about their starting over. "Yes, I know."

Jess's hand clasped hers and her eyes held a sparkling light, what seemed to be excitement. Her voice was even light when she said, "Maybe we can do something sooner? Do you think Eric would do a photo shoot of us in our lingerie?"

Elena's chest loosened a little. It was promising to think that Jess was picturing her in her lingerie. Even more so, she was thinking about Eric taking pictures. Sipping her coffee, she took the moment to breathe and not get overly excited. Finally she said, "Dress up does sound like fun."

They'd played dress up from the treasure chest in the playroom before, but those were costumes. Elena couldn't wait to see Jess in lacy lingerie specifically suited to her creamy skin and fit figure. She swept her gaze over the woman, head to toe. "Would you like to call the shots?"

"Maybe?" Jess said, finally lifting her lips from the cup rim.

Elena saw a dreamy spark appear in the other woman's green eyes. Eagerly she kept hold of Jess's hand and led the way into the store. "Let's go."

Jess held up the pink filigree lace bra cup, viewing it against her skin. She decided it was too light for her. But she liked the vision in her head of it against Elena's darker skin. She lifted her gaze and searched the nearby racks, looking for Elena.

Elena moved her hand through a selection of garters in a dark rainbow of colors and shades. While still dreamily fingering the lace, Jess drank in the other woman's appearance.

Elena's curves were outlined in a simple spring-green dress. A shiny belt in the same color accented her waist. The dress ended just above Elena's knees and showed off her bare calves and low slingback heels.

Jess inhaled and exhaled to avoid a telltale flush to her cheeks as her internal heat rose. She remembered the sexually charged atmosphere of the elegant dinner club and how it had enhanced the intensity of holding Elena as they danced, before they slid together on the tiny couch. A million fireworks had exploded in Jess's body. Then the proposal—no, *the invitation*, she corrected—had struck her heart so sharply, so startlingly, dangling an impossible future, she had reacted automatically to protect herself.

"Hey." Elena's voice made Jess's heart race. She jerked her gaze up from the woman's calves to meet her eyes. "Hi," she went on. "You like that?"

Jess dropped her head to follow the nod Elena made and saw the lace in her hand. "I—uh." *Not for me.*

"I think this could be lovely on you," Elena said, swapping the garment with one in her hand. The electricity of their touch set Jess's heart racing even faster. "I'll try this on."

Brown eyes held hers as Elena's hand remained on Jess's a moment longer. Gradually her heart returned to a normal rhythm. "Yeah." Those brown eyes squinted slightly as full lips pulled into a big smile. "Yeah," she repeated.

Elena's smile widened and her eyes crinkled. "OK."

While in separate changing rooms, Elena talked to her through the wall panel. "Will you show me if you like it?"

"You mean step out?" Jess asked.

"You sound scandalized. No. Just use your phone." Elena tapped her phone. The text message that beeped on Jess's phone read, "Send me a selfie."

"I've never taken a picture," she realized.

"It's easy," Elena said through the wall. "Look for the camera icon. Click. Click." Elena's voice was light. "I'll show you mine if you show me yours."

In the changing room, Jess looked at herself in the mirror. The green lace did look nice against her skin. "All right." After finding the right icons on her phone, she snapped a few pictures of herself in the lingerie and sent them to Elena's phone. Soft pings sounded in the next changing room.

A moment later her phone pinged. The message, *you are stunning*, was followed by a cat with hearts for eyes.

Elena's next message was two pictures of herself in the lacy lingerie Jess had picked out. The woman seemed even more beautiful than she remembered. Dark hair and dark skin contrasted with the cream-pink lace. And the way her breasts bulged a little over the tops of the bra cups... Jess licked her lips and fumbled to type with her thumbs. Backtracking twice, she nearly dropped the phone. Finally, she settled on a simple reply. *Wow.*

Delighted laughter erupted and Jess thought the sound even more beautiful than the woman herself. Elena might want to make her laugh more often, but Jess was fast deciding Elena's laughter worth the effort, too.

They didn't buy those things, leaving them instead with the changing room attendant to place back on the display racks. But the outing had reawakened Jess's attraction to Elena to a degree she wasn't sure she'd felt before. Absence makes the heart grow fonder? Maybe. But she also felt like this time they were approaching each other differently.

Elena linked her arm around Jess's and led the way to Macy's. A few sensible packs of underwear and one new bra later, Jess sat in the passenger seat of Elena's car being driven back to the Caliente. "Thanks for the trip. I had a good time. Tell Eric I hope everything went well at the doctor."

"It was just a check-up. I'm surprised he didn't call already," Elena said.

Jess worried her teeth at her bottom lip. "Would he be trying to give us time together?"

"I wouldn't put it past him. He was sincere about just dating you until you get comfortable."

"He really is like no guy I've ever known."

"He'll appreciate knowing that," Elena said. "You haven't had much luck with guys before."

"No, I haven't. Eric was the first in a while."

"He wants to be a good man," Elena said.

"Why would he be worried about that?"

"His father was...not." Elena's explanation abruptly ended there as her phone, on the center console beeped. She glanced down. "That's him now."

"OK."

"I'll see you later?" Elena asked.

"I'll text."

Elena reached over and grasped Jess's hand on the open car window. "Please."

Jess was warmed by the soft brown of Elena's eyes and the gentle tilt of her smile. She stood in the parking lot until the car had disappeared out of sight and around a corner.

CHAPTER SIX

LEAVING THE Diligent Air crew area, Eric texted Elena that he was back in town, but would catch an Uber home after stopping by the club to visit Jess. Next he called Jess. One p.m. on a Thursday he hoped she might be free for a date like he'd promised.

"Froyo?" he asked. "It's not a far walk."

Jess sounded all smiles when she answered. "I can do that. You want to meet me?"

"I'm getting an Uber," he said. "I'll just ask and we can either walk from the club, or have the driver take us."

"OK. I'll meet you out front."

"Don't wait there. I can come get you."

"Can you get in when the club isn't open?" she asked.

Eric had only tried once before, and he'd had business with Hector at the time. "I'm sure it'll be fine."

"OK."

Hanging up, Eric went into the ridesharing app and entered his location and destination. A car was only three minutes away, a benefit of being at the airport where a lot of the rideshares got their business. He saw Val, his head cabin steward, exiting the terminal and heading toward the parking lot. The redhead already had her uniform tie loosened and held her heels in one hand and dragged her rolling luggage with the other.

She spotted him, too. "Eric?"

"Hey."

She walked toward him. "Elena busy?"

"No. I'm catching a ride."

"I can take you home. It's been a while since I've seen Elena anyway."

"I'm not going straight home," Eric said. "I'm headed over to Caliente."

"I didn't know the swingers club had daytime activities."

"They don't."

"Oh."

"I'm picking up a date."

"Oh?"

"Yes." He paused, then asked, "Do you remember a blonde? Jess. At the house party in November?" She shook her head. "Well, anyway. I have a froyo date," he finished just as he saw a car pulling toward the curb. The dash held an Uber sign. When the car had stopped he leaned in. "Tanner?"

The driver, a gray-haired woman, nodded. "Yes."

"Thanks." He looked at Val. "My ride. See you Monday."

"See you Monday." She frowned.

He put his case on the back seat. Closing that door and slipping into the front seat, he asked the driver, "Hey, you mind a bit different destination?"

"You still going to this hotel here?" the woman asked, pointing to her GPS where, he presumed, the Caliente was already entered.

"Yes. But there'd be a pick up and a drop off at a froyo place about two blocks from there."

"As long as we enter the second trip so I'll get paid."

"Sure. No problem." While she drove, he entered the froyo shop, and she told him her driver number. Just like that he had organized his first real date with Jess. He chuckled and set aside his phone.

When they got to the hotel, he asked the driver to wait; he'd be right back out.

He was pulling open the front door to the main part of the hotel, not the club doors, when he saw Jess stepping out from a corridor. "Hey." He smiled. She walked quickly to him. He only had a moment to take in that she wore jeans and a green top that hung off one shoulder, showing a black bra strap. On her feet were some well-worn cross-fit sport shoes.

"Hi," she said.

He held open his arms and she let him wrap her up. He breathed in the soft scent of her hair and then pulled back. "Ready to go?"

"Yeah. Are we walking?"

"No. Got a car out front." He laughed, holding the door. "That sounds like some *Pretty Woman* line," he said.

"I feel kinda like Julia Roberts," Jess said. "You're all dressed up."

He loosened then removed his uniform tie. "Better?" She nodded. "I'm not Richard Gere, but I can show you a good time." Her laugh sounded wonderful. He grasped her hand and said, "Come on."

Eric helped Jess out of the car at the curb in front of the Menchie's. He pulled his luggage from the Uber's trunk where he'd moved it when Jess got in the back seat. "Thanks," he said, pressing a good tip into the woman's hand on top of what he'd paid in the app for the original ride.

Turning back to Jess, he held out his other arm. She stepped into it, turning around, and he squeezed her shoulder. "Welcome to the promised land of froyo." She chuckled again.

Inside they collected the paper cups and he noticed she selected one flavor–chocolate–and served herself only a small swirl. He stopped her before she headed toward the add-ons counter. "You can get more if you want."

She looked over at the wall of dispensers.

"You don't have to, but you should know I don't count it as a date if you're counting calories."

She seemed startled, eyes widened and then dropped. He recognized contrition. "I wasn't." He wondered what she *was* doing if she wasn't counting calories.

"So you're not very hungry?" He doubted that; he saw how robustly she ate whenever they had food at the house. He nudged her toward the Cake Batter he'd just gotten himself. "Think of it like a sundae. At least three wildly different flavors."

She added another small swirl of the Cake Batter, he thought simply to placate him. He lifted an eyebrow at her then put a sizable swirl of Mint Chocolate in his bowl. But that was as far as she was willing to go. She had eyed the banana and caramel combination, but in the end she walked over to the add-ons counter and poured a spoonful of rainbow sprinkles on top.

He added several toppings to his and dropped a cherry on top of hers as she passed behind him. "Because I can't take your cherry," he whispered when she cocked her head in question. "I'll give you one." She laughed.

The clerk looked up as they approached the counter. "Together?" the young man asked. He looked young and gangly. Probably the kid's first job.

"Yes," Eric answered, putting his down and taking Jess's from her hands to put it on the same scale.

"Ten-ninety-four."

Most of that was definitely his bowl. He resisted a sigh. Swiping his debit card, Eric returned Jess's bowl to her and picked up his own. "You wanna sit inside or outside?"

"Outside is nice. It's nice weather."

"It is."

"I haven't been in Miami in January."

"That's right. You had only gotten here in August?"

"Yes." Jess sat down at one of the small plastic tables and the plastic chair creaked under him when he sat down across from her. She looked around, holding the pink spoon in her mouth. When she removed it, she pointed with it. "I think I broke down just off that intersection there."

He looked over at the road, at least six lanes approaching the intersection from all directions, and thought about Jess alone, knowing nobody, sitting on the side of the road. "You couldn't fix it?"

She shook her head. "No money, no car." She looked around and he followed her gaze to a dense patch of woods. "Slept in there a couple nights until I worked up enough nerve to approach the hotels."

He let that tidbit sink in while he ate a couple bites of his froyo. "Now that you have a job, have you considered getting another car?"

"The public buses are pretty good. Gus lets me borrow his car occasionally."

Eric accepted that Jess wanted to manage her own situation. "Well, still, if you wanted to go...say, to the beach, how would you get there?"

"Never thought about it."

"You can't be in Miami and not go to the beach."

"It's January," Jess replied, sounding like it was ridiculous.

"And you just pointed out it's a nice day for January."

"Compared to snow, of course."

They'd talked somewhat about other places she'd passed through in her travels. He certainly couldn't say she'd lived in those places. "So you've been someplace where it snows in January."

"Most everywhere snows in January," Jess replied.

Through a playful smile, he pointed out, "Not Brazil. It's summertime for them."

"Have you been to Brazil?"

"Yeah. It has been a few years though."

The sound of a scraping spoon caused Eric to look down and see Jess finishing her treat. He was a little sad their date was ending, but he'd had a good time getting to know her some more, which had been the point. "Walk you back to the hotel?"

CHAPTER SEVEN

JESS HUMMED as she worked behind the Caliente's bar. Elena had called and said she and Eric would stop by the club that night to socialize. They said they knew she was working, but looked forward to any break time she was willing to give them.

"You're looking happy," Gus said.

"Elena and Eric are coming tonight." She blushed. "To see me."

"Ten-fifteen, you can take a break." He smiled and patted her on the shoulder before he moved away down the bar to see one of the waitresses, a curly haired African-American woman named Janae.

She glanced through the haze from the smoke machines and tried to separate individuals from the surging sea of dancers among the light show, everyone and everything moving to the frenetic beat of the music. It was "80s Night," and Jess recalled it as one of Eric's favorite themes.

"Looking for someone?"

Jess turned and smiled big when she saw Eric leaning casually against the bar. He was half-turned toward her, elbows canted back onto the surface kept him balanced.

"Not sure you could see anyone clearly in all this haze," he said, turning now to look at her. "And those lights?" He gave a waving gesture toward the ceiling. "No one is anything but silhouettes really."

She moved closer to him and wiped at the bar top before leaning forward to speak. "Hi."

He was smiling as he reached across the freshly cleaned surface. Catching her hand under his own, he held her gaze and said, "Hello." Looking down at the space separating them, he then looked up and added, "Perhaps I can ask for a hug later?"

"Gus said I can take a break at ten-fifteen."

"Do you want to find a quiet spot to talk?"

Jess appreciated Eric's earnest look. "There's a green spot out past the dumpsters."

"Upwind, I hope."

She chuckled; she found herself doing that a lot around him. It was a nice feeling. He found her hand on the bar's top and lightly caressed the tips of her fingers. Exhaling her anxiety, she nodded. He cupped her fingers then kissed the backs of her knuckles. "We'll see you then."

She decided he didn't need to leave just yet. "Can I start you off with drinks?"

"Something with not too much octane."

Preparing a couple light cocktails, Jess passed them across the bar. "Are you and Elena staying on-site again?"

Eric handed her his credit card for their tab. "We might have a set of room keys by the end of the night."

Jess smiled. To secure a room, he would need the credit card, so giving it to her, she felt, was a subtle way for him to say he and Elena planned to come back and get it, and to ask her to join them. He brushed her hand as he accepted the drinks and repeated, "Ten-fifteen," before walking away.

Following Eric's progress as best she could through the miasma of light and noise, she finally saw him sit down next to Elena on a low leather couch in a mostly dark corner beyond the dance floor.

Elena accepted the drink from him and then his kiss on her cheek. She said something and Eric replied. Elena's ruby-red lips drew Jess's gaze like a beacon as the couple continued to talk.

"Can I get a drink, please?"

Jess looked at the man who spoke. "Yes, of course, what will you have?"

"Whiskey." She was surprised; he didn't look to be a hard drinker.

"How about a cocktail?" she suggested.

"Just the whiskey," he said.

"All right." She poured it and collected his cash payment. He was gone when she came back with his change from the till. Tucking the two singles in her pocket, she moved to take a drink list from Cerise, another waitress, who also handed her a credit card. "Open a tab, table 12."

A tray full of the requested drinks later, Cerise moved away under Jess's watchful eye. The waitress was new, but there had been an increase in club-goers over the holidays, so they definitely needed the extra hands. Cerise herself had told Jess that a couple televised series released through streaming services had increased people's interest in swinging. When Jess asked if she had tried swinging, the woman had replied, "Yep," popping her 'p' like she was popping bubblegum back in high school.

Cerise had her own apartment, but she stayed here many club nights after the bar closed, enjoying the attentions of multiple men at the same time, a gang bang. Jess remembered Elena said she had done a gang bang before, but remembered the outcome had been less enjoyable than she expected.

Jess couldn't imagine it. She had been plenty busy when she and Eric and Elena had gotten together. She remembered the house party but also remembered that she'd not even had sex with Eric at that event. They'd just grinded while watching Elena with the other guy whose name she'd couldn't now recall.

They'd always been so careful with her feelings, she realized. Feeling guilty that she hadn't been brave enough to reach out, she was now beginning to feel like it might be possible she could learn how to do this relationship with the Tanners. They hadn't gotten back to sex yet, but she was happy with the way the intensity increased each time she and Elena had hung out. She and Elena had gone from holding hands to massage. Then she remembered how good it had felt just talking with Eric over froyo, and the walk back here that afternoon had been nice, too. When he touched her fingers tonight, she'd felt the familiar tingle; his mustache and lips brushing her knuckles had generated a familiar heat.

Looking up from her thoughts, she saw Eric and Elena crossing to a space on the dance floor as a new song started up: "Wanna Be Startin' Somethin'." The two rolled into the high energy song and soon were at the center of a full crowd of bodies rocking to the popular Michael Jackson tune.

Elena and Eric, separately and together, gyrated with new partners, laughing and singing. They did seem to be reconnecting with a lot of friends. The way Eric had spoken so earnestly about not wanting her to feel it was all her responsibility, she was starting to believe that they honestly cared for her. Love was... well... Too many people had thrown that word around in her life and in the end all she'd gotten was hurt.

She groaned when she remembered Gus telling her there was seldom sex without feelings. And damn, yes, sex with Eric and Elena had *felt* so good. She wondered if their belief that they loved her would change the sex. Unfortunately that thought always cast her mind back to her boyfriend. Ex-boyfriend, she corrected.

Sex had definitely changed in the week after they moved into the apartment. He had said, "I love you," a lot but he'd stop after he came, tell her to shower, and be asleep when she got back to their bed. Like he didn't need to work to keep her anymore. The "thrill of the chase" was gone.

With Elena or Eric, or both of them, it seemed they weren't satisfied until she was.

To cool herself down, after wiping down the bar top, she moved to check the stock. "How can I tempt this again?" she asked for the umpteenth time. She remembered how low she felt at the Diligent Air party. Then there'd been the super-high on the dinner date, only to crash again. It had been a roller coaster. Was she really going to get back on?

A memory of brown eyes and blue eyes looking at her across the dining table made her nod her head. "Yes, I do want them," she confirmed. The heat from her face slid into her chest and then down lower.

Elena sipped her seltzer water with lime and tried to listen to Cris and Caitlyn on either side of her at the cocktail couches. The couple had been busy since attending the Tanners' house party back in November.

Both women were blonde, former Navy officers, and married. For their fourth anniversary in late December, they'd booked a swingers cruise out of Port of Miami.

"It was Bacchanalian, I tell you," Cris said, a husky quality to her voice. "A bounty of bodies. I could've happily slept my way through most of that company." She leaned back and sighed with happy dramatic flair. Elena laughed.

"But we didn't," Caitlyn said, gently laying a hand over her wife's knee and teasing at the hem of her coral blue-green cocktail dress. "Found a lovely foursome that welcomed two more. We saw a couple of the shipboard shows, went dancing, gorged on incredible food. And yes," she added getting a raised eyebrow from Cris. "Yes, we also attended several themed parties."

"I'm so glad you enjoyed it," Elena said. She wanted to find out more about the cruise and its organizers. She made a mental note to email Caitlyn during the week so she could get the details. Cris wouldn't remember much beyond the flesh-filled good times. She looked away from the two women and spotted Eric on the dance floor with Jane and her husband Brian; the two were dancing in a conga line, grinding around and between other club members as everyone worked up their appetites before going to the playrooms.

Caitlyn murmured in her ear, "You look ready to make a move on someone."

She turned and met the ice blue eyes with surprise. "I do?"

"Yes, so...let me guess." Caitlyn's eyes drifted around the club. "You've got more of a first-time hunt look in your eyes, so who has caught your attention?"

Jess hummed and Elena found herself bemusedly listening as several new faces were described. She shook her head at each of them though.

Caitlyn finally deduced, "It must be that delicious new waitress, the redhead." Then she frowned. "You're not usually into redheads."

"I am not," Elena confirmed; she shook her head. "No, I'm not interested in the redhead or, really, any of them."

"So will you and Eric come play with Cris and I?" Caitlyn asked.

Elena considered their history. The couple had been among the small number invited to the house party precisely because they were close, familiar, easy playmates. A playroom session tonight would definitely be familiar.

Eric walked over to the couch at the beginning of another song; Jane was now on his arm. "Hello, ladies," he greeted, then he kissed Elena, Caitlyn, and finally Cris on a cheek. "Planning the next part of our night?"

Cris looked up at Eric through her mascara-laden lashes. "I'm more than ready to shed these layers." Considering she wore a sequined cocktail dress, four-inch red stiletto heels without hose, and probably only the smallest possible lingerie underneath, *layers* was a bit of an exaggeration. Everyone laughed.

Any ice effectively broken, Jane waved over her husband, Brian, who was a dark-haired reed-thin thirty-year-old. Everyone around the small couch and table had played together in many different configurations over the years. Eric took Elena's hand as they followed the other four toward the private part of the club.

Catching sight of Jess at the end of the bar, Elena saw her heading toward a back corridor. *Her break*, she realized. She tugged on Eric's arm. "Eric," she said.

"Hmm?"

"Jess just went on break."

"Oh, is it that time?"

From Eric's other side, Cris asked, "What time?"

Elena grasped Caitlyn's hand next to her. "I think we're gonna go."

"Before playtime?" Cris asked.

"We saw someone we'd like to talk to," Eric said.

"Oh. You sure about that?" Cris grasped his hand. "We *have* missed you."

"Later," he said, kissing her cheek.

Elena accepted a kiss from Caitlyn then grasped Eric's hand and headed in the direction she'd seen Jess go.

The corridor she followed went out to the back of the building, into a dark area at the corner of the courtyard of the hotel. Jess looked up through the trees following the moonlight up to the full moon. The bar had not been particularly hectic, but still she felt a release of tension as she briefly let work leave her mind.

"On break?"

Jess turned to see Elena, who had spoken, and Eric emerging from the building's shadow. "Yeah." In her properly fitting black suit, Jess tucked her hands in her pockets, leaned against the wall, bending her knee to put her heel up against it, and steadied her stance. "You look good."

Elena looked down and briefly brushed at the skirt of her dark blue cocktail dress. She then passed her small clutch purse from one hand to the other. Finally she shrugged. All the while, Jess simply drank in the woman's form. Thirst made her lick her lips; she did indeed want to resume sex with Elena.

Tearing her gaze from Elena, she looked now at Eric. He also looked handsome in a hunter green sport jacket over a tan button-up with the collar open. While she watched, he took the jacket off and draped it over his arm. "Bit warm out here."

Jess shivered and a thread of heat licked up her throat as her body reacted to the luminous attention shining at her from his blue eyes. "Yeah, I guess."

"But it isn't really upwind," he added.

She winced. "Sorry."

"Is there another place we can go?" Elena asked.

Jess turned to catch Elena's gaze flowing slowly over her as she stepped closer. Under that admiration, she felt as warm as if she were standing in a sauna. "I—well, there's not really meant to be a lot of people outside except by the pool."

"We could do that," Eric said. "We're just going to talk."

Jess nodded. Leading the way around the corner of the building, she stopped at a high chain-link fence threaded with green fabric for privacy. Using a key, she led them back into the club area.

The pool deck was quieter than the club, but it was not empty. A few members were naked in the Jacuzzi. The pool itself was empty and the deck seating at the far side, closer to the hotel rooms, was also quiet. They settled into three chairs at a table engulfed in shadows. The hotel breezeway lighting filtered toward them but didn't reveal them as more than silhouettes.

Eric sat back and lost himself in simply watching Jess. His hand tingled with the memory of touching hers at the beginning of the evening. "Most people on break drink or smoke," he said wryly, noticing Jess's fingers tangling together. "You need a drink?"

She shook her head. "I-I just don't know what to talk about. I did just see you a few days ago." She visibly brightened suddenly. "Oh, wait, you've been flying. See anything interesting this week?"

He shook his head. "Same old, same old."

"Oh." She shrugged. "I guess." She turned to Elena. "How's the business building?"

Elena smiled, as Eric knew she would. He'd already been privy to a couple happy developments. "I secured two more sponsors and have started a swag bag."

"What's a swag bag?" Jess asked.

"Freebies for tour guests. Some are useful items. Others are just fun, but all are branded to advertise corporate sponsors."

"Useful items for an adult resort tour. Like the hotel's toothpaste, toothbrush, mouthwash, shampoo," Eric said.

Elena added, "Also condoms, sample sizes of flavored lubes, and discount cards for mail-order items." Jess blushed; Eric chuckled.

Jess asked, "Do you special order those or do the companies just give them to you?"

"Both. I'll have boxes shipped in a few months once the sponsors agree on what they'll provide and I have enough reservations to make the tour."

Eric said, "Then you'll need some help putting the bags together."

Elena shook her head. "Won't be for a while yet. I'm only part way there."

"You'll get there." Jess reached out and cupped Elena's hand just as Eric had done for her earlier.

"Maybe when the tour is made, Jess can help with the bags," he said.

"Work for you?" Jess asked.

"Help me anyway," Elena said. "There's not any pay."

"Yet," Eric encouraged. "Think positive."

Jess nodded at him then at Elena. "He's right. Think positive."

Elena cupped Jess's hand back and her smile widened. "As long as you do." When her gaze moved from Jess to Eric, he knew that the message wasn't about the startup, but about *their* restart. "One step at a time," he said.

"Right."

CHAPTER EIGHT

ERIC BUSSED Elena's cheek after he had replaced his suit jacket from the club room lockers. Quickly looking inside the dark recessed space for anything they'd forgotten, he asked, "Got everything?" He turned to see her smiling and just lifting her head where she sat on the bench. She tucked away her phone then put on her heels.

"Yep," Elena replied. She removed the locker key on its stretchy ring from around her wrist and handed it to him before she picked up her clutch from the seat beside her.

After replacing the key in the locker, he held out his hand for her to take.

"Are you leaving?"

Eric turned to find Hector, Caliente's owner, standing at the corner of the bank of lockers, wearing a white cotton robe. "Yeah, time to get home," he replied.

"Gianna and Rohan are coming to our suite and continue the fun. You should join us."

Elena lightly squeezed Eric's hand as she took it; when he saw her face, he saw the unspoken 'no' in her eyes. He shook his head at Hector. "Thanks, but we're all played out...for tonight anyway," he added with a quick smile to soften the blow he saw land in Hector's eyes as a shadow.

By the time he and Elena had gotten back inside from talking with Jess on her break, Jane, Brian, Caitlyn, and Cris had been enjoying each other quite thoroughly. So they hadn't intruded, instead having sex, just the two of them, in a quiet corner.

"We're going home."

"My door is always open," Hector replied. "Elena, it was wonderful to see you again."

Elena nodded at him. "Good to see you, too, Hector." She took Eric's hand and turned to leave. So he didn't look dragged, Eric moved quickly as well.

"Everything OK?" he asked when they were alone walking down the corridor from the playrooms toward the front of the club.

"Yes, I'm fine." She smiled. "I'm going to use the restroom."

"I thought we were going home?"

"I may have a surprise for you," she replied. "Just wait here a minute."

Elena disappeared into the small ladies restroom. Eric leaned on the wall outside and looked around. The place was empty. The bar had been closed a couple hours ago and its lights were dim. He didn't even hear the clatter of anyone cleaning up.

He thought about the times they'd waited here to take Jess home with them. One time, he remembered they'd taken her home only for her to fall in bed between them and fall asleep as he stroked her back. It had been nice, better than nice, even.

"Eric."

He turned toward the voice at the same time he registered Elena emerging from the restroom behind him. Jess stood just past the end of the wall where he leaned. She wore a simple button up peach blouse and jeans. The tumble of her blonde hair was down from the bun she had while working. Fancifully he thought of her as an angel, giving off her own glow. He searched her face as Elena took his hand and squeezed his fingers softly. Jess dipped her chin briefly then smiled. His cheeks pulled his lips into a wide smile. "Hi, Jess."

She cocked her head at him. He held out his other hand and she took it, stepping forward. He felt the heat of her body inches away. "You done for tonight?" Jess asked.

"We were just heading home," he said.

"Elena texted me." Jess held up her cell phone where presumably Elena's text was displayed.

Eric didn't care; he was enamored with Jess's face. Her smile was open and warm. The blue of her eyes sparkled. He'd missed it. A lot. First their froyo date, and now this. It was sweet, soft, and he felt like they were meeting again for the first time. She looked to Elena then back at Eric.

"Are you working tomorrow?" she asked. "Today?" she corrected.

"Not flying again 'til Monday," he replied. "You?"

"Not until late." She looked past him briefly to Elena.

He looked from Jess to Elena. "Are you...?" He trailed off and stepped forward then stopped, watching her for any hesitation. "Would you like to have breakfast with us?"

Jess finished closing the distance. Her hand brushed his chest with a warm welcome pressure. She lowered her hand to touch his. The light squeeze seemed to be her favorite form of silent communication. Leaning forward, she pressed her lips to his. *That was another good message*, he thought, smiling into the contact but letting her direct.

The way her lips molded to his, their warmth, the soft searching touch... Eric groaned and his heart thumped harder while his groin warmed. A few moments passed. He kept his body still and moved only his lips tenderly in their mutual kiss. Slowly she lifted away until their mouths were parted an inch. Her breath warmed his face.

Gaze holding his, her fingertips soothed over the hairs at the gap of his shirt collar. Her green eyes twinkled. "I'd love to spend time with you," she replied.

Eric's chest was so full he couldn't speak. He nodded and she tucked herself under his left arm. Elena tucked into his right side. The three of them walked together out into the parking lot.

It wouldn't be light for a few hours, even at three in the morning when the trio arrived at the Tanners' home. Eric asked if Jess was hungry; she wasn't. They walked to the living room instead and sat. The idea of watching a movie became a discussion of cinema and no movie was ever selected. Around four a.m., Elena prepared three coffees.

Sipping on coffee from a cartoon-printed ceramic mug, Jess leaned back on the couch. Eric had taken his shoes off and put his sock feet up on the coffee table, sitting on her left, his shoulder companionably against hers. Elena, who had commandeered the remote, had curled up on Jess's other side.

"I liked *Captain America*," Jess said. "Peggy Carter was hot."

"Did you know there was a TV series with her?" Elena asked.

"No? Really?"

"Yeah." Eric chuckled. "Elena binged it." He sipped his coffee. "I'm partial to Ant-Man, actually. I know he's not a big gu—" His words cut off when Jess elbowed him in the ribs.

"Really, Eric?" Elena chuckled.

"He was big where it counts," Eric protested. "His heart."

Jess chuckled. "True."

Eric's hand slid from the back of the couch to her shoulder. "Is this OK?"

She nodded. "Yeah, I'm...this is nice."

When he leaned the small distance and kissed her temple, she sighed happily.

CHAPTER NINE

WHEN DAWN finally arrived, Jess sat on the pool deck sipping a mimosa from a champagne flute. The sound of the pool circulation system could just barely be heard. Elena had led her out here, then kissed her before she said she would help Eric bring out breakfast. The sound of the sliding glass door moving drew Jess's gaze from the trees where she'd been searching out the birds making all the noise.

It wasn't super warm, but a small battery heater under the table and Elena giving her a blanket over her shoulders had made it reasonably comfortable. Of all the other places she'd spent a predawn January morning, Miami was certainly the warmest. *And not just for its weather*, she thought.

Elena slid quickly onto the bench after putting on the table a tray of fruit salad bowls and crepes covered in powdered sugar. She kissed Jess's cheek. "Hey."

"Breakfast is served," Eric announced proudly. In his hands he carried a tray filled with bacon, eggs, and pancakes, all still steaming fresh from the griddle. He slid onto the bench on her right, placing the platter in the middle of the table directly in front of her. Steamy aromas rose from everything and despite herself, Jess's mouth watered and her stomach rumbled.

She lifted up the corner of her blanket; Elena took the invitation and snuggled up to her. Looking from one to the other, she lifted her flute. "A toast," she said.

Elena's eyes were soft and curious as she lifted her glass. Eric's blue eyes were almost the same color as the sky overhead as he looked at her. He asked, "To what?"

"I didn't get a chance to wish you a happy new year," she said. "So I'm going to do it now. Here's to 2020. May it be as clear as its name suggests."

Eric's smile told her he appreciated the sentiment. Accompanying the clink of all their glasses in front of her, Elena nudged and then kissed the back of her shoulder from the other side. *Yeah, it was going to be a good year.*

Jess could point to several things that made this visit with Elena and Eric feel like a first time, but it also felt brand new. Just as they had the first time, they were eating on the pool deck. She sat next to Elena, but she was quiet instead of talkative. She didn't appear to feel the need to carry the conversation as she had before. Now Jess leaned easily into Elena's shoulder, both of them listening to stories Eric told about his work.

"Thank god, the drones are FCC-controlled now. I get wanting aerial pictures, but a flight path is no place for that shit," Eric said.

"What happens when you hit one?" Jess asked.

"It can screw with the engine. Mostly though it pops up in your sight field, and you think it's something else for a moment. Damn distracting."

Jess grasped his hand on the table. "I'm grateful you aren't easily spooked."

He smiled. "Me too."

They each had one more mimosa before Eric announced the last of the champagne. Jess nursed her drink slowly, not needing the alcohol for liquid courage like she had for their first get-together.

Finally it seemed necessary to clean up; all the food had been decimated. Flies were investigating the remains and everyone swatted the air as often as they each tried to add something to the conversation.

Jess grabbed one tray and started piling everything she could onto it. Elena picked up several containers and serving plates. Eric collected bottles and glasses on another tray. It was an easy division of labor and they walked toward the sliding glass together. Eric opened it. Elena and he kissed before she entered. Jess found herself naturally leaning toward him and kissing him when she started across the threshold.

He nibbled her lips and it was playful; her stomach fluttered pleasantly. When he backed up, her heart thumped and she was pleasantly aroused.

"C'mon," he said, adding a smile before he kissed her temple. "It'll only take a moment to get this stuff out of the way."

In the kitchen, Jess saw Elena turning away from the refrigerator, hands empty. Taking the tray from Jess, Elena said, "I've got these. It all just goes in the dishwasher." She started sorting the items into the top and bottom racks of the appliance. Jess turned to the right and found Eric already filling the sinks with soapy water and sorting pans, skillets, and cooking utensils.

She had to take a step back to get out of their way, looking at the couple moving around one another. Eric stepped aside when Elena went under the sink for a dishwashing tablet and then he passed Elena a few utensils and glassware that could still fit. Looking around, Jess saw a drying towel hooked through the handle of the refrigerator.

Snatching it up, she said, "I can dry."

Eric smiled and nodded when he put a large flat pan into the drain rack on his left. Jess quickly lifted it and dried it. Turning from setting the dishwasher cycle, Elena took the dry pan from Jess's hands and slid it into a cabinet next to the stove. Jess tried to remember where the pan had gone as she turned to collect another from the drain rack.

The entire task was done quickly and Eric took the drying towel from Jess's hands after she passed a mandoline grater to Elena to put away. "Thank you," Elena said.

"No problem," Jess replied. They walked into the living room together and settled to different parts of the couch. "What now?"

Eric lifted his digital camera from a shelf by the television then put it back down with a shrug. "Can't do a photo show like our first date," he said. "I haven't taken any new pictures since the holidays."

"Nothing? Really?" Eric had sounded matter of fact, but Jess thought it must be disappointing. "You enjoy photography." She remembered viewing the sexy boudoir pictures of Elena and then the ones of Elena and herself on that very first date. Eric had been all smiles showing off his art. "You should get back into it."

He hesitated as he was sitting back down on the couch, looking at her.

"Now," she said, standing up. It was a strange feeling standing above them, but when Eric and Elena looked up at her, their hands simply resting on their knees, Jess realized *she* had just sounded too insistent. Their expressions revealed a mix of emotions; she felt the need to check in. "Is that OK?"

"Don't doubt yourself now," Eric said, standing up. A smile pushed his cheeks wide. "I have been waiting for take-charge Jess to make an appearance since we first met." He stepped until their bodies were flush and lifted his hands to her face. "Is this all right?" His palm was strong and warm.

She tipped her head into it. "Yes," she said when he didn't continue.

"I am so glad to see you," he said. Then he cupped her cheeks and kissed her.

Jess felt no hesitation, no throttle on his passion. Eric was turned on and pressing his body against hers so she could feel it too. She hummed into his mustache and his tongue brushed over her lips.

Breathing rapidly when he released her, she turned to find Elena moving to her side. Elena's fingers cupped her chin. "Jess? Or no?"

Jess nodded. Elena's kiss was just as passionate. Warm and soft, with occasional urgent presses with the pads of her lips, the kisses mixed with Elena murmuring Jess's name against her throat and ears before reclaiming her mouth.

She nudged the other woman backward until she dropped once again on the couch. Grasping Elena's hands, she spread them out wide with their fingers interlaced. When Elena arched, their chests slid against each other. Her nipples perked against the inside of her shirt, and she felt Elena's do the same. When she moved between Elena's thighs, the bottom of Elena's dress hiked up and her legs rose around Jess's hips.

Holding Elena's gaze, Jess throatily said, "Eric, get your camera." She reveled in the breathlessness of her own voice and noticed how Elena's pupils widened.

"Right here?" Elena asked. Her full red lips were smiling though and Elena's tone was teasing; Elena knew very well Jess didn't have any intention of breaking the momentum by moving very far.

"Yes. Though I do have a request."

"What do you need?" Eric asked.

"Condom?" Jess asked Elena, tangling their fingers together on Elena's stomach.

"Right here," Eric replied, opening a drawer in the side table.

She smiled and took the foil-wrapped package with her free hand. "Lay back."

Elena rearranged on the couch so she lay full length on it. Jess untangled their fingers and drew her left hand up Elena's arm and then down her side. With quick movements, she unrolled the condom down the two middle fingers of her right hand.

"You've been very patient with me," Jess said.

"I've missed you," Elena said.

"Let's see how much." She grasped the bottom of the dress with her other hand. "Hmm?" When Elena nodded, Jess kissed Elena hard. She pushed her fingers inside Elena's underwear and finally inside her center.

Elena was soaked. Jess toyed with her clit and rubbed between her labia for long moments, eagerly enjoying Elena's writhing.

"Jess!" Elena gasped. Her Spanish accent edged in and pushed Jess' desire for her to another peak. To meet the other woman's need, Jess curled her fingers up against the top of Elena's channel and rubbed her thumb against Elena's clit.

Green eyes locked with brown, Jess watched Elena's pupils dilate and contract as the woman spiraled on the sensations. Proud of herself, Jess sought to push deeper, feeling inner walls fluttering.

Elena clutched Jess tightly when she reached orgasm. Her head fell back to draw in breath. Jess kissed then sucked at a spot where shoulder and throat met until she tasted the heat of Elena's blood under her tongue.

Crying out her pleasure, Elena shouted, "Jess! Si!"

Nuzzling Elena's throat, Jess continued pumping her fingers inside Elena and kissing her. She noticed Eric moving toward Elena's feet and lifted a brow at him when she saw he was without the camera.

"Video." He grinned and pointed. She glanced over to see the camera on a tripod set up about three feet off the ground. She had been so focused on Elena that she hadn't heard him setting up.

After speaking, Eric leaned over the back of the couch and, to Jess's delight, gave Elena a matching hickey on the other side of her throat.

"Eric," Elena moaned and grasped his shirt. With a little

maneuvering, she splayed her legs wider and used one foot on the floor to push herself up and onto Jess's fingers. Her desire leaked around the condom when she came a second time, wetting Jess's hand.

Eric leaned forward. Jess closed the space and the two of them kissed in front of Elena. Her center tightened a third time around Jess's fingers. "Oh, god."

Removing her fingers slowly, Jess massaged Elena's inner thigh with her other hand before leaning back and smiling at her. The three of them undoubtedly made quite an erotic picture: Eric, in a now slightly askew button up shirt and tie, held his naked sweaty wife in his arms as she lifted her chin to meet him in a kiss, her dark legs splayed, and her swollen center visibly dripping.

Licking her hand as she removed the condom, Jess hummed in pleasure. "You taste so good."

Dropping the latex in a small can by the end table, Jess got to her feet. Eric straightened where he stood behind the couch and his hard cock was easily visible, trapped in his pants. He walked back to the camera tripod. Intercepting him, Jess pressed against him and kissed him, but he put a hand over hers when she tried to work his buckle free.

"You don't have to," he said.

"I want to," she replied.

He nodded. "Get another condom."

Jess stepped away and opened the same drawer she'd seen Eric use. Out of the corner of her eye she saw him sit on the couch. Elena helped him out of his pants. She considered the array of choices in the drawer then chose two. Stripping out of her clothes, she returned to her lovers who eagerly pulled her between them.

"Two?" Elena questioned when Jess handed them to her.

"One for you and one for me," she said simply.

"I'm up for that." Eric took one and unrolled it over his cock.

Jess straddled Eric's legs and together they played with her clit which made her pussy throb. "I know you are."

Elena watched as her husband's cock disappeared slowly inside their lover. Jess was teasing Eric, lowering then lifting only an inch at a time. She brushed Jess's shoulder, causing Jess to turn her head, green eyes heavy-lidded and lips smiling. "I'm so glad you're here," she said before leaning in to kiss the woman's lips as she began moving in earnest on Eric.

Taking a momentary pause in kissing Jess, Elena glanced at Eric's face. She remembered seeing him and Jess kissing over her satiated form a moment ago. His expression was similarly adoring. Her husband breathed steadily, but his wide pupils had almost completely edged out the blue irises as he watched Jess above him. He must have sensed her looking because he dropped his gaze and met hers while shifting his hands to Jess's hips. His expression didn't change. The adoration was equal for both her and Jess.

Jess grasped Elena's hand as she turned. With green blissed-out eyes, she kissed her. Feeling a mix of stunned, blessed, loved, and turned on, Elena leaned into the kiss. They really were doing this once again. *God, it felt so good.*

CHAPTER TEN

JESS STEPPED quickly out of the passenger side of Elena's car when the woman parked. Stumbling a bit in her new heels on the asphalt, she managed to stay upright. She hurried to the driver side, intending to take Elena's hand as she emerged from the car. They were really on a proper date. After everything, she and Elena were moving forward in a romantic relationship. She adjusted the mask over her hair and face.

Movement in the doorway to the club a few feet away startled her and she froze with her hand on the open car door. Jess stared at the couple lowering their masks, showing their ID, and paying their cover charge to the door guard. She fingered her mask, which blocked most of her face and even some of her hair.

"Help me out?"

Heart racing with nerves, she realized she was blocking Elena from getting out. "Sorry." She held out her hand.

"Don't worry, I've got our tickets." Jess exhaled as Elena's hand slid over her upper arm, rubbing soothing circles on the skin above her costume's arm band.

For the Caliente costume party Elena had suggested they would go as She-Ra and Catra. The two of them had binged the show over the last two weeks. The tickets were originally for Elena and Eric, but he had been called to replace a sick pilot for a flight. He suggested Jess go with Elena instead.

"Everyone has to take their mask off to get in the door."

Elena gave her arm a squeeze. "This is your night off." Jess leaned into the kiss pressed on her cheek and let the words fill her with confidence. "What can they say to you? What you do with your time is your business."

"Are you planning to go to the playrooms tonight?" Jess asked. Looking delicious in the skintight red Catra costume, Elena almost certainly would be frequently approached.

"Only with you." Elena kissed her cheek and traced her palm down Jess's throat to cup one breast. "Now come on. It's late, and I'm sure the dance floor will be crowded."

"It's easier to get lost in a crowd," Jess said.

She fingered her helmet and adjusted the gold mask. It wasn't a typical part of the costume, but she was determined to go unrecognized. Looking down, she smoothed the torso of the white costume dress with its gold trim. Filled with nerves she flexed her hand, suddenly wanting the sword, too.

But then Elena took her hand, opened her fingers, and interlaced hers. Feeling a little more secure, she squared her shoulders. Jess's heart slowed its rampant pace and she sighed. "All right."

Elena stepped up first to the door. Withdrawing the tickets from her bag, she showed them to the door man.

"Good evening, ma'am."

"Elena Tanner and guest," she said, lowering her mask and holding up her ID.

The door man, Brett if she remembered correctly, checked his reservations list and looked at her ID. "Eric?"

"He's out of town. This is Jess." She gestured and Jess lowered her gold mask part way and held up ID. The door man took it from Jess's fingers.

"This is an expired Georgia license," he said, handing it back to her. "You local?"

"Sorry. Last place I owned a car," Jess answered, taking back her ID. "I...yeah."

"She's with me," Elena said, not bothering to clarify that. Brett seemed to find that sufficient though and waved them through. Inside the Caliente, she took Jess once again by the hand.

Jess moved to Elena's other side as they approached the bar's doors. The action put Jess directly in front of her, so Elena kissed her.

A voice sounded a few feet away. "I do think they make a great couple."

Elena nudged Jess aside and looked at a pair of women who had apparently stepped out of the ladies restroom to the right of the bar entrance and spotted them. She looked closer as one adjusted a Harley Quinn mask. The other was dressed up as Ivy, complete with a scarlet red hair wig, but there was something familiar about the blue eyes and tilt of her head looking at them.

"Hi," she said and guessed, "Caitlyn?"

The Ivy mask didn't move but the other person lifted their hand and removed the Harley Quinn mask.

Elena exclaimed, "Cris!"

"Hello, Elena," Cris said.

Caitlyn lowered her Ivy mask, but she was silent, still studying Jess. Finally she asked, "You're definitely too thin to be Eric."

"Eric's working." Elena smiled. "This is Jess. You met her at our house party."

When Jess had lowered her mask, Caitlyn grinned. "Oh yes. Hello. Nice to see you again."

Jess took the hand offered. "Hello again." Elena couldn't read Jess's expression but her tone seemed cool. She couldn't determine why that might be before Cris spoke up again.

"You two have fun," Cris said to Jess. "Please tell Eric we missed him," she added to Elena.

"I will. You, too."

Caitlyn tucked her arm around Cris, mirroring Elena holding Jess. The two women headed into the dancing area.

"Shall we?" Elena asked, watching Jess adjust her mask.

Like any other night, Elena headed for the tables and couches along the wall. Absently, she asked, "Would you go to the bar and get us a couple drinks?"

Jess stopped moving. Elena sat down. Jess looked toward the bar then back at Elena. "Do you really need a drink?"

"You do," Elena suggested, reading the stiffness in Jess's shoulders.

Jess didn't relax and her gaze swiveled to the bar.

"Oh." She stood quickly, understanding Jess's reluctance. "You sit. I'll be back."

Jess took her spot on the couch and Elena crossed through the dance floor. Reaching the bar, she leaned on it. "Drinks?" she asked the gray-haired man rubbing a glass clean.

"Hello," he said.

"Gus, right?" Elena asked.

"Yep."

She removed her mask. "I'm Elena. We've met before."

"You're the woman seeing Jess."

"Yes." She looked at the assembly of alcohol on the shelves behind him. "Would you pour one of whatever Jess likes then make a Mai Tai for me?"

"She doesn't drink much."

"She's enjoyed a wine or two with me, but maybe something not alcoholic?" Elena added. "I want her to relax."

"She will. She likes you," he said.

"I like her a lot too," Elena confirmed. She pulled out her wallet and retrieved her credit card. "OK."

Gus took the card and nodded. "You wanna start a tab or close out?"

"Tab's good." She eased onto a stool and watched him work.

A few moments later, Gus slid across two glasses. She recognized the Mai Tai and the other was amber. He pointed. "Mai Tai and a non-alcoholic cider. I'll comp her as the DD. But you don't need to tell her that."

The consideration touched Elena; Gus seemed to already know how Jess would feel being singled out for favor. "I won't."

Stepping off the stool, Elena took the drinks and walked back toward the couches, this time moving on the side of the dance floor to avoid spilling.

A male voice called from the side. "Hey, Catra, wanna wrestle?"

She turned her head to see a pretty accurately dressed pirate. He wore a headband and black hair wig to complete his costume rather than any mask. With a square jaw, he was handsome enough, but she was only interested in kissing one jawline tonight and it didn't have stubble. She shook her head. "Dance card's full up," she replied.

"OK, but... if you change your mind..." He trailed off, leaning back; she walked away.

Last call at the bar had been an hour ago. Costumed swingers had been disappearing to the playrooms since just before midnight.

Jess and Elena had danced a conga line with a dozen other people to several songs then done a shimmy shake—Elena leading and Jess lagging as she tried to pick up the movement—while attempting a chorus kick line. After taking an entire hour to sip her cider, Jess finally had accepted a glass of white wine from Elena. Elena said she closed out their tab after getting the wine.

Energy flowing all around her, Jess could feel her own draining away as she tried to keep track of too many things. So she focused on Elena's ass rubbing into her belly and the heavy bass in the music rumbling through the floor and up her body. Wrapping her arms around Elena's chest she simulated fucking her from behind with several hip thrusts. She squeezed a breast through the costume and kissed Elena's throat between her words. "You're so fuckably hot."

Elena's hand slid to Jess's thigh, pushing up the short costume skirt. "Ready to take me to the playrooms?"

"As long as I can keep on my mask."

"Catra getting fucked by her princess will make quite a show." Elena turned in her arms and pressed full length to Jess's body as she lifted the skirt and squeezed Jess's ass cheeks, which were conveniently bare due to the thong Elena had gotten her to wear.

"Mm hmm," Jess murmured, kissing her.

The playrooms were busy, but after they left a few items in a locker, Elena quickly found them a spot in a room painted to look like a jungle.

She nodded to the couple on one of the two beds. "Mind if we join you?"

"We're not swapping at the moment," the man said when he lifted his head from giving his partner oral.

"No problem," Elena replied. "She-Ra and I just want the other bed." She nodded toward the further empty one.

He lifted a brow, then shrugged. The woman looked them over as she ran her hands lazily through her partner's hair. "Oh, I do enjoy watching a little kitty licking."

Jess moved toward the other mattress where there was a small bright blue wedge pad. Helping Elena out of the catsuit, she discarded her costume with it, piling both on the floor in the corner.

Wrapping her arms around Jess, Elena pulled them down on the mattress with hungry kisses and trapped her with arms and legs.

Jess balanced on one arm and stroked Elena from throat to

breasts with the other. Pushing down the cup of her tan lace bra, she latched onto a thick nipple with her teeth. Strong fingers clutched her hair and she grinned at Elena, making her laugh, before she switched to sucking at the breast. Nipping all around the areola, she rocked her hips so that her mound continually stimulated Elena.

Elena wrapped her legs around Jess's hips. Reaching down between their bodies, Jess pushed aside the crotch of Elena's lace underwear, and fingered her while they kissed. Their masks butted awkwardly and Elena laughed.

"You don't have to hide me from their eyes," Elena murmured. "So fuck me over that wedge like you mean it."

Jess grabbed the wedge and arranged Elena face down over it. Kissing down Elena's back to her upraised ass, Jess fondled each cheek and fingered her open pussy until her hand was sloppily wet. Elena wiggled her ass invitingly, filling the air with groans and pants.

When Jess noticed the other couple watching them, she slowed, deliberately showing off how open and wet Elena was. She nudged apart swollen labia, curled and twisted her fingers inside Elena, while listening closely to her lover's pleased moans.

When Elena reached behind her blindly seeking, Jess hugged her back and wrapped one arm around her chest, kissing her shoulder and neck. She continued to stoke Elena's passions until the orgasm rushed through Elena in uncoordinated shivers and she cried out, "Jess!"

Elena limply rolled onto her back, pushing the wedge out of the way. Jess kissed her and brushed the dark damp hair out of her eyes. Peripherally she saw the man and woman leaving. "You wanna go somewhere else?" she quietly asked Elena.

"Hmm?" Elena hummed into Jess's throat and stroked Jess's breasts, then she wrapped her arms around Jess's back. "No. We've now got this room to ourselves."

"I did enjoy making you orgasm with them watching." Jess nuzzled and lightly kissed full soft lips.

"Oh, mmm." Elena rubbed Jess's clit, making her squirm. "And I loved it. But, I do believe it is your turn." She licked and sucked lightly at the sensitive skin where Jess's shoulder and neck met.

Lower Elena dipped a finger inside her, no doubt finding how wet she had become.

"Here?" Jess asked, though the short thrusts of Elena's finger were beginning to short-circuit her thinking.

"You got off on fucking me publicly, so now it's my turn." Elena pushed her fingers inside Jess only to withdraw and lick them.

Jess smiled and laid back as Elena shifted on top.

Elena delighted in Jess's responsiveness to her touch. Chasing goosebumps around the pale skin with her fingers, she nuzzled Jess's cheek then her lips. When she returned her fingers to Jess's center, she drank in the increasingly heated and urgent moans.

Grabbing Jess's legs to pull her center to her mouth, out of the corner of her eye Elena saw people pausing in the doorway. She knew Jess would close her eyes once she had her in her mouth, so she dove in. Jess's hips gyrated, which brought her center more fully against Elena's tongue. "Fuck," Jess said and her fingers threshed through Elena's hair.

Eating until Jess reached orgasm, Elena enjoyed the shudders and groans of her name as Jess continued coming on her tongue.

"El, El, oh, fu—mmm, ungh!" Jess's back arched as she hit another peak. "Elena!"

She continued to lick. By rubbing her thumb against Jess's clit, she pushed her into and through another peak. She loved the sound of Jess's pleasure and it thrilled her to be the cause of it.

Lifting her face from Jess's folds, Elena turned her cheek into Jess's hands caressing her hair and face. "God, fuck," Jess gasped.

"Mm hmm," Elena said. "Jess." Catching movement in the doorway, she recognized Maya. A slender Black man stood behind her.

Whether anyone would recognize her and Jess in their costumes was a moot point now. Elena Tanner, club regular, had just made the Caliente's beautiful blonde bartender repeatedly come in her mouth.

She arched an eyebrow at Maya but the club co-owner said nothing and finally moved away. Turning away from the door, she saw Jess wearing a frown. "No," Elena insisted. "You're on your own time."

The orgasmic glaze was gone from Jess's eyes. Instead, her expression was worried. "Can we go now?"

Elena sighed but nodded. She helped Jess dress, but diverted them to Jess's room instead of her own car in the parking lot.

"You still have jelly legs," she teased, kissing her neck when Jess leaned on her. They walked out and Elena retrieved her bag from a locker before they walked down another hall and exited through an 'employees only' door.

CHAPTER ELEVEN

THE NEXT morning, awakening in Jess's arms on the single hotel bed, Elena sighed happily. Through the darkness she could just make out where they had tossed their costumes in a renewed desire to be naked and wrapped around one another.

"Hmm," Jess murmured, her breath warming Elena's head.

"Hmm," Elena replied, lifting her head and kissing the collarbone under her cheek.

"What time is it?"

"Too early," Elena replied. There was almost no light seeping in around the drawn window curtains. "It's still mostly dark out."

"We should get you back home," Jess replied.

"Not right now," she protested and rose over Jess, letting the sheets fall from her shoulders. Straddling wide hips, she palmed Jess's nipples. She slid one knee between Jess's thighs, pushing it against Jess's center, feeling the warmth and the soft hairs. Inhaling, she sighed when Jess lifted her knee, putting welcome pressure on Elena's core.

Slowly they rocked together. Jess's hands gripped Elena's hips and held their bodies flush. Elena fell into the rising pool of sensuality and she let her world focus down to just her and Jess.

Elena felt Jess's thigh getting slippery and warm with her own juices even as her knee was quickly coated in Jess's desire. Pushing each other, they gradually climbed to the peak of pleasure and fell over with exultant shouts.

Elena sat down on the bed, then suddenly moved aside. Jess noticed the wet spot from their sex. Leaning against the wall, she indulged in watching Elena tug a white towel closer around her breasts and tuck the corner so it would stay in place. Midnight dark damp hair curled around her face and throat. The only sound was the A/C fitfully cycling in the background.

She didn't want Elena to get dressed, but knew their time was rapidly coming to an end. Still only in her jeans, Jess went to the chair where she'd overlaid Elena's costume the night before and found it full of wrinkles. "Maybe I should've taken the time to hang it up."

"Don't blame yourself," Elena said.

"We only came back to sleep," Jess said.

"We did more than that. And it was after I gave you jelly legs," Elena reminded. "I'm rather proud of wearing you out," she added.

Jess continued to finger the wrinkled fabric, velour if she wasn't mistaken. It needed dry cleaning.

"Too bad we already showered. The wrinkles might come out if we hung it in there." Elena took the costume from Jess's hands.

"I'll get it dry cleaned." Jess held on tightly.

"It's a rental. They'll handle that." Elena took it from her hands.

"OK, but you can't walk through the club wearing a wrinkled costume."

"I didn't bring a change of clothes." Elena hugged Jess and her lips pressed to Jess's jawline.

Holding Elena in the circle of her arms, Jess knew she was right. Despite her desire to be unrecognized, she easily remembered seeing Maya's sour expression in the doorway to the playroom.

"You know Maya will say she saw me with you," Jess protested. "What abou—" she started. "Everyone knows you and Eric."

"Now they'll also know about me and *you*."

"But—You—We-" Jess stuttered until Elena put her hand over her lips.

"Yes, absolutely. This is a swingers club, Jess. *You*, my beautiful Princess of Etheria, were *my* date last night. I'm lucky no matter what anyone says."

"The whole reason we started meeting at your place was because I work here and you're a member guest."

Elena's brows drew together in what Jess read as frustration that was proven by her next words, tight and growling. "And I'll explain again that it was your night off."

Sitting down on her bed, Jess fretted. Elena hugged her to her naked chest. With her face nestled between warm breasts, she did feel her shoulders loosen. Lifting them, she wrapped her arms around Elena's waist, surrendering her worries to the other woman's assurance.

"So we're agreed. We are *good* together, Jess." Elena released her, bent down and kissed her, caressing her chin as she leveled their gazes.

"I–" Jess faltered. "I just..." She looked helplessly at Elena and her shoulders slumped. "OK, so what will you wear?"

"How about I borrow something?" Elena walked over to the chest of drawers that, in many hotel rooms, was practically for show and never used. In this space, however, the top and second drawers contained Jess's few clothes. After looking through the contents, Elena pulled out a blue cotton circle-neck T-shirt with an outdated Marino 13 Miami Dolphins picture. She tossed Jess a second Dolphins logo tee. Next she grabbed a pair of cotton gray drawstring shorts. The cut-off style shirt would have barely covered Jess's breasts, and it still showed a slice of Elena's midriff. Her ass, more ample than Jess's, was just barely covered by the shorts.

"You make my clothes look good," Jess said, pulling her T-shirt down over her head and tugging her long blonde hair free of the shirt collar.

Elena chuckled. "I feel sexier than I did in that catsuit last night."

"Not possible." Jess scoffed. "You were super hot."

"But this"—she pointed out their coordinated look—"makes it clear I'm with you." She grasped Jess's hand, twining their fingers. "Walk me out?"

Jess looked again at their shirts. It did make her feel like they were a pair, too. "Yeah?"

"Yes."

Parting briefly after that, Elena and Jess both walked around and collected Elena's other discarded items. Her clothing went into a plastic bag Jess grabbed from under the sink. The last thing Jess picked up was her room key off the TV stand, which she tucked into the front pocket of her jeans.

Finally she held out her elbow to Elena. Her palm settling against the curve of Jess's forearm sparked a warm feeling in her chest.

CHAPTER TWELVE

ON MONDAY, in preparation of doing errands and laundry, Jess asked Elena to call ahead. She would meet her at the street corner off hotel property. Maya had been giving Jess strange looks ever since the costume party. When she came by on Monday to collect the linens for the staff's once weekly laundry, she had said, "You getting up and up." Jess took that to mean Maya thought she was "uppity."

So she tried to stay out of the woman's way the rest of the week.

Jess's day off—what she'd come to call errand day—dawned rainy and promised to continue wet and miserable.

A knock sounded on the door. Jess had been quickly sorting her things, prepared to run to the corner and hide under the cover at the bus top until Elena arrived.

"Something you need, Gus?" She opened the door still speaking. "I gotta ge—Elena?" Her voice trailed off at the sight of the woman standing in her doorway. Wearing a long light overcoat and with an umbrella hooked over her arm, she also held out a pair of coffees in a carry box that read *Cafes Lindas*. "Elena?" she repeated, mystified.

"I thought you could use a dry escort today," Elena said. She held out the coffees. "And a warm up."

After looking up and down the corridor Jess quickly pulled Elena inside her room.

Elena sat down on Jess's bed next to the growing pile of laundry. Putting her coffee to her lips, she sipped then sighed. "This is crappy weather. I don't want to sit in a laundromat or the library," she said. "Let me take you back to the house?"

Finishing stuffing the clothes bag and tying it off, Jess looked at the clothes then Elena's earnest face. She exhaled. "OK."

Elena kissed her then grabbed Jess's coffee. Hefting her laundry bag over her shoulder, Jess followed her out of the hotel. Elena held the umbrella up to protect them both on the short walk to the car.

"Oh," Elena said as she put the key in the ignition but then stopped, "I need to call Eric."

"Oh? Is he home?" It was Tuesday, so it was odd that Eric wasn't working. "Is he sick?"

"No. He took time off. He's putting together some new photography equipment that came in."

Jess leaned on the car's window, looking out the front windshield. "So he's been able to get back to his photography?"

Elena nodded. "He's shooting for another fundraiser."

"I saw the signs and wondered." In the front office and in the bar, Jess had seen the signs advertising a new gallery event. She thought about the pictures that had first introduced her to Elena. "Has he decided what to shoot?" It warmed her to think that her encouragement that he get back to it might have played some small supporting role in his decision.

"He has some ideas."

Jess lifted her hand and placed it over Elena's on the phone. "I have some too. Let's surprise him."

Elena put her phone down. "Ooh." Jess blushed.

"I think I'll start with that," Eric said, pointing to the large faux leather pirate chest. "Move it over there," he continued, pointing to the harem mattress. "That will clear a lot of the corner traffic-wise. I can store the light boxes and tripod along the wall."

Said light boxes and tripod lay beside Jess where she and Eric had put them at the bottom of the basement stairs a few minutes earlier. Jess dusted her hands together and started toward the chest.

Eric's voice called her back. "What are you doing?"

She shrugged. "Helping you."

"You don't have to. I know you've got laundry to do."

"My last load is in the dryer. Elena said she needed to work on her business plan some more. If we both work on this, you can be done faster too." Jess lifted the chest with a soft grunt. "Then we can have some real *down* time."

Jess was pleased when Eric moved quickly toward her. But his words weren't sexual. "Wait, let me help you with that."

She shook her head at him, already walking, legs spread to more effectively center the weight. "You move the other stuff you need out of the way. I've got this. I'm stronger than I look, you know."

When she set the trunk down it made a bit heavier thunk than she'd planned. She covered her wince before turning around. Eric had his hands on his hips and stared at her.

"Oh, I know," he said, finally. His smile, coupled with the warm light in his blue eyes, made her quickly counter with her hands on her own hips. "What's next?"

"Really, I got this." He moved toward the next thing he planned to move. She followed him.

Already bending over, she said, "You don't have to do this by yourself. I don't mind helping."

He frowned. "Why so determined to help me?"

"Elena told me you were planning a new photo shoot. I wanted to help with your photographs." He had awakened after Jess's arrival about two hours ago and eaten a cream cheese and jelly bagel with a large black coffee before heading to the living room where several boxes had been partially unpacked. He had said hello to Elena and Jess sitting in the living room reading and occasionally talking.

Jess had sat and talked with him a little while he assembled the contents from the various boxes, but she had stayed out of his way as the assembly was something she knew nothing about.

"Oh. I think I'm beginning to see." His eyebrow lifted.

"You'll see a lot more if we finish this." She laughed.

"Got it. Let's get this done then." Eric gave her a side hug and she laughed again.

He really had already spent time planning exactly where each piece of equipment would be best placed because when they moved a backdrop canvas, Jess saw crossed bits of tape, forming an X, on the floor right where he said, "Put it down."

On another X they positioned a strobe light stand. In all, he had them move four reflectors and two light boxes, along with several backdrop canvases.

When he declared all the equipment positioned properly, Eric tugged Jess's hand and took her with him, flopping down onto the playroom's biggest mattress. Breathing just a bit heavily, she toppled next to him and landed with a giggle. She looked him over, taking in his dusty blonde hair and the soft features of his face.

A now familiar feeling of affection mingled with her satisfaction of having helped put the smile on his lips. His brow and cheeks glowed with a light sweat. After a moment meeting her gaze— a moment in which she thought maybe he would kiss her—Eric leaned away and stripped his sleeveless cotton t-shirt off over his head.

Lifting her head up onto a bent elbow, she reached out her free hand toward Eric's chest. She trailed her fingers lightly through his chest hair. Inhaling deeply, she became absorbed in listening to both their breathing, deep and full, replenishing a depleted energy that slid heat into her center. While tracing a line with her fingertip through a sweat trail down his shoulder, she studied him. Out of the corner of her eye she spied a large boxy air conditioner and chuckled lightly. "You have A/C down here."

He glanced over his shoulder toward the unused machinery then rolled back to face her, blocking the view of the air conditioner as he mirrored her pose. "Uh, yeah, but..." His blue eyes captured her and his fingertip trailed over her own sweaty cheek. "Sweat can give a sense of the action. Did you want to pose for me?"

"I do." Steadily, she returned his gaze.

"OK." He rolled closer and while his fingers traced a line of sweat on her skin, his gaze silently asked permission. She shivered pleasantly at the contact. When he tilted his head, she nodded permission to the silent request. Then he kissed her. When he pulled away, he asked, "How about we test out the new lighting arrangement?"

Jess looked around the space and stretched. "Sure."

His hand met hers on the bottom edge of her tank top, stopping her from immediately pulling it up and off. "Let's start with the tease," he said. "Take things slow."

She smiled and dropped her hands from her clothes. "OK."

"Good. Over on the chair first, I think. You decide the poses."

The chair was a wood frame mahogany ladder back stained black walnut; the seat was crisscrossed leather strips. While Eric went to get his DSLR camera, Jess looked down at herself, crossing her arms, and considering how to make her sweat-stained shirt and shorts appealing. She turned the chair around and sat down straddling the seat. Crossing her arms over the top of the back, she leaned forward. Her shoulder muscles appeared in vivid relief and her legs, what she often thought of as her best feature, looked sculpted where they partially wrapped around the chair legs. She remembered the photos where Elena spread her legs, showing off her glistening center. Though hidden partially by the chair back, if she pulled off her shorts it could make quite a tantalizing image.

Looking up at footsteps, Jess saw Eric pause. "Oh, I like that," he said. He handed her a gray card and told her to hold it up over her shoulder. Then he snapped the shutter a couple times. After examining the digital previews, he put the camera down on the floor. He walked to the light stand closest to the chair and adjusted the panel angles before retrieving the camera. Again, he snapped two pictures and checked the screen.

"Yeah, that's perfect," he said and took back the gray card. "Now, follow me with your eyes." He stood off and behind her left shoulder. She curved her head over her shoulder and smiled up at him. *Click. Click.* She turned her head to follow when he moved parallel to her shoulder. *Click. Click.* Finally, he stood in front of her.

Licking her lips, she tasted sweat droplets at the corners. The camera clicked and a light burst from the stand draped his shadow across her. "Damn. Gorgeous. Angel."

Jess heard the desire in his changed breathing and licked her lips again. Rolling her shoulders prompted Eric to click again. "Will you take photos of fucking me?" she asked.

He moved to her right side, shooting down now, across her chest toward the chair. "You sure?"

"I knew we could end up here when I offered."

"You want to be part of the collection?"

The idea of being on display at the club as sexy, wanton, nude, in pictures being fucked by Eric and Elena made Jess throb with lust. She recalled dancing with Elena at the club last week. Yes, fine. Maya had not been happy seeing her with Elena, but... Jess looked down to see her nipples had hardened, slightly peaking the fabric of her tank top. The conflict certainly was no longer affecting her body's reactions. "Can you hide my identity?"

"Mask. Blindfold. I can also just carefully frame and crop." The camera clicked. When he brushed his fingers through the back of her hair, she felt tingles all the way to her stomach. "Only you and I will know they're you."

She looked up at him. "And Elena."

"And Elena," he agreed. "You can preview and decide which ones I'll transfer to canvas."

She reached for the bottom of her tank top. He didn't stop her this time as she stretched and pulled it off over her head. While her face was obscured she heard the camera click several times. Desire flushed hotter through her body. She stood and pulled off her shorts. Eric's brow lifted over his blue eyes. "I want to try something."

He stepped back as she sat down in the same position as before.

"What do you think?" she asked, turning out her knee and lifting her foot up which drew his attention down.

"Tempting," Eric agreed. "You sure?"

"You help me feel pretty confident."

He chuckled and leaned forward, pressing his lips to hers softly. "I'm glad."

She watched him walk over to the chest. When he returned he handed her a gold mask, the one she'd used with her She-Ra costume. The entire outfit must be in the treasure chest. She thought Elena had rented them. Eric tugged a few of her long curls out and sifted them over the mask elastic so they draped in front of her shoulders.

He went back to shooting her, this time focusing on her breasts and shoulders. She flexed and brought the muscles in her arms and shoulders into sharper relief. Spreading her elbows lifted her breasts a little, too, the nipples pointed and hard.

As Eric moved around her, Jess watched his cock grow thicker inside his shorts. Her center was warm and getting wetter. She squirmed and glanced down a couple times to make sure she wasn't actually dripping onto the chair's leather seat.

He walked around her twice more clicking away. Jess decided she was done teasing and ready for Eric to be inside her. Lifting a hand from the chair back, she put it on his thigh. "Stop."

Immediately, Eric lowered the camera. She stood, flipped the chair around and sat back down on it. Grasping her thighs, she spread her legs and showed him her soaked center.

"Done?" he asked.

Remembering how he had told her he appreciated 'take-charge Jess,' she said bluntly, "One more shot like this then I need us to fuck."

When Eric got on his knees, Jess decided she liked that. She heard the mechanisms whirring and realized he had set a zoom. Her heartbeat thrummed harder in her ears.

"Here," he said and shifted forward to show her the digital preview. "Delete it?" he asked.

She looked at the shot. Her folds and center were darkly colored, flushed with arousal, and shined with wetness. "Keep it," she said.

"OK." Eric stood and put the camera aside on a small table. He stripped out of his sleeveless shirt. When he unzipped his cotton shorts, his cock spilled through the flap in his jockey shorts.

Jess stood from the chair and Eric lowered again to his knees when she dipped her head. He had been thrilled to see her take charge and was more than willing to do anything she wanted. Yes, he was hard. Yes, he was interested in burying balls-deep inside her. But there was also the fact that he had been snapping up close beautiful shots of her increasingly wet pussy.

He licked his lips as she stepped forward. Her legs were a little long for him to either sit flat, or rise to his knees and still easily eat her out.

He looked up. "Will you sit on my face, madam?"

Her green eyes glinted. "I think that can be arranged. On your back." She tried for a haughty toss of her hand and head, which only led to a bit of her hair tumbling forward over her shoulders.

It was far from intimidating, but it was definitely enticing. Laying back on the floor, he looked up at her dripping center. He inhaled her scent and licked his lips. Cock twitching, he felt precum dribble.

"Get protection from the box," he said.

His gaze followed her over to a small box by the treasure chest where he and Elena kept their safer sex supplies. She moved with confidence, but not swaggering, still largely unaware of her body's beauty, rounded hips, wide but delicate shoulders, trim legs with power enough to squeeze possessively around his hips... He snapped his attention away from the daydream to the very real woman as she walked back to him and placed her feet to either side of his shoulders, she showed him a condom, which he reached up and took from her fingers. Then she held up a dam. "Which would you prefer?"

"Dam," he replied, setting aside the condom, sure he'd need it before they were finished. Tearing open the foil-wrapped dam, he smirked. "Now, please come sit on my face."

She lowered slowly, those powerful legs holding her balanced. With eager fingers, he pushed the dam inside her and smoothed the edges of it over her labia. Each stroke of his fingertips through the thin latex made Jess squirm with pleasure. Satisfied with placement, he finally said, "OK."

She lowered all the way to her knees and adjusted, a hand tucked over her stomach to look down at him, until her center hovered inches above his mouth. When her green gaze found his looking past her tight abs, he smiled at her. She threaded her fingers in his hair and nodded. Grabbing her hips, he pulled her against his mouth and stimulated her clit with his mustache. When he thrust his tongue up inside her, she groaned and grasped his head harder, a silent *stay right there.*

The hard bud of her clit was easy to find and he sucked at it. Her groan turned to moans and she rocked over his shoulders until she reached orgasm. Protecting her head with his hand, he rolled her under him to the mattress. He tossed aside the used dam. Then, kissing down her chest, he hunched over his cock and rolled on the condom.

Jess spread her legs and welcomed his full-depth first thrust. He exhaled, trying to slow his urge for immediate release, but she was still having after-shocks from her orgasm and her inner muscles throbbed around him. Burying his face in her shoulder, he kissed the soft warm skin. He drew the sensations out for both of them, moving his hips as slowly as possible.

When she locked her ankles behind his ass, he dribbled, then spurt, and his cock continued to pulse. His orgasm wasn't overwhelming, but the release drained his muscles and left him exhausted. Jess rolled over atop him once again and wrapped her arms around his neck, sliding up until she held the back of his head in her hands. They kissed leisurely while he softened inside her.

Elena lowered her glasses from her nose when she heard Eric and Jess outside the door to the second bedroom where she was working. She looked at the time. They'd separated to different tasks about two hours ago with Jess offering to help Eric take his photography equipment to the playroom. Standing, she walked to the door and opened it to see Eric entering the master bedroom.

Jess was beside him. Both of them were nude. And Jess wore the She-Ra mask. He stepped back for Jess to enter first.

"All set up?" she asked before they disappeared.

Eric's blue eyes were light and his lips smiling, so was Jess. "I've also got some new pictures," he said.

The flush on both their bodies told Elena it had been quite a vigorous shoot. She grinned. "I bet you do."

"Yep," Jess said. She clutched her clothes in her hands in front of her crotch, but her shoulders were proudly back, lifting her breasts up.

Altogether, the signs said Jess had a great time. "I'm glad you had fun." She walked over and pressed up against Jess, brushing the bundle of clothes aside with her arm so she could feel firsthand Jess's wet center. "Will I get to see pictures?" she asked, pulling back and watching green eyes blaze anew when she slipped her finger inside.

"Jess wants me to get some of you together," Eric said.

She looked between them and now noticed Eric had his DSLR in one hand. It touched her that they intended she join them.

"Now?" Elena definitely had felt arousal start between her legs the moment she saw Eric and Jess naked, but the idea of getting to fuck Jess, or be fucked by her, so soon after Eric made her body heat even faster.

Jess kissed her and the intensity in that kiss told Elena that she was the one about to be ravished.

Jess held Elena in her lap as they sat together on the bed, Elena's back tucked into Jess's chest. With her arms wrapped around Elena's chest, Jess could caress Elena's thighs, breasts, belly and center with her fingers. Elena moaned and groaned, and writhed.

Eric stood in front of them, snapping pictures.

She traced soaked labia and circled before curling one finger inside. Elena arched into her hand squeezing a breast. She could happily finger Elena like this for hours.

But Elena demanded more. Two fingers became three, then Elena was begging for her mouth. "Suck me."

Jess rolled them both down across the Tanners' king size bed and kissed her way down between Elena's legs. Eric worked carefully with his framing and the angle and the mask helped, but he would probably have to do some blurring. Jess was just having too much fun licking and sucking on Elena's hot, wet folds.

Elena grasped the back of Jess's head and held her tightly in place while Jess fucked her with her tongue.

"All right, then," Eric murmured when he sensed Elena's orgasm approaching. He stepped back and decided to work on full body shots.

While seeing Jess's lighter coloring and Elena's darker coloring unfiltered was quite appealing, Eric decided he would push the colors and lighting in his darkroom app to get an even more dramatic contrast. Or maybe he'd go black and white... Classic.

Abruptly, Elena threw her head back. It was clear from the sounds that she was squirting and Jess eagerly lapped it up. A moment later, Jess slid up between Elena's quivering thighs and the two women kissed. Their sweaty bodies slipped breast to breast and belly to belly.

Eric got a wonderful angle on Jess holding herself above Elena, fingers and palm teasing a breast. He also zoomed to fill frames with the couple's tongue kisses, Elena's pointed and Jess's more rounded providing another delightful contrast.

CHAPTER THIRTEEN

AFTER THE photo shoot, Jess more happily spent each of her days off at the Tanner home. Eric wasn't always home. Flu season it seemed caught a lot of the pilots unaware and he was filling in last minute on a lot of flights. Today, after tossing her laundry bag in the trunk and kissing Eric in the passenger seat, Jess had hopped into the back. Elena and Jess dropped Eric at the airport for another last minute flight coverage. Then Jess moved to the front seat and agreed to accompany Elena to the grocery store.

With each bit of conversation—asking her which brand of yogurt or noodles she liked and tossing in the cart a bottle of Jess's preferred shampoo—Elena hoped she was making a connection for the younger woman that she did fit perfectly in their lives.

Taking them to a small sidewalk cafe for lunch, Elena enjoyed watching Jess devour her sandwich. Elena bit into a corner of her wrap and chewed slowly. She'd noticed before, and again now, that Jess tended to hunch over her food and eat quickly. Occasionally Jess jerked her head at a passerby, someone moving to another table, and got this mulish look on her face before that would vanish into a distressed expression.

She didn't talk to Elena, or even look up, until all that remained on her plate were crumbs.

"Some dessert?" Elena asked. Her wrap was mostly finished, but her bag of chips remained unopened.

"I—no, no, it's OK. I'm good." Jess patted her stomach. "I'm good."

Elena studied her lover for a long moment. "You sure?"

Jess visibly hesitated, looking away and then back at Elena. She asked, "You stopped here. Is there a dessert you like?"

"No, no. I just thought maybe—you..." Elena gathered her thoughts. "You ate really fast. I thought maybe it wasn't enough and you were still hungry?"

"Oh." Jess looked at her plate and then back at Elena. "I'm OK."

"If you're sure?"

"Yeah, I'm sure."

Elena nudged her bag of chips off her plate as nonchalantly as possible with the back of her hand when she went back to eating the remainder of her wrap. She followed a swallow of sandwich with a long sip from her soda. By the time she had put the cup back down, Jess had taken the bag and was eating the chips. Elena said nothing as she considered how to ask for what she wanted.

It being early in the week, making for a slow night at the club, Jess didn't have a shift at Caliente, so Elena hoped they could continue together for another night. She wanted to suggest a Netflix movie and hoped that it would become a romantic night in. Maybe they could use the edible body paints she'd gotten several years ago. Jess had also enjoyed the massage oils, so maybe offer that again?

She pictured Jess lounging in her underwear on the couch at home, flipping through Netflix. Elena wanted to prove to the younger woman that they worked, *this* worked. They could share every day and be happy.

Just as she stood to collect their trash, Jess's cell phone rang. The old style telephone sound caught Elena off guard. Used to being the one to call or text Jess, she realized she'd never heard the other woman's ringtone before. She also wondered who was calling. Waving Jess to sit back down, Elena collected all the trash herself so the call could be handled.

Headed back to the table, she saw Jess still sitting and holding the phone to her ear. She was obviously listening more than talking. Her expression seemed confused. Elena slowly moved forward.

"You want me to say that?" Jess shook her head. "I don't know that I can even get there."

"What's up?" Elena asked. She didn't sit down, torn about

whether or not she should put her hand on Jess's which she saw tightly squeezing a napkin. She was definitely worried about something.

"Gus–from the Caliente bar–he's going to the ER." Elena hadn't needed the refresher on the man's connection to Jess. She remembered the gruff man who'd closed the whole bar so Jess could spend the entire Thanksgiving weekend with the Tanners. He had also been amenable to working the bar alone so Jess could be Elena's guest at the club's costume party.

But Jess's words were worried. "He says he felt short of breath and feverish."

"Do you need to go into work for him?" She tried to keep her disappointment out of her voice.

Jess looked surprised and shook her head. "He wants me to go to the hospital, tell them I'm his daughter so they'll let me stay with him."

"Doesn't he have family?"

"No, his wife's been dead a while, and they had no kids."

"Oh." Elena exhaled. "Well, OK. I'll drive you to the hospital."

Jess didn't know what to expect at the ER, but asked for Gus at the check-in station. She only nodded when the nurse asked if she was family. As long as she didn't sign something she figured she was OK. She was let back. Giving her a light kiss, Elena promised that she'd wait outside.

"Jess," he said, his voice echoing underneath the oxygen mask. He waved her over to his gurney.

She grasped his hand. "Gus."

The older man looked drained and thin. Sweat beaded on his brow.

"You got here quick. They only just finished hooking me up."

"What's wrong?"

"It felt like flu, but I got some funny tightness in my chest like pneumonia. They've drawn some blood to see what's what."

"You need me to work the bar?"

"No. Hector and Maya said they'd find someone else."

Jess inhaled. That sounded very much like she would find a pink slip when she got back to the Caliente. "I should go in."

Gus shook his head which dislodged something and made him cough again. When he got his breath back, he said, "Maya angry with you for some reason?"

"I think I got involved where she thinks I don't belong."

"I thought you were with that lady and her husband?"

"Eric and Elena used to play with Maya and Hector. I don't think they do anymore."

"Oh. Spending all their time with you?"

"Yeah." Jess sat down in a chair and, still holding his hand. "I really like them, Gus. I might…" She hesitated, but then figured he was safe, and added, "I…uh, you know, might even love them."

"What have they said?"

"They're being so welcoming. Yeah, there's sex, but… Listen, she wanted me to do my laundry *at her house*. You saw…she went with me to the laundromat and we hung out, but finally, she…We also go shopping, her stuff, my stuff. It's all just time together. We were eating lunch at a sidewalk cafe when you called. We do have sex sometimes while the laundry's going. But we also just talk or read books sitting together on the couch. Eric's got a weird schedule, but he and I talk and snuggle even when there's no sex."

"So you caught feelings?"

Jess blushed. "I-I guess. You know I was Elena's date the other night at the club. It was fun, but it's like…it's different. Deeper." Gus chuckled, then coughed. Jess helped him shift and ease the pain in his chest but she blushed, too. "Not like that."

Gus turned his hand around and gripped hers instead. "It's all good."

"Yeah, I think it might be."

CHAPTER FOURTEEN

"HEY, GUYS." Jess was wiping down the bar at Caliente when Eric and Elena arrived. Elena wore a skintight red cocktail dress so short she called it her "cock-tease" dress because of how high it was cut. Only the slightest bend at the waist would reveal whatever she wore underneath. She was obviously looking to be fucked and fucked hard tonight.

Jess smiled at Eric as she pushed their drinks across the top of the bar and he put bills in her tip jar before handing over his credit card. "How's it going?" he asked. Elena walked off with her drink, settling onto a couch already occupied by a man and a woman. The trio started chatting and Elena set Eric's drink on the small table in front of the couch and waved over at another couple who lifted their glasses toward her. It was clear to Jess that Elena was planning the orgy she'd come for.

"Jess?" Eric prompted.

Turning away from watching Elena, Jess realized she hadn't answered Eric's question.

"It's light tonight. Gus should be out of the hospital by the time the big Friday and Saturday night crowds are here."

"Well, at least they realized they still need you."

She had told Elena, who obviously told Eric, that Hector had manned the bar himself instead of calling in Jess. One night had been apparently too much though, so they'd called her in "until Gus gets back." The tone Hector had used had been grudging and Jess was becoming more and more certain that a pink slip was in her near future.

"What happened?"

Jess remembered Eric had been out of town on his flights when she got the call and Elena took her to the hospital. It surprised her that Elena hadn't mentioned it.

"Pneumonia."

"I'm glad he's on the mend," Eric said.

She nodded; she'd been using Gus's car every day with his blessing to visit him in the hospital and then coming back to work the bar. Jess looked toward Elena when she heard her laugh even at this distance and in this music-filled space.

"There's probably no way you can take a break with us tonight," Eric said.

"No," Jess said. She turned to a man walking up to the bar. "Yes, sir?"

"What's on tap?" She told him. "Bud Lite," he said. She served the beer and passed him his drink, telling him the price. "Tab," he said, handing her a credit card before walking away.

Jess turned back from placing the card on the register to find Eric still standing there. He reached across the bar and brushed his fingers over her hand holding the rag, making her fingers tingle. "See you again soon?"

"Yes," she assured him, touched by his attention.

"All right."

Eric walked over to the couch where Elena had settled with a Black couple. He recognized them but their names escaped him. But he did recall enjoying a swap with them in the past.

"Hey." Elena looked up at him. "You remember Mike and Malia?"

"I do." He lifted his drink from the small table and extended his arm a bit in a toast before he sat down to the outside of Malia. "How're you doing?"

Malia nodded toward Elena. "Swapping stories," she said with a slight laugh. Eric nodded but said nothing, suddenly realizing he didn't feel in the right mood for the innuendo to be funny. He glanced back toward the bar to see Jess taking an order slip from a waitress. She laughed a bit with the redhead and the two chatted about something while she put the drink order together.

"Eric?"

Elena's voice drew him back. "Yes. Sure."

She stood. "Let's dance."

He put down his glass and held out his hand.

When they were on the dance floor, she asked, "What's got you distracted?"

He shrugged. "Jetlag maybe."

"You slept five hours when you got home today. Are you sure?" Her eyes scanned his face. She brushed her fingers over his cheek.

"I'm not sick," he said. "Just..." He trailed off, querying his body. It wasn't physical exhaustion. He glanced around again, seeing the crowd around them, and listened to the music. He liked the song, but... "It just feels..." It wasn't crowded; Jess had been right about that. But it felt.. or he felt... "Off."

"You're not in the mood?" Elena bit her lip.

He knew she was; that's why they'd come. But he had to be honest so he shook his head. "I don't want to stop you."

"I know you wouldn't," she said. "And I am still feeling horny, but..."

"I thought you were looking for a bang."

Elena's reply was slow. "I thought so, too."

That surprised him. "You changed your mind?"

She frowned and nodded.

"Is it Mike and Malia?"

"No. It's nice to see them, but..." Elena now turned her head and Eric watched her expression shift softer with an edge of yearning. He knew before he turned his own head where she was looking.

At the bar.

At Jess.

"She's working all night."

"I know. Her friend's in the hospital."

"So you said," Eric said. As the current song ended, he held her close. "Do you want to play or just wait for her?"

"It'll be hours."

"Sounds like you'd rather go home."

"Would you mind?" Elena asked.

"No."

They walked toward the door.

Walking through the main room, they turned toward the front door to leave.

"Elena! Eric!"

Elena turned on Eric's arm and saw Hector and Maya walking in from the play rooms. She glanced up to see Eric also had noticed the club owners.

The couple stopped a few feet away in front of them. They wore robes and it was clear they were both naked underneath. "Come with us to the Jacuzzi?" Hector asked.

"We were just leaving," Elena said.

"Did you get to the playrooms at all tonight?" Maya asked. "We didn't see you."

"Not tonight. Guess I'm tired from flying," Eric said. "We just danced, had a few drinks."

"The bartending not up to standards?" Hector asked. "The girl is filling in for our regular man."

"We heard he was in the hospital," Elena said.

"Yes, ambulance and everything, but it is just pneumonia. Man is old."

Elena felt slighted on behalf of Jess and Gus as Maya and Hector continued to leave their names unspoken. "*Jess* is doing fine." Eric's hand on her low back shifted. She swallowed and smiled tightly. "Good night."

"Come sit. Come to our suite," Maya said. "VIP guests tonight."

Hector added, "We got the Jacuzzi working again."

"It's a little cold," Eric said. Maya's eyes widened with clear surprise. "We're just going to call it a night."

Hector stepped back and cleared the path to the door. Elena bit her lip, but then shook herself and walked for the door. Her hand met Eric's on the cross bar and they both pushed their way outside.

"That..." She trailed off and shook herself again. "Let's just go home."

Jess turned the lock between the bar and the rest of the club, having sent the last customers out to the playrooms. She'd long since cleaned the machinery and sinks because the one remaining couple had nursed waters, clearly just sobering up before they headed home. She'd been able to watch all the comings and goings easily because of the light crowd. This last couple had danced and necked a little on the couches, and they'd gotten drinks from people obviously trying to entice them. But they'd never gone to the playrooms. She had seen Eric and Elena leave the dance floor and assumed they had headed to the playrooms to get Elena what she'd come for. After all, the Black couple they had been talking with followed only a moment later.

She put the last two glasses inside the dishwasher and then went to the register.

"Finished?"

She turned to see Hector in a loose shirt and shorts standing in the doorway to the kitchen. "Just about to count receipts," she said.

"Slow night."

"Yes," she said. She printed the sales report and began sorting the register contents, reconciling it to the sales.

Hector walked around behind her and she watched him go to the tips jar. He looked over his shoulder at her, shrugged, then moved off to lean against the bar and watch her. "You done."

"Not yet." She started the count of bills again in her hand, but this time aloud. Hector seemed anxious for the till.

"No, you're done."

"What?"

"When Gus comes back you go find another job."

"What?" She knew she was repeating herself, but nothing else was coming to mind. Even expecting this, she'd thought it wouldn't happen in the middle of the night.

"You know Elena and Eric Tanner?"

Jess nodded. "The couple are regulars."

"No. You see them. You are having sex with them."

No use denying it, she thought and nodded. "We've been seeing each other off and on."

"They left here without playing tonight. You know why."

"No, I–they did?" Jess frowned. "Why would they do that?"

"That's what I asked you."

"I have no idea."

"I know you pose for him. Have sex with them. Eric makes pictures of you with his wife."

Jess bit her lip. She hadn't had a chance to walk through the photo gallery yet. But she had seen the shots Eric had decided to use. She had agreed she wouldn't be recognizable.

Hector's eyes narrowed. *Guess not*, she realized. Again truthfully, she said, "Yes."

"Maya tells me you were at the costume party."

"As Elena's guest. I arranged the night off with Gus."

"I pay you, not him."

"But he sai–"

He interrupted her, slashing at the air with his hand. "You will not work here. When he gets back, you go."

Jess swallowed, refusing to let the tears burning at the back of her eyes come forth. "Yes, sir," she said quickly. She backed away from the till, the receipts not finished, and walked into the kitchen doorway. Once she was out of sight, she ran quickly to her room.

She found her phone where she'd left it on top of the drawer chest. She couldn't have taken any calls anyway while working alone behind the bar.

A message alert flashed on the screen when she picked it up. From Elena: *Went home. Hope to see you soon.*

Arms suddenly weak, she dropped her phone on the bedding where she'd half-crouched. Staring at herself in the bathroom's mirror she debated telling the Tanners about being fired. She shook her head and decided against it. Aside from the fact that it was the middle of the night, the couple couldn't help her anyway. Leaving the text unanswered, she set the phone down on the side table. Looking around the room, she sighed, stripped, then crawled under the covers. She swiped at the base of the lamp and plunged the room into darkness.

CHAPTER FIFTEEN

JESS DIDN'T have time to call in the morning before Elena called her. She wanted to see how her night went.

"I got fired," Jess said.

"What? Why?"

"Hector said I'm too close to you."

"God." Elena fell silent.

In the silence Jess heard a knock.

"I'm sorry," Jess said. "There's someone at my...the door. Gotta go."

"Jess, don-"

Jess set the phone aside then stood. "Coming." At the door she asked, "Who is it?"

"Gus." His voice was quiet.

She opened the door and looked up into his benign features. He lifted his shoulders and dropped them. She felt tears gathering. When he lifted his arms, she moved forward into his embrace. "Gus," she murmured. "You're back. I..." Her lower lip trembled.

"Hey, I'm gonna be fine."

"It's not fine. He-" She cut herself off with an inhale to keep back the tears. She rubbed her face. "Hector, he told me to get out when you came back."

Grasping her shoulders, Gus moved them both back inside

and shut the door to the hallway. "You tell me everything."

She sat on the bed; he sat in the chair. Haltingly Jess relayed what Hector had said to her.

"So he thinks I'm the reason they're not playing as much," she finished.

Gus reached out and cupped her hand between his. "Did you call them?"

"I was just on the phone with Elena."

"Call her back."

"I can't go over there with nothing."

"So where will you go?"

"Shelter, I guess. I've lived in 'em before."

"Where? Certainly not here. There aren't residential shelters 'cept for battered," he replied. "The homeless is first come, first serve. One night at a time."

Jess sighed.

"You say they're friends. Friends can do this. Call."

She reached for her phone and hit redial on her recent calls list. Putting it to her ear she waited for the line to open. "Ah, yeah, hey. Sorry. It was Gus at the door. I...I need a place to stay."

"Elena texted me what happened."

"What are you doing here?" Jess asked. Eric stood only a few feet away from the table at the back of the bar where she'd holed up. "I thought you were flying out today."

"I called in sick. Thought I should be here."

"You won't get in trouble?"

"I'm more worried about your trouble. I've got paid time off and sick leave and all sorts of options."

Jess's brow furrowed and she winced. "Options."

"Are you OK?"

"No. I don't know what I'm going to do." She hunched over.

He slid onto the booth seat next to her. "Hug?" he asked. She nodded and he put his arm around her back, brushing his lips against her temple. "I'm sorry."

"Nothing you did," Jess insisted.

"Elena sai-"

"I know. She reminded me we did nothing wrong; it was all off property or off the clock. But they do have the right to fire me for any reason."

He looked frustrated on her behalf. "It's not right."

"Maybe not, but I'll figure it out."

"Do you have...someplace?"

Jess could hear Eric treading carefully with his words. She exhaled. "Elena said I could stay with you."

He smiled then, but it wasn't triumphant, just kind. "I wasn't going to presume. We can probably help you find an apartment."

"Until I find another job, I can't pay for an apartment." She didn't want to lose her independence.

"OK, so it's just until you find a job."

"Yeah. I'll start looking tomorrow."

"Well." His attempt to restrain his smile failed. He grinned widely. "I'm sure Elena said it already but...*mi casa es su casa.*" While Elena's Spanish made Jess melt, Eric's accent was so terrible it made her laugh. She fell into a hug with him. Against her temple, he said, "Let's go get your things."

As she stood up, she glanced across the room to Gus standing at the bar. He looked at her and smiled. She tried to feel brighter, but it was hard.

Eric's arm around her shoulders moved up and down then he rubbed her back. "That Gus is a good guy," he said.

"Yeah, he is."

Eric hid his feelings about the situation from Jess, but Hector and Maya's actions had him livid. Jess had a tendency to feel that strong negative emotions of others were partially, or entirely, her fault. He'd seen her react to a grimace by retreating, and become tentative when something moved wrong during intimacy. He already knew that agreeing to move in, however temporarily, was straining her sense of self-reliance.

No, he thought, kissing her cheek as he took one last box from her hands to ferry to the car. His anger was aimed in a very specific direction.

Emerging from the employee wing, he saw movement out of the corner of his eye and squared his shoulders at the same time Hector's voice rang out. "Eric! What brings you by?"

Pleasure in the voice vanished from the man's fleshy face when Eric stopped mid-stride and turned to face the Caliente's owner. "Helping Jess move."

The man lifted his hands but then dropped them to his sides, a fruitless gesture. Then he tried another smile, obviously planning to try and placate him. "Did she tell you I found her till short?"

Jess had not said anything, but Eric wasn't inclined to believe Hector in any case. She had said that they gave a reason to fire her, but he knew what they said would've made them liable for wrongful termination. So they probably wrote down this till business to make it seem legit.

The woman was taking this firing as her fault because of Hector and Maya's petty jealousy. "You're a liar. She's not a thief," he replied. "You can't accuse her of something that isn't true."

Dropping the pretense, Hector said, "She was not good for business."

Eric put down the box. Hector took a step back. "She has filled in *every* time you've asked."

"You know this because she was with *you*," Hector replied. "You were good members, around a lot. Now, you come, you drink, maybe you dance a little, but you leave."

"Because we weren't in the mood to play."

"You and many others lately. I'm losing business. She only makes drinks. Others do more."

"Do more?" he asked sharply, feeling his eyes narrowing and his temper rising. "Like what?"

"New staff work to keep people coming back. They talk to them, keep them interested in playing here."

"So, what are you saying? You're getting more money because they what? Are they having sex with members in the rooms?" Eric recalled telling a guest that there were not "those" kinds of services here. For fuck's sake it was why he and Elena had decided it was better to have their time with Jess off-site. "You're firing her because she's playing with us, but you're getting a take when other employees play with members? You're a fucking hypocrite."

"Everyone consents," Hector said, sounding defensive. "Club members rent rooms, buy food and drink. We make money." He shrugged.

Eric didn't hide his disgust. "This used to be a classy place."

"If we don't move with the times, we die."

"And if I called the vice cops?"

Hector narrowed his eyes. "You will not."

"Maybe I should."

"I will say you lie."

"I can get the names of the girls who are sleeping with club members from Jess."

Hector's eyes went wide. *Stalemate,* he thought. Turning his back on Hector he picked up Jess's box. Over his shoulder he said, "I'll be back to cancel my membership and collect my unsold canvases." He wondered if he should check to see if Hector had been making the donations to the charity which he'd said the event supported.

Arriving at the Tanner home, Jess carried a large duffel bag inside, while Eric said he'd get the boxes. She found Elena in a back hallway by following the sound of thumps. Elena was just setting a picture on a tiny hanger newly applied to the wall. She looked away from the beach photograph and then took in the room itself. "What's this?"

"It's now your room. You can put your things in the closet there." Elena gestured to an open space framed with bi-fold doors. "This is your bed." Elena straightened from adjusting the mattress on a steel-framed futon about the width of a loveseat. The cover was beige and a stack of white sheets still in their store packaging lay atop a thin green blanket at the far end of the cushion.

"What was in here?"

Pointing at a filing cabinet and small table against the wall under the window, Elena said, "The household accounts."

Jess looked toward a box on the floor by the door with what looked to be some files and desk supplies. "And your business stuff."

Elena put her hands on her hips. "That's going into our bedroom."

Jess picked up the box and put it back on the desk. "I won't take up space. You should keep the things you need here."

"But..."

"Where do you want these?"

Jess turned to see Eric behind her, carrying her two small boxes.

Elena said, "Hang the clothes in the closet and put the other things on the floor in there."

"Guys," Jess tried to interject.

"You're not sleeping on the couch," Eric said. "One, I intend to still have movie nights, and two, the leather couch isn't nearly as comfortable as this," he added, nodding to the futon.

Chastened but also warmed by his care, Jess moved out of his way. Elena's hand clasped her shoulder while they both watched Eric remove Jess's work suits from one box and hang them up. He straightened after pushing the other boxes into the empty space under the clothes. "Thank you."

"You're welcome. Now, let's go make dinner."

Stepping toward the door, Jess looked up into his face and insisted, "I'm cooking."

Elena and Eric exchanged smiles then she grasped Jess's hand. "Lead the way."

CHAPTER SIXTEEN

IT SEEMED the Tanners were determined to make Jess feel, at least this first night, that it was little different from any other date night. Following dinner, Eric washed the dishes and Elena told Jess to pick a movie in the living room.

Emerging from the master bedroom, Elena wore a knee-length peach silk robe and she carried a dark blue silk robe which she handed to Jess. "Go undress for bed," she said, giving her a light kiss on the lips. She pressed Jess's hand against the warm skin at the gap in her own robe.

Jess took the cue to leave everything in the room, including any remaining inhibitions. When she returned to the living room wearing the robe, Eric was just sitting down on the couch. He wore a gold robe with white trim that looked to be a cotton blend instead of silk or satin. "My Rocky threads," he joked.

Elena patted the cushion between herself and Eric, encouraging Jess to sit down. When Jess had settled, Elena stretched out and lifted a red and green holiday tray from a side table filled with broken chocolate chunks. "It's almond bark," she said.

Eric then drew her attention to the TV table in front of him and lifted up shot glasses filled with something orange. "Orange liqueur," he said.

"A toast," Elena said, holding hers up. "To new beginnings."

"New beginnings." Jess sipped then hummed at the sweet smooth taste.

While she had enjoyed the movie nestled into Jess's shoulder as the romantic comedy played, Elena decided she liked this choice of after-party activity much more. She sat on the coffee table and dipped her fingers into the bowl of melted chocolate. In front of her, Jess's robe was open, revealing the breasts she had only glimpsed from the side during the movie.

Eric's palms moved up Jess's ribs, lifting Jess so she more comfortably straddled his legs. He then lifted the small pert breasts up. "What do you want?" he whispered in Jess's ear while meeting Elena's gaze.

"Your mouth," Jess replied. Her green eyes blazed with need as they grabbed Elena's.

"As you wish," she teased, quoting a line from the movie. Eric hummed and returned to kissing Jess's throat.

Elena swirled one chocolate-covered fingertip in a pattern around a taut nipple. Grasping Jess's waist with both hands, she left chocolate prints. She licked in circles moving closer and closer to the tip. Jess's deep breathing filled her ears and she licked until she had cleaned away the last of the chocolate. Then she latched and sucked languidly on a turgid peak.

When Jess tried to hold her head, Elena instead leaned back, drinking in the sweet sight of pale skin streaked with chocolate. Eric's hands still cupped her breasts. Jess's long lean legs were spread open across Eric's lap. Her husband's condom-covered cock slowly pushed up into Jess. Looking up from her husband's tight balls, she met his eyes across Jess's shoulder where he was kissing Jess's throat.

"I love you like this," Elena murmured.

Jess reached for her, pupils wide with arousal. Elena kissed her fingertips and leaned into the touches. "Love..." Jess breathed. Then she gasped and Elena felt Jess roll her hips and Eric wrapped his arms completely around her chest and hugged her. Jess's groans sounded deliciously raw and needy. "God..."

"We've got you," Elena encouraged. "Let go."

Eyes rolling back in her head, Jess closed them, a sign she was overcome by the intensity of their connection. Elena leaned forward and breathed in Jess's panting, warm breaths. Sealing their lips together, she tasted her. Jess's belly quivered under her palm, the stomach muscles rippling with her orgasm. Eric groaned against Jess's throat, a sign of his struggle to hold back.

Jess's orgasm, when it came, was a quietly powerful moment. Nuzzling into Jess's breasts, Elena languidly licked and sucked at her nipples and listened to Jess's heartbeat gradually slow.

CHAPTER SEVENTEEN

DESPITE THE bedroom she'd been given, Jess awoke the next morning, laying between Elena and Eric in their king-size bed. While the three of them had enjoyed sex on the couch after the movie, the move to the bedroom had been strictly for sleeping. There was room enough for all three to have comfortable space. During the night Elena had slipped an arm over Jess's waist and curled around her back. The intimacy was comforting. She turned her head a bit and buried her nose in soft, sweet-smelling dark locks.

A warm foot slid up her ankle and thick legs rubbed against her calves. Jess eased her head back around and whispered, "Morning, Eric."

Through the shadows she could just make out his blue eyes. She felt his fingers at her shoulder, then her hair lifted and warm breath preceded his lips pressed to her shoulder blade. "Morning."

The bed shifted so she started to move, realizing Eric was getting up.

His hand slid to her hip. "Stay in bed. I'll make breakfast."

"You sure?" Jess asked, grasping his hand.

"Let him do this for you." Elena's fingers slid over her hip and drew Jess's gaze back around to see blinking brown eyes.

"You just don't want to lose my warmth," she teased.

"Mmm," Elena replied. "True."

"All right," Jess agreed. She let go of Eric's hand and instead grasped Elena's on her stomach. The door to the bedroom opened and closed, then she felt Elena nuzzle into her hair. Closing her eyes, she dozed.

Jess scanned the want ads in the paper most of Saturday and Elena helped her create accounts on two online job boards. Eric disappeared into the playroom, shooing Jess out when she would have followed him. "I'll show you later," he promised, kissing her. "You get busy figuring out your next move."

Eric's tone was encouraging, not pushing. He wanted for her what she wanted for herself. When she encouraged Jess to talk about the want ads she found, Elena also only reflected Jess's thoughts back to her. Jess was left with simultaneously the weirdest and most amazing feelings. Someone—*two someones*—supported her. Gus was right; sex aside, Elena and Eric were her *friends. True friends.*

Glancing away from the paper, Jess took a moment to watch Elena working. Seated at the far end of the couch, she had her box of business papers at her feet and her laptop in front of her on a small folding TV table. She had tucked a pink highlighter behind one ear and held a pencil in her teeth while writing something in pen on a yellow legal pad. Every now and again she would set down the pad next to the laptop and scan between that and the screen while typing. It was a nerdy look and completely adorable, causing Jess's body to warm.

She glanced down at her own notepad filled with information about a dozen businesses to contact on Monday morning. Looking ahead to the start of the week, she had to admit she was filled with hope. Elena had agreed to drive her out to several bars, to see if there were any openings since that had been her most recent work. However, she had also gotten Jess thinking about office work and she had signed up with a temporary staffing agency. Though Jess had no idea how she would measure up—high school typing class felt like ages ago—the agency had online assessments and Elena said Jess could use her laptop to complete them when she was ready.

Her stomach rumbled and Jess looked down sheepishly. Elena said, "Maybe it's time for a lunch break." Elena's eyes crinkled at the corners and her lips held a bemused smile. "Soup and sandwiches?" she suggested.

WE FIT | 107

"I'll get Eric," Jess said. Both of them set aside their things and rose from the couch.

The trio sat at the dining table eating the lunch Elena had prepared. Eric smiled around his own bite as he watched Jess finish off the soup lifting the cup to her lips. He'd noticed the enthusiasm Jess had with most meals. She thanked him and Elena often for the simple meals they prepared and insisted on making things for them as well, like breakfast the other day. As much as she appreciated food, she had a relatively lean figure. Her curves were a little fuller than Elena's but she was also more muscular. She did seem to have excess energy to burn, so perhaps her metabolism was simply higher than average.

"What have you been doing down there?" Elena's question drew Eric's gaze from watching Jess finish the second half of her sandwich. He smiled when he saw his wife had spoken from behind her glass of iced tea.

Leaning forward over his sandwich, he took a bite before setting it down. Chewing gave him a minute to phrase what he wanted to say. After he had swallowed, he answered, "I'm arranging a gallery to sell my photos."

Elena's brown eyes widened a little with clear surprise. "How many did you talk to?"

Eric shook his head. Her confusion, though, was to be expected. For her own business development, Elena was calling physical agencies around the greater Miami area. He was less likely to sell his photos that way. "Not physical galleries, an online one," he clarified. "There aren't many places in Miami that showcase nude or explicit photography because of zoning." He sipped his iced tea. "Anyway, more business is done online with this kind of art."

Jess asked, "How does it work?"

"I set up a seller's page, wrote a bio, and uploaded thumbnails as well as the high quality images behind a paywall. The host provides all the sales scripts, securely processes payments, and arranges delivery. The images will be printed and shipped to them, or they can download digital files for a price I set."

"How do you get paid?" Elena asked. "What about taxes? Shipping charges?"

"The storefront handles all that, processes the product orders, and charges the buyer for shipping. I set up an online wallet to handle the rest, protecting our bank account information."

"That simple, huh?" Jess asked. She lifted her soup cup and sipped.

"Yeah. You wanna see?" He looked between the two women. "It can be pulled up on a smartphone."

"You're not using any of the pictures with our faces, are you?" Elena asked; she'd already taken out her cellphone.

"Nope. Though I have a few with the backs of your heads. Just like we showed at Caliente." He gave Elena the website address.

Jess brought up the page on her phone. "You really think you can make money selling these online?" she asked, moving her fingers on the screen that suggested she was zooming in on an image.

"Maybe not a lot, but it is just my hobby. And right now for charity." He stood. "I do have to have model releases included on my account, but they've got those too in PDF. I'll print them on the office printer and we can all sign them."

"You're uploading some photos with you, too?" Jess asked.

"Yep. Check the smaller digital prints gallery," he said, directing them to a list menu on the left side of the screen. "I uploaded a few stills from our videos. They're still high quality, but they're smaller, so they'll be downloads or available only to print on smaller items, not as art canvases." Elena looked up. "But I'm not selling the videos," Eric assured. "I want this to be about the *art*."

"But someone soon could have an original Eric Tanner photograph hanging in their bedroom."

"Yeah," he said, an amazed sigh finishing the word. "It's kind of wild to think that."

"Will they tell you when something is sold?"

"I'll get alerts for all physical product sales and a monthly report summarizing digital downloads. Also there's an annual report sent out each January for tax filing."

Jess looked up from her phone. "Some of the other sellers have drawings."

"There's some completely digital art, yeah. Others use filters on their photographs to create 'chalk' or 'cartoon' versions. I'm playing around with it."

"Oh, it says how often the various pictures have been downloaded," Elena said. "There's a 15 under this one. And a two under another one."

Eric leaned toward her and she turned her phone to show him the screen. "They did say there were algorithms that would make the most popular downloads appear in ads."

"So they track all that," Elena concluded. "How did you arrive at these prices? I thought you were auctioning them for more through the club?"

"I was, but I had to cover purchasing canvases and ink for the printer. This is just about paying for my time and some equipment wear. I'm also trying to be competitive. I looked at some of the other photography art pages to see what they charge."

"Are any of these ones you already sold through the club?"

He shook his head. "I put those in digital downloads only. The canvases will continue to be unique purchases which will help them maintain, or even increase, in value for the buyer."

"Like real art," Jess said.

"Yeah."

Jess got to her feet and came around the table to stand next to Eric. When he looked up at her, she bent and kissed him. "I'm impressed."

"You're the subject in a lot of these. It's more likely the beauty of my models attracts the buyers."

Jess looked at Elena. "I can agree with that. This all got started because of my attraction to your model."

Elena laughed. "You've gotten horny just viewing our photos."

"How can you tell?" Jess asked, arching her eyebrow.

Elena gripped the swing's velvet ropes, adjusted her legs in the loops, and settled back to enjoy her lover's attention as Jess's hands settled on her ankles. Face obscured by a golden mask, Jess had stripped to her boy shorts. The sight of Jess's uncovered breasts, nipples peaking, caused Elena to lick her lips in anticipation.

Inhaling and exhaling slowly prolonged the sensations of Jess's hands moving up her calves, then knees, and finally nudging open her thighs. Bright green eyes held her in thrall, leaving her unable to look down and anticipate where Jess would touch next. She quivered at each touch, to the sides of her breasts, the stroke of a nipple, a tickle along her ribs. Then Jess took a firm grip of each ankle. The soft command, "legs around my hips," sent a thrill through Elena as she complied, crossing her ankles over Jess's back. The move opened her knees and pulled Jess forward.

She could only move as much as the swing allowed, but her hips canted upward, and she felt her soaked center parting. Jess's fingers softly stroked her swelling and heated flesh. Slowly one finger slid inside, adjusting the dam inserted in her pussy. Closing her eyes, absorbed in the deep pleasuring caress, Elena moaned, "Fuck me."

Jess's one finger became several and she used both hands to stroke her intimately. Fingers moved from Elena's center to her lips and her pussy parted over Jess's belly. Then she was tickled by the light hairs that covered the other woman's sex. Licking her own flavor from Jess's fingers, Elena rocked into Jess's mound, rubbing their centers together. A gradual delirium stole over her senses listening to Jess's hitched breathing and soft moans formed around Elena's name. Her own breathing was steady, but her pussy clenched repeatedly, rubbing her essence against Jess's belly before it dripped down her own ass.

One of Jess's hands stole around Elena's back and lifted her in the swing. Breasts pillowed against one another, she and Jess kissed languidly. Jess eased her other hand between their bodies and curled several fingers inside Elena.

After a moment, Jess murmured against Elena's lips, "That's three. You're soaked. Ready for four?"

"The dam won't do." She felt Jess remove it, tossing it aside to a bin. "Lube?" Elena asked.

"Right here. Gloves too," Eric said.

"It's been a couple weeks. We know we're all clean." She opened her eyes to see her husband holding out the lube bottle. "I think we can forgo the gloves."

Eric and Jess exchanged smiles. Jess lifted her hand to Eric and directed, "Just lube then."

Once her fist was covered, Jess resumed kissing Elena. She was distracted by the sensation of Jess's touch, without the latex between them, and enjoyed Jess's teasing, playful nips at her lips. Jess whispered, "You're so soft with four, I'm tucking in my thumb now." Delicious anticipation flooded Elena's belly.

Without reservation, Elena kissed Jess and consented, "Yes. Fist me."

It was hardly a stretch at all. The bridge of Jess's hand rotated and slipped inside her. She'd known that Jess's hands would be smaller than Eric, who had never managed to fist her fully, but the actuality of it, the ease of it, gave her such joy. Her inner muscles throbbed around the slowly rotating fist.

"Hey," Jess's lips brushed her eyes and cheeks. When her gaze returned to Elena's and they resumed kissing, Elena tasted the slight saltiness of her own tears. "How are you doing?"

Worried Jess might take the tears wrong, Elena assured, "I'm OK. This feels *so* good-God, *so* amazing. I love it." She lifted her head and pressed her lips to Jess's before continuing, "I love *you*."

Jess's eyes shifted from flecked hazel to a warm green. She nodded and kissed the corners of Elena's lips. Then, pressing their cheeks together, Jess began moving her fist in strokes. She whispered in Elena's ear, "Love you, too."

The throbbing intensified with each rotation of Jess's wrist. Elena got so wet that she smiled when she heard the slurp and suck sounds made around her lover's fist. She couldn't recall the last time she'd gotten this wet and the thought made her arousal shoot to another level. Throwing her head back, she groaned as her pussy squeezed Jess's hand. Jess moaned and her kisses moved slowly down from Elena's face.

Both her breasts were given lavish attention even as Jess's fist continued shifting inside her. From the tightness of her nipples and the way Jess chewed the peaks before sucking in the mass, Elena relished the idea she would have several hickeys come morning.

Jess shifted between her legs and lifted one over her shoulder, opening her even more. Her fist seemed to slip deeper. The changed angle shifted the pressure and Elena felt herself starting on the journey toward her orgasm. Inside it became so tight, it felt like her pussy conformed to the exact shape of Jess's hand. Her knuckles, fingers, the heel of her palm... She felt like she could distinguish it all. The tiniest twist made Elena groan.

"Oh, God, more...fuck, Jess, mmm..." The throbbing started rising from her pussy to her belly. "Oh, damn, I'm gon-na...ungh, God..."

"Damn, Elena," Jess murmured, her lips pressed to the inside curve of Elena's hip. "You're so tight. Fuck."

Jess adjusted her thumb. The twitch threw Elena over into orgasm. Every muscle tightened for an endless second. The release triggered her squirting. Jess pulled her hand free as soon as the muscles released which set off a cascade of tremors in Elena's pussy. "God, ungh, uh..." she panted.

Lips and tongue pressed between her legs, lapping and sucking, bringing forth more tiny tremors. "God, you taste *so* good."

Hearing Jess's delighted laughs Elena threw her arms across her eyes. It was only then, in the background of the fading roar of her racing heart, that Elena heard the faint clicks from Eric's camera. She looked forward to seeing the pictures for herself. "I get you next," she said to Jess.

"You've got me." Jess's breath wafted across Elena's still quivering clit.

She sighed with pleasure at the small after-shocks rolling through her belly. Jess rose and softly kissed her while caressing her temple and hair.

CHAPTER EIGHTEEN

AT THE airport, in one of the public booths, Eric made a phone call he'd been thinking about for more than a week. Jess had been denied unemployment, the office telling her the business hadn't paid into the unemployment fund. If they weren't going to act like a legitimate business, he was going to make sure they were closed. An anonymous tip to the Crime Line about pimping going on at Caliente adult club and he hung up. Grabbing his flight bag, he hurried to his plane.

"Hey," Val greeted him.

"Hey," he replied.

She took his flight bag as she usually did, to stow it with the other bags belonging to the flight crew then paused. "You upset about something?"

"No," he said. Carlos stepped into the plane behind him. "Carlos, go start the checks."

If the co-pilot was surprised at the lack of greeting, he didn't show it. "Aye, Cap," he replied easily and moved away into the cockpit.

"Eric?" Val asked.

"Yeah."

"Yeah? You want to talk when we get to New York?"

He frowned thinking instead that he wanted to call Elena or Jess. "Nothing's wrong. See you for the lunch break."

"All right."

He stepped back into the terminal, finding three bars, and texted an emoji heart, first to Elena then Jess.

Elena looked up from her phone to see Jess looking up from hers. They'd both received text beeps a moment apart. "Eric?" she asked as she looked at the heart.

"I wonder what that's about."

They were in the car driving to Jess's first interview of the day. Elena had confessed she wanted to drive Jess to each of her job interviews because she wanted to be the first to congratulate her when she found her new job.

Though, because she thought it would make Jess more anxious, she didn't share that it felt important to be there in the same way she was beside Eric for all his company parties or sharing a celebratory meal about a promotion or raise.

When it came to Jess though, Elena knew the only gain she got out of Jess finding work was she would stick around Miami. The intangibles were more enticing though. She got to see the woman's smile as she entered a business and the way each report of positive interaction lifted Jess's shoulders when she got back to the car. Just as Elena had predicted, the collared green cotton button-up and black slacks with the flat pumps complemented her figure. The office-friendly attire gave her a relaxed, professional look where her black suit and white shirt suggested "wait staff."

Elena felt she was present at the beginning of something and wanted to see it through. At the same time though, she disliked the way Jess's shoulders sagged when each message popped up on her phone indicating the "position for which you applied" had gone to someone else. She felt Jess could find good work at something other than tending bar, but the greater Miami area didn't seem to want to provide it.

After Jess's interview, Elena returned them to the house for lunch. Jess changed into shorts and a t-shirt because she said she didn't want her "fancy clothes" to get stained.

"What about a service desk?" Elena suggested. "You dealt with the public at Caliente."

"Where?"

"Anywhere." Elena pushed her laptop toward Jess.

Jess input the words on the job search site. "Fingers crossed." Her phone dinged, the noise signaling a text message. She lifted it and read, "Appointment confirmed for eleven tomorrow at Admin Temps."

Elena leaned across the small space between them and kissed Jess's cheek. "Congratulations."

"I don't have a job yet."

"I have faith in you."

Cheeks turning pink, Jess said, "Thanks."

The dress Jess wore was borrowed from Elena's closet. Dark blue, it hugged her figure and stopped just above her knee. Sleeveless, it had a jacket which didn't quite fit, so Jess had that folded over her forearm in her lap. A way to present that she could look more formal if the employer didn't consider bare arms appropriate for the workplace. Though, Elena had assured her, this was Miami. The perpetually hot spot had created a different style for business because of its consistently tropical weather.

Jess stepped out of the car onto the curb, adjusting her stance in her heels.

Elena leaned over the passenger seat. "I'll meet you at Vice City Bean."

Nodding, Jess recalled seeing the sign a couple blocks back down the street. She flashed Elena a thumbs up.

"Good luck." Elena blew her a kiss.

"Thanks." Keeping her hands together under the suit jacket, she entered the office building and headed for the elevator bank where she checked the directory sign and mouthed, "Floor four."

"Looking for office work?" A redhead whose look clearly came from a bottle stood nearby in a sharply tailored red skirt suit. Jacket on, Jess noticed.

"I-yes, I am." As she replied, she tucked an errant lock of hair back behind her ear.

"Bit of advice then. Lift your chin and don't play with your hair."

Jess pinched her lips together, lowered her hand, and turned away to face the bank of elevators, hearing a ding. *Right.* She sighed and entered the opening elevator, pushing the button for the fourth floor. She exhaled as she heard the echo of clicking heels and saw the back of the woman disappearing around a corner. Her confidence was now completely shot to hell.

Entering office suite 402, she looked around. A lone clipboard rested on the horseshoe desk dominating the center of the space. Several people sat in padded chairs along the walls. The woman behind the desk looked up as the door clicked closed. "Sign in, please."

"I have an eleven o'clock appointment," Jess said, determined to sound confident and positive. This place felt less inviting than the free clinic she had visited with Elena. She clenched her left hand into a fist at her side, then reached out with her right and signed the next open line on the clipboard.

Two hours later, Jess stepped out of the Admin Temps office and rode the elevator back down to the lobby. Frustration and anxiety weighed down her shoulders. She hadn't been able to get a read on the recruiter. The questions all sounded canned and she had no idea where her experience, or lack of it, ranked her in their general candidate pool.

Walking down the street, she stepped aside from the many people rushing past her in the opposite direction. Continually she looked up to check street signs and how close she was to the coffee shop where Elena had promised to wait.

Jess dwelled on the frown she'd received when she answered no to the question, "Do you speak Spanish?" Probably not a good thing in a place like Miami where half the population spoke it as their primary language.

Entering Vice City Bean, she walked over to the table where Elena had settled. The woman had her laptop out and was rapidly typing away. *That would be her good news first*, Jess decided. "I tested at 52 wpm for typing," she said.

Elena looked up and the smile Jess received soothed her roughed up self-esteem. "Hey," she said. "So, you're done? How'd it go?" She pulled back the chair to her immediate right and patted the wood seat.

After putting the suit jacket over the back of her chair and laying her purse on the table, Jess sank onto the chair. Elena passed her coffee. Cupping her fingers around the paper cup's heat guard, Jess inhaled the aromatic steam. "Thanks. They had all these assessments. Basically they redid all the tests I took online."

Brown eyes flashed with disbelief. "What was the point of the online tests then?"

While taking a sip from Elena's coffee, Jess shrugged. After a moment she exhaled and said, "I have no idea."

CHAPTER NINETEEN

THIS WAS crazy. It was *February*, yet Jess reclined on a lounger beside the pool in the backyard of the Tanner home. Eyes hidden behind big sunglasses, wet blonde hair braided and resting across her shoulder, she was half asleep soaking up the 80-degree sunny day. Occasionally she peeked at Elena and Eric splashing and making out in the waist deep water by the pool's steps. She exhaled with a feeling she might just call contentment.

In the week since losing her job at the Caliente and moving in with her lovers, Jess had struggled with feelings of worthlessness. She was repeatedly told how happy they were to have her here. They raved over meals she insisted on making to earn her keep. Elena had driven her around to several interviews, but so far she had received mostly "we'll call you" responses to many job applications.

Unfortunately, the "will calls" became "we're going with someone else. Thank you for your time." Thinking back over each interview, Jess became more certain that they balked at her last employer being an adult club, no matter she was only a bartender. Or they had decided not to risk it because of her record. She did still have the application at Admin Temps. She had tested well for the temporary agency. Crossing her fingers, she hoped a job offer might come by Monday or Tuesday next week.

Eric's work for Diligent Air continued with a semi-regular schedule of four days on and three days off, though they frequently changed his first and last flight times, so he was not truly on a consistent schedule. He had returned from his latest circuit before dawn that morning. Elena currently worked from home, still angling to get her adult vacation travel business off the ground.

"I think Jess's become sun-addled, Eric."

She opened her eyes at the closeness of the voice and saw Elena looking down at her with her hands on her hips, eyelashes sparkling with droplets of water around her brown eyes. "Maybe it's time we take her back inside." She winked when Jess's eyes met hers. The invitation was clear.

Jess smiled. They didn't have sex *all* the time. But the couple was adventurous and spontaneous. The things they encouraged her to do felt good—even great. More important though, they made her feel good about herself.

Eric had once explained that he and Elena had both gone into the travel industry to see and experience as many new things as possible. Jess began to see her own nomadic life to this point as a positive rather than a negative. She was who she was because of what she had seen and experienced, and the Tanners appreciated that about her. Maybe, as she had told Gus, this was what love was supposed to feel like. She was definitely starting to think there wasn't any other word to describe the way she felt about both of them. She'd even spoken the words a few times and they no longer felt so awkward. The couple made her feel welcomed and accepted exactly as she was. It was an incredible feeling. Incredibly tempting.

Standing over her now, Elena and Eric were not naked and Jess felt a desire to remedy that. Eric did look amazing in a navy blue Speedo clearly showing off the outline of his cock. Elena's bikini was three tiny white triangles strategically held together by thin strings. Water from the pool still beaded on their bodies and sparkled in the sun.

She licked her lips and struggled with the desire to kiss the water off every exposed (and not so exposed) patch of skin. Her fingers flexed and her center became heated and wet. Closing her eyes a moment, she shifted her thighs together to ease her rising arousal with a little pressure.

Eric chuckled, obviously aware of the move. Jess's belly muscles tightened pleasantly at the sound. A cap clicked, then she felt Eric's cool, lotion-covered hands sliding up her feet, calves, and thighs.

The touch was relaxing. She continued to feel just a little crazed though, with her nerves sparking under the attention of his big and gentle hands.

"Definitely time to come inside. You're going to burn." Jess looked down to see Eric's fingers on the side tie of her bikini bottoms. "You're already quite hot."

Before Eric stepped back, he brushed his palm across Jess's center. It could have been an absent stroke, but his gaze held a smirk when Jess's hips jumped and tried to follow. She couldn't stifle her groan. "Damn."

Taking Eric's extended hand, Jess stood and enjoyed a brief hug against his chest. Elena led them downstairs to the playroom. When Eric flipped on the wall switch, Jess considered the many options, knowing they would ask her. A traveling trunk decorated as a pirate's treasure chest had been filled with roleplay costumes. The sex swing she'd used several times hung from four points in the ceiling. Multi-colored pillows, cushions, and sheets of satin, cotton, and silk, covered in cotton blankets made several other love nests on the floor.

Soft fingers lightly tangled with her own. She turned to look into brown eyes. "We'd like to both take you," Elena said. "What would you like?"

"Bump and grind," Jess replied. Eric kissed her.

Going to a boom box, Elena started some music. The beat was a slow building one without vocals. Jess felt her heart gradually shift its beat and thump in the same rhythm.

"Anything else?" Eric moved behind Jess and wrapped his arms around her torso, pressing his chest against her back. His damp skin was a cool counterpoint to her heated body and she sighed into the contact. While he untied her bikini top, Elena lowered to her knees, making Jess's belly quiver with her kisses while untying and removing her bikini bottom.

"I don't want to come too soon," she requested before she couldn't think clearly at all.

Sensuously Eric's hands palmed and pulled on Jess's nipples. Both he and Elena let the music's beat govern the pace of their touches on her skin.

Jess lifted one arm up and curled it back around Eric's neck. As his mouth lowered to meet hers, she dropped her other hand onto Elena's head, sifting through the dark brown locks as the woman pressed apart Jess's thighs. The woman tongued through her labia and hummed. The sound of her delight and the wetness pooled in her center pulled moans from Jess's throat.

Elena rolled onto her back, licked her lips, and enjoyed the lingering taste of Jess's essence. She hummed her pleasure as Eric's fingers slid strong and warm into her soaked center. Jess might not have wanted penetration, but Elena had demanded it. Sitting up next to her on the pile of pillows and blankets, Jess reclined. She'd been eating out Jess only a few moments ago.

Lazily, she combed through long golden locks while she and Jess tenderly kissed. When she shifted to sparring with her tongue, Jess laughed and dueled with her. Elena groaned. Pleasure rippled through her as Eric's thrusting fingers pushed her closer and closer to her peak. Still focused on green eyes, she felt Jess's fingers join Eric's playing around her folds.

"My turn," Jess said. After a parting kiss, her lips moved away from Elena's and trailed warm open-mouth kisses down her chest.

Elena arched into the lips pulling at her nipples and teeth abrading on the swells of her breasts, then Jess's tongue dipped into her belly button. She writhed into each sensation, head rolling back and then forward so she could watch Jess's face. Jess's expression radiated such bliss that Elena cried out with joy of her own. "Jess!"

Testing Elena's wetness, Eric and Jess slipped their fingers in and out, one-two, wide-thin, and her heart pounded hard to the unusual rhythm. Her arousal rose like a car on a roller coaster's hill, teasing her with the promise of the sudden rush of orgasm to come. Finally Jess moved between her legs and arranged them over her shoulders. Jess sucked her essence from Eric's fingers while Eric's bright blue gaze met hers and he blew her a kiss.

"Now put those in me," Jess told him. Eric's pupils had gone wide, proving he was extremely turned on. It thrilled Elena to know that Jess wanted more.

Eric and Jess kissed, their tongues slipping over and under each other. When he leaned back, Elena couldn't see what her husband was doing to Jess, but the way Jess's expressions shifted, eyes rolling slightly in her head, she definitely approved of his technique. Cupping Jess's head between her palms, she drew the green eyes back to look at her.

"Hey," Jess said. Her pupils, like Eric's, were wide from her arousal.

Jess dipped her head and a moment later Elena felt Jess's

breath then tongue slide across her clit. Already hypersensitive, she jumped. It wouldn't be long before she reached orgasm.

"Oh, not yet," Jess said and shifted her attention to Elena's opening, sucking now on each fold, lingering, before slipping her tongue inside. Her desire, which had begun to boil, shifted to a simmer.

"You're going to make me wait?" Elena asked, slightly breathless, grasping Jess's head, threading her fingers through soft locks. *God, she was so ready for this.*

"You've taught me patience is *so* much better." Jess kissed just to the side of Elena's clit and then, just when Elena started quivering, her hips were held down and a thumb brushed across the ridge of nerves.

"Fuck!" Elena felt a jolt in her groin that traveled to her chest, racing her heart, but it left her teetering on the edge, not falling over. "No," she whined.

"Yes." Jess chuckled and the warm breaths across her clit felt like another shot to Elena's nerves.

She threw one arm over her eyes but gripped Jess's head more firmly with her remaining hand. "Oh, God. Damn," she agreed. "Yessss..."

Eric had been raised in a home with very rigid gender roles. Since they'd met, Elena had insisted on a more equal give and take and he found being cherished by a woman didn't make him feel less manly.

Currently being given oral attention by two gorgeous women, Eric felt fantastically cherished. Elena guided his cock into Jess's mouth and Jess enthusiastically took the head to the back of her mouth, bobbing up and down on the shaft. Her talented tongue stroked against the underside of his head where his nerve endings appreciatively fired away. His groans felt like they were pulled from his toes curled into the sheets and he tried to keep a grip on reality.

From the start of their relationship, he had loved sinking into Elena's body, feeling almost as equally possessed as possessing. But Jess gave the most amazing head. He patted her hip, silently conveying he wanted to return the favor. His cock never leaving her mouth, Jess rearranged her arms and legs until she straddled his head. Pulling her hips down, he brushed his mustache against her clit. She rewarded him by quickly grinding down onto his face. When she gasped, her hot breath surrounded him. She sucked on his cock after that. When she finally pulled back, the suction created a *pop* when she released him.

Before he'd learned better control with Jess as a new partner, the sensation had often made him orgasm earlier than he liked. Jess always looked so pleased when he lost his finesse, but he wanted to be a considerate lover and that meant keeping up as long as possible. He thought about her request not to be penetrated earlier. The fact that she enjoyed oral as much as he did meant that foreplay could last quite a while.

He pulled down on her hips again and licked her clit, making her writhe on his chest, grab his cock, and suck harder around the head. *Now who's losing control?* he thought with delight.

Elena smiled down at him from above Jess's back. Sweaty disarrayed brunette hair framed her face; she looked thoroughly fucked and ridiculously happy.

"Having fun, flyboy?" She massaged the cheeks of Jess's ass and the intensity of Eric and Elena attending her made Jess groan and then cry out.

Juices soaked Eric's chin. He thrust his tongue inside to lap it up. Jess shuddered over him again, then she took a deep breath and a small break from sucking his cock. When she started again, his cock was more perfectly fitted to her mouth somehow and he couldn't hold back any longer. He pushed up his hips, curled his back, and his cock jerked as he came. When he opened his eyes and saw her face, a little cum had dribbled out over her lips. Smiling, Jess licked it away at the same time she took hold of him in a firm fist. The sight and feel of her pleasure made him spurt into her hand several more times.

"Elena." Jess's call moved Elena to help her suck and lick the cream off him. The edges of his vision darkened. With the change in blood pressure as his cock throbbed in Elena's and Jess's mouths and hands, Eric's eyes rolled back in his head.

He wrapped his arms around Jess's back, trying to hold on to some small bit of awareness while his body drifted on endorphins. Both of them covered in sweat, Jess's body slipped slickly against his. Both Elena and Jess laughed while kissing around his cock. *So. Damn. Good.*

Chapter Twenty

SETTLED ON the couch reading her library book, Jess startled when her phone buzzed. The text gave an appointment time with another temporary agency. Unwilling to let the opportunity escape, she quickly texted back "yes" and confirmed. But when she read the appointment time more closely in the follow up message, she jumped to her feet in alarm. She had agreed to meet in one hour.

"Elena," Jess called over to the dining room table where Elena had settled with her phone and laptop. Seeing the other woman on the phone, Jess fretted for a moment. Quickly she scribbled a note on her notepad and slid it toward Elena's left side.

Pausing her conversation with a quick, "Excuse me, I need to make a note," Elena scanned the message, looked up at Jess, then down at her phone. Distress drew a furrow in her brow, but she exhaled, reached to her feet for her purse, rummaged, and finally tossed Jess the car keys.

Jess caught them. Elena smiled and gave her a thumbs up. The silent message: *take the car and good luck*. She ran into her room, changed into a button-up, slacks, and flat pumps.

"I'm back," Elena said, returning to her call. "Yes, I think that will work. I can join your team's meeting on Friday at the Maplewood office."

Stepping onto the street from the temp agency's office building, Jess wondered how to tell Elena she had not passed the temp agency's background check. They wouldn't send a person with a record of petty theft into lots of different companies. She had reported her arrest on the application last week, and the woman who took her paperwork at the time had seemed unconcerned, simply putting the application in a pile with several others.

She started toward the Tanners' car in the parking garage, only to remember she hadn't received a parking voucher when she'd left the agency. She contemplated going back up to the agency's front desk, but she didn't want to face the ladies there again with them knowing what they knew about her.

The car would be safe enough, she decided. She had the cash to pay for the parking, even the maximum if she left it there all day. She needed to clear her head with a walk. Besides, maybe it would be better for her to look for work the old-fashioned way. Surely someone still posted "help wanted" signs in their windows.

The temp agency was located in a densely populated business district. Office buildings rose six and ten stories around her. Their first floors and a few in-between buildings housed retailers and restaurants that busy workers patronized during their lunch breaks or in a rush before heading home. Just in this block she saw shipping services, tailors, dry cleaners, fast subs, pizzas, and a not-Starbucks. She laughed when she looked again at the knock-off sign, a green circle, but a cup of coffee adorned with wings occupied the center.

Standing at the corner in front of the coffee shop, she looked in all four directions. Down to the right she saw more office buildings, but down to the left, she saw more shopfronts and a surprising number of Pride flags hanging from multi-colored awnings.

Deciding to investigate the shops and patronize a friendly business or two, Jess adjusted the shoulder strap of her bag and crossed the intersection with the walk signal in the middle of a small cluster of people.

She passed a store featuring lamps and lighting first. She paused at the window display of the next shop, seeing a tooled black leather vest, leather pants, and a studded belt on a female mannequin. Briefly she enjoyed the mental image of Elena wearing that vest—and nothing else. Tinkling accompanied her opening the shop door. *Just wanna browse.* She hoped that the shop owner wasn't one of those pushy types. There was no way she would be able to buy anything right now.

Within a minute of her entry, a man stepped out from the back. He wore jeans with a leather apron hanging low from the weight of tools in the pockets. Over a white short sleeve t-shirt, he wore a leather vest with the store's logo stamped on the front.

He asked, "Anything I can help you find? I also do cosplay commissions."

She shook her head and he shrugged, lifting a tool from his pocket, and resumed working holes into a strip of leather. He said nothing to her for the next fifteen minutes while she browsed the bracelets, watchbands, and headbands. She headed for the door still wistfully imagining Elena in the leather vest.

"Thank you," he said. "Hope to see you again."

"Yeah, thanks," Jess replied. Stepping back onto the street, she leaned against the brick wall and considered where to next.

She glanced at her phone to check the time and saw a missed text from Elena. She'd obviously sent it so as not to disrupt Jess's interview: *Hope it's going well.*

The niggling voice in her head told her to call Elena. Instead she texted a neutral *having lunch,* still unsure how to tell her ever-hopeful lover that she had failed to qualify for yet another job.

She looked up at the awnings and signs for ideas. Right in front of her was Face to Face, its logo a silhouette of two women's faces. The middle white space with the bar name in stylized script looked like a fancy stem wine glass. One of those visual illusion things. The front windows of the place were dark and the Pride flag swinging from the awning had three other flags under it. Not up on all the different flag patterns, she wasn't sure which orientations were represented, but as she approached the door to check the hours, she could just see inside the windows. It looked nice, even cozy.

Loveseats with small coffee tables were set along the walls, but the floor was dominated by the typical square tables and foursome of chairs found in storefront diners. At the far left was a stage which suggested the occasional live music, or at least a DJ. Maybe it was one of those Spoken Word places. She glanced over the computer-printed signs in the windows announcing "Trivia Tuesdays" and "Meetup Mondays." "Speed Dating" was scheduled for Valentine's Day. That sign had been covered in hand drawn pink, red, and purple hearts. On the Saturday after, a live band had been scheduled, notably "all women."

A car engine cut behind her and Jess turned to see a redhead woman getting out of the driver seat of a dark red SUV. The rear door started to rise and the woman ducked into the trunk area to collect something.

She huffed and dragged, and finally wrestled into her arms, a box that was just a little too large to carry comfortably.

Jess asked, "Could you use a hand?"

The redhead looked around the box, gaze traveling briefly up and down Jess's body. She adjusted the box at the same time, gave a shrug of her shoulders, wrestling keys into view. "Get the door for me?"

"Sure." Taking the keys, Jess turned around, worked the lock, and pulled open the bar's front door. She followed the woman inside all the way to the bar, noting slim-fit black jeans and a red-collared short-sleeved polo. The box went atop the bar and the redhead went behind it. Using a box cutter, the redhead opened it and started removing the contents: a variety of liquor and wines. "What's your name?"

"Jess." She slid the keys across the bar top where the redhead collected them and stuffed them back in her jeans pocket.

"Thanks for the assist, Jess. Can I get you something to drink?"

"I was more hoping for a bite, but since you're not quite open yet..."

"I can be if you give me a few minutes. Menu's over there." She pointed to a laminated card sticking up from a condiments caddy.

Jess slid onto the stool and plucked out the card. "I'll just ha—" she started, only to cut herself off when a glass of ice water was slid toward her on the bar top. "Ice water, thanks."

"We don't usually end up with a big lunch crowd."

"I was just exploring when I saw your sign."

"That's about the size of it. We prefer word-of-mouth around here."

"You've got all the flags. I thought the area would be friendly."

"Yeah. This area's what we like to call 'Alt Alley,' or AA. Most of the business lunch crowd eats on the main street out there. We do get hopping once the high rises clear out for the night."

"That's kind of the way my last job worked. Opened at noon to a trickle. But things got busy later." Jess looked down at the menu. "Can I just have a cold cuts sandwich?" The redhead nodded. "The

Subbie Club then."

"Sure. Anything else?"

"Bag of plain chips. I can nibble on those."

"All right." The redhead turned away. "Be right back."

"Thanks—what's your name?"

"Monica. Face to Face is my place."

The information made Jess smile. "Thanks, Monica."

The woman walked past a button pad on the wall and tapped a few keys. Music filled the silence while Jess drank her water.

CHAPTER TWENTY-ONE

AFTER SHE ended the call, Elena cursed floridly in both English and Spanish.

That was her thirteenth dead lead today. She looked over her pitch script again. What the hell was wrong? She'd get the signal to make the call to an upper exec, then, after "hello, I'm Elena Tanner," and "Your assistant told me you might be interested in partnering on a Central American vacation package," she'd get a firm "no thank you." Sometimes they just hung up while she was speaking. This one had been yelling for his assistant before he ended the call. Elena winced, feeling guilty for the man's assistant getting caught up in his anger at Elena.

After placing her notes for that company atop the growing "dead end" pile, Elena turned to grab another lead generation printout from her printer's tray. A moment later she turned at a knock on the door.

"Yes?" She winced as she heard her own abrupt tone.

Jess pushed her way inside the office before Elena could speak again. "Hey." Green eyes warmly reached out to Elena as she held out a mug. "Fresh coffee?"

"I'm pretty caffeinated already," Elena lamented. Then she considered, "Maybe I was too forceful."

"About what?" Jess came forward and handed her the coffee.

"It's decaf anyway. You've been in here three hours. Just take a few minutes break."

"Forget it." Elena sat back with the coffee, humming with a little relief as the flavor and aromas did a lot to make her feel more centered. "What have you been up to while I've locked myself in here?"

"Reading the newspaper."

Elena knew that meant the want ads. Jess was being so diligent about her job hunt and it was really disappointing for her not to have found something yet. She wondered why the temp agency hadn't called. "Maybe the local Starbucks is hiring." She sipped the coffee again. "It's good...for decaf."

Jess said with a wave of her hand. "I didn't think you needed more stimulants."

After another sip of her coffee, Elena asked, "You have some?"

"No. There's more in the press for you."

"You made it just for me? What are you doing to keep the stress away?"

"Taking care of you." Elena felt her cheeks get warm. Jess admitted, "I was prepping the coffee already thinking you needed a break when I heard you curse."

Elena frowned. "I'm sorry."

"Forget it. I'm here. So, tell me, what's wrong?" Jess perched on the top of the small filing cabinet by the door which reminded Elena that her "home office" was now an eight-by-three folding-door closet. She might have continued to use Jess's bedroom if she'd started her home business a couple years ago, but when Jess moved in she hadn't fully settled the space. Now, warming under Jess's concerned green gaze, she was happier with that turn of events than almost anything else in the last year.

She nodded toward her phone face down next to the computer's keyboard. "That last call. My thirteenth dead lead."

"Oh. Unlucky thirteen, but maybe lucky fourteen, right?"

"I think it's something in the script."

"I really liked what I read."

Elena shook her head. "Good on paper maybe, but it's not working for me." She sighed. "I should get back to it."

"No." Jess held out a hand. "C'mon. You won't sound anything but tired if you try to talk to someone now. Take a break. Let's have lunch. It's already noon."

Elena looked at the papers and exhaled slowly. "I don't know.

Maybe this isn't what I should be doing."

Jess straightened up, lifting herself from atop the filing cabinet. Putting her hand on Elena's shoulder, she said, "You'll make this happen. I believe in you."

When Jess's warm lips pressed to the corner of her mouth, Elena did feel her mood improve. She suggested, "Probably most of the offices are at lunch, right? I guess eating something would be good."

"Eating was on my mind too," Jess said, a smile dancing on her lips. "But I also thought we could take a dip in the pool?"

The backyard pool did sound inviting and, with all the neighbors at work, Elena considered they could go without suits. Her body perked up at the idea and she replied in full flirt mode. "That would leave me all wet."

"And naked," Jess added. She took Elena's hand and pulled her up from her chair. "So, what do you say?" Their bodies were flush. Jess's heartbeat pounded hard enough that Elena felt it against her own chest. She stretched into the touch of Jess's hand on her back sliding up under her top.

Feeling her body heat rising with her arousal, she stepped out of Jess's hold and into the hall. "Let's go."

Their path to the sliding glass back door of the house became strewn with clothes. Miami's tropical sun warmed their skins quickly. Taking Jess's hand, Elena led the way down the steps and into the shallow end of the pool.

Squirming with delight and moaning her appreciation, Jess caressed the back of Elena's head as the other woman hummed and licked through Jess's folds. Her nipples tightened and her pussy begged for something to fill it. "El," she whined. "Please. Fuck."

Water moved around her ankles and Elena's shoulder pressed against her inner thigh. A soft kiss caressed her clit and, finally, fingers pressed inside her. She stretched and moaned. "More." At the same moment her pussy flooded and eased Elena's entry.

"Love your taste," Elena murmured, licking Jess's pussy thoroughly before complying. "Three," she said. Elena shifted her licks to Jess's clit as her fingers pushed and twisted, curled up and stroked her G spot.

Thankfully the towel Jess laid on protected her back and shoulders from the pool's deck as she writhed. She wrestled herself up onto her elbows and drank in the sight of Elena sucking on her clit, brown eyes almost black as pitch as they met her gaze. The woman toyed with her, continually twisting and thrusting her fingers, and filling her gloriously full. Needing to connect again, she slipped her fingers into the dark hair falling across Elena's cheek. "Love you," she murmured.

Elena lifted her face from Jess's center, turned her head and kissed Jess's palm while her fingers shifted deftly inside Jess's pussy. The sudden intensity of the stroke against her clenching muscles made Jess throw her head back and cry out as she came.

Clutching Elena's cool, damp body pressing down gently on hers, Jess turned her head to meet Elena's kiss. Their tongues slipped softly around one another and she sighed. Elena massaged Jess's pussy with flat fingers. Elena slid lower to suck languidly on Jess's pulse in her throat and then each of Jess's breasts. She stroked her pussy with the same languid pace, drawing Jess's orgasm out in rippling aftershocks.

Bliss. It was the only word Jess could think of to describe her emotions and the sensations as she sank back against the towel, everything tingling like she was fading away.

Elena's lips drifted over Jess's chest, her shoulders, her belly, then up to her cheeks and forehead. Each touch raised more tingles. When they were tenderly kissing once more, Jess wrapped her arm around Elena's shoulders and hugged her as tightly as her spent body would allow. "I was supposed to help you relax."

Elena nuzzled Jess's throat, at the spot where her jaw met her ear. "I'm very relaxed. I feel perfect," she assured. "I love you, too."

"Yeah?"

"Mm hmm."

"Hello!" Eric's voice came from the foyer.

"We're in here," Elena said. She motioned and Jess paused the streaming movie. Elena looked over the back of the couch toward the front door. Sitting up from where Elena had been stroking her hair while her head rested in her lap, Jess realized the special effects had covered up the sounds of the car arriving and the door opening.

"Close your eyes, both of you." Eric's voice was clear, but there were a bunch of sounds, like paper rustling.

"Eric?" Elena asked.

He didn't come into view. Instead he answered, "Humor me. It's Valentine's Day."

Jess looked at Elena and they shrugged at one another. "OK,"

Jess replied. Then she turned to face the television and closed her eyes. Next to her Elena did the same.

Mustache-topped lips brushed Jess's cheek then moved to her ear. "Open your eyes."

Jess opened her eyes and smiled to see him standing over her. When she dropped her chin she saw his arm move in front of her holding tissue-wrapped flowers, pale tangerine-colored roses mixed with golden daisies. A tiny golden bear charm clung to one of the stems. Jess gathered the flowers to her chest. A glance to her left revealed Elena smiling softly at her.

"Thank you," she said to Eric. Her smile widened and she knew her cheeks were warm and pink from pleasure.

He kissed her head. "You're welcome." He straightened. "El, eyes closed."

Jess laughed when she saw Elena roll her eyes before closing them once more. Eric moved to the other side of the couch and more rustling occurred. Jess held her breath as she watched him move around with another flower bouquet, red roses mixed with purple flowers. He dropped to one knee to present them.

"OK, open your eyes." Jess watched Elena's eyes open and saw a bright light enter the soft brown gaze before Elena gathered in the flowers to her chest. Burying her nose in the bouquet, Elena suddenly lifted her head out, wearing a frown. She rustled in the center of the bouquet with her fingers and withdrew a foil-wrapped nugget on a stick. Elena squealed, "Dulce Tipicos!"

"What's that?" Jess asked.

"Puerto Rican traditional candies. This is Pilones Ajonjoli, lollipop with sesame." She held it out to Jess. "Doesn't it smell wonderful?" Jess sniffed and smiled at the faintly nutty butter-sweet scent. Removing the wrapper, Elena popped it in her mouth, lips closing around the stick.

"I take it these are hard to find?" Jess guessed.

Since Elena's mouth was full, Eric explained, "The ones here are OK, but these I found on my last flight circuit. We branched out with a Puerto Rico leg from and to LaGuardia."

Elena smacked his shoulder. "You didn't tell me."

"I kind of like it. I'm home earlier." He held open his arms as if to say 'see'. "I didn't do Chicago or St. Louis this trip. It was Miami, New York, San Juan, New York, and Miami. Lots of business bookings looking to expand their market."

"Wow. So when can I come along?"

"I'll have a new round of family allowance next month."

"We have to go."

"We can plan that later." He pulled out his phone. "However, I also made reservations for you and me at La Taberna Tapas for dinner tonight."

Elena passed Jess another of the candies. Unwrapping it, Jess pressed it against her tongue. Satisfied by the flavor which matched the nutty and sweet smells, she continued to suck on it.

"What time's our reservation?" Elena asked.

"Seven," Eric replied. Elena kissed him again then got up from the couch and disappeared into the bedroom.

"She'll be in there until we leave," Eric said as he sat on the couch next to Jess.

Leaning back, Jess took the candy out of her mouth. "This is good. Was it hard to get reservations at this Taverna place?"

"Oh, yeah. But I've had them for a while. Since we missed getting in for our anniversary. The candies were a treat, not her gift."

"Wow. OK. You guys have a great time. Thanks again for the flowers."

"Oh, I have more for you," he said. He picked up the bear and Jess realized as he pulled it apart that it was a pin. She nodded when he gestured to her shirt's collar. "Would you like to see a Panthers hockey game at the BB&T arena in a couple days?"

She lifted her head, giving him the space to place the pin. "I'd enjoy that."

His fingers smoothed down the collar and, cupping her chin, he kissed her cheek.

She touched the pin and brushed it with her fingers. "Thank you."

Eric asked, "What are you doing with Elena for Valentine's Day?"

"Damn, I haven't had a chance to ask her." She walked to the master bedroom door. After knocking, she called through it, "Elena, would you like to go to a concert with me Saturday?"

Through the door, Elena asked, "Who?"

"Face to Face has scheduled an all-woman band."

Elena opened the door, letting both Jess and Eric see her barely wrapped in a towel. "You want me to go to a lesbian bar with you?"

"You've heard of it?" Elena nodded. She hadn't been sure if Elena knew the place. Jess twisted her hands together nervously.

Elena reached out and grasped her hands, stilling them. "Not for many years. I'd love to enjoy it with you."

Jess brightened. "OK. The show starts at eight tomorrow."

"That sounds perfect." She kissed Jess. "Now I have to get ready." She closed the door. A moment later Jess heard the shower start up.

She laughed and walked back over to Eric, sitting next to him again on the couch. Eric wrapped his arm around her shoulders and asked, "What's this place?"

"It's called Face to Face. It's down in an area they call Alt Alley. Monica is the owner." Jess leaned back. She looked down at her hands and then up at Eric. "I've hung out a couple times now between job interviews."

"Seems Elena knew of it. Probably from before we got together, so it's been around a while."

"I also think maybe I can get a job there. Monica said she has a waitress who will be moving upstate to care for her mom."

"Do you really want to get back into bartending?" He rubbed her shoulder and she leaned into him. "Have you thought about getting some training? Move on to something really stable?"

Jess frowned. "I–haven't told Elena, but I didn't pass the temp job's background check. I've been going door to door down there."

"Oh, OK. I get that. We did agree you can stay here as long as you need. It's our fault you lost the job at the club."

"Elena said the same thing, but I really don't think so. Gus had already strong-armed Hector and Maya a couple times about me. I just didn't fit there."

Eric nodded and kissed her temple. Jess leaned into the touch briefly before he lifted his arm from around her and stood up. "OK. Just laying out my thoughts."

She smiled. "I know. Thanks."

"You're welcome."

"Go get ready for your date," Jess told him.

CHAPTER TWENTY-TWO

ERIC HELD the door at the restaurant as Elena entered. The crowd around them looked hopeful to get in on a cancellation at the restaurant. He straightened the line of his suit jacket when he saw people giving him and Elena lingering looks. Brushing his lips against her temple when she passed close to him through the doorway, he put his hand on her bare back. Yeah, it was a 'possessive' move, but she *was* his, and she looked stunning in a 'grab em by the throat' crimson strapless red dress.

The style hugged her body, ending mid-thigh, and emphasized her curvaceous figure. Her flawless almond skin was on elegant display in the low-backed dress. She wore a bracelet on each wrist and a glittering diamond drop necklace rested in the space between her collarbones.

As they crossed through the small waiting area, he loved the sense that the hum of conversation hushed as they neared, heads turned, and their appearance was noted.

"Tanner," he said to the maître d' standing at the podium.

The man's eyes dropped to a list and he responded quickly, "Yes, sir. Right this way." He spoke to a young brunette woman in a demure cocktail length black dress. "Table 22." Following the young woman, Eric stopped watching the crowd and instead watched Elena.

Her eyes slowly scanned the crowded restaurant. When they reached their table, their escort stepped back and Eric reached for a chair to pull out for Elena. She breathed against his ear and kissed his cheek. "Love you."

He tucked the sides of his jacket close together and kissed her cheek. "Love you, too." Sitting down across from her, he looked up at the young woman.

"Your server, Gabriel, will take your drink orders."

"Thank you," Elena said and the young woman withdrew.

Despite the fact they had been to this restaurant several times for special occasions over the years, Eric took it in once again. If he wasn't mistaken the sconces mounted on the walls had been replaced, the shape more flowery than he recalled. And the table shape was circular, not square. The effect meant that there were almost never going to be large parties. They'd gone all-in for the intimate dining experience.

"They've refurbished," Elena noted.

"I was just thinking that. It's catering more exclusively to couples now, I think."

"There are larger tables in other rooms. I saw a few foursomes over the dividing walls as we walked through."

"Is this still your favorite special date place?" he asked.

Elena lifted her menu. "We'll have to see if they've changed their menu. The Gilded Age may be my new favorite."

"The food was passable." Eric recalled the meal there only vaguely. Food hadn't really been his focus that night.

"Perhaps. But the memories are unforgettable," Elena said, meeting his gaze.

They had both been taken back to that memorable night with Jess. He agreed. "It was special."

Gabriel arrived and Eric told Elena to select their wine. She chose an understated Riesling and from that Eric had his answer for her expectations for the evening ahead: quiet.

After they had looked at their menus for a few minutes – he'd quickly chosen pincho moruno – Eric asked, "How's your business building going?"

Elena shrugged. "I have had a few bites. I need to make a few more connections, though, for the package numbers to really work."

"You want me to share a few pamphlets at work?"

"You can't post this in the airport lounge."

"Why not? Maybe not the DA pilots lounge, but I can put stuff up in the general airport."

"You'd do that for me?"

"I'd do that for you." He sat back. The server had arrived with the bottle. When the cork was popped, Gabriel held it out to Eric. He waved it to Elena instead. "What do you think?"

She inhaled the wine's scent from the cork and nodded. "Mm hmm," she told the server who then proceeded to dispense an ounce into a wine glass and hand it to her. She smiled at Eric then tipped her head up, giving him a lovely view of her throat as she sipped, swirled and swallowed the taste. "Excellent." She put it down and said, "Two glasses and leave the bottle."

"Yes, ma'am." The young man's voice was filled with obedience and Eric smiled.

Elena's face was flushed when the server withdrew. Eric knew it wasn't the wine though. She was "feeling her power," just as he'd intended by making sure she was the one the server dealt with about the wine. "Better?" he asked as he lifted his glass and reached it toward her for a brief clink.

"Thank you," she said and tapped his glass. "I don't say it often enough. Thank you."

"You're welcome," he said. "You will make this tour package. And another after that." He sipped his wine. "I always have believed in you."

"I sometimes think I should have stayed with Diligent. The paycheck was at least reliable."

"But the conditions sucked. I agreed with you then and I still do. I do what I can to create a protected space on my teams, but not all pilots do."

The server returned, this time asking if they were ready to order. "Ensaladilla rusa," Elena ordered after Eric requested his dish.

Eric picked up a bite from the complimentary patatas bravas. "You don't usually worry about money. What's up?"

"Jess is really sensitive about it."

"Mm hmm, I've seen that."

"She's adamant to make her own way."

"And it's making you consider maybe you're not contributing the way you should?" Her brown eyes leaping up to his in surprise told him that he'd hit the nail on the head. "When you quit DA, what did I say?"

Elena's lips pursed, but she answered him, holding her wine glass in front of her lips. "You told me don't find my next job, find my passion."

"Your passion. Right." He reached across the table and, with a small twitch of his fingers, invited her to take his hand. She did. "I still believe that, El. This tour package excites you. So it's your passion. Let me take the flyers and pamphlets to distribute. You'll find your bookings fill quickly, I bet."

Her answer was slow, but she accepted his words with a small nod. "All right."

Their meals were delivered, interrupting the flow, but after a few bites, Eric made sure to answer Elena's question.

"About the other thing. If Jess wants to give you some money for the household expenses, you don't *have* to spend it. Put some or all of it away. Maybe we can use it later to give her something she'll need."

"What do I tell her?"

"Thank you." Eric nodded as he thought back over his own knowledge of Jess. "I don't think she's heard that enough in her life."

"You are scary accurate about people, you know?" Eric nodded. Elena added, "I've missed clues about Jess all along, though I am absolutely crazy in love with her. How do you do it?"

"I listen. You say you love that about me."

Elena exhaled. "And I talk too much."

"Being involved with Jess has changed that," he said. "It's how I first figured out you were in love with her, not just attracted to her. You do a lot more thinking ahead than you used to."

"I didn't even realize," she said, her voice trailing to silence. "I thought since I blurted I wanted her to move in, it meant I'd pushed."

"Well, you were trying to solve a problem. You were afraid she'd leave. Now she's living with us though, so that's not really an issue."

"I still need to listen more."

"Yeah. Jess is a deep thinker and a habitual loner. Other than that old guy at the club, I'm pretty sure we are her only friends."

"Should we try to help her find new friends?"

Eric remembered, even if she was networking for a job, Jess said that she had made friends at that girl bar. But he wouldn't break Jess's confidence. Certainly if she and Elena were going on a date there, Elena would see firsthand how friendly, or not, the women were with Jess. He shook his head and finally answered Elena. "Just keep listening to her."

They finished their meal in companionable quiet and declined desserts. After Eric paid their bill they strolled out to the street.

"Thank you, Eric." She kissed him. "I love you. So much."

"Happy Valentine's Day," he replied. "I love you, too."

"What's next?"

"Movie. Theater's just a short walk." He tucked her into his side since the wind had picked up a bit. "But we could get the car if you're not warm enough?"

She circled her one arm behind his back and rested her other hand on his shirt over his stomach. He was comfortable for the moment, but if she continued circling her fingers like that, he'd be sporting a tent pole quickly.

"You fed me," Elena said. "You deserve dessert."

"I don't deserve anything," he said, then added with a smirk, "but you know how much I enjoy the taste of cream."

The theater was crowded, since everyone else seemed to be doing the Valentine's dinner and a movie date night, too. But there were fourteen screens. While Eric knew Elena was excited for the idea of public sex, something not super-popular would have fewer people. He wanted to fulfill her fantasy, but it would be depressing to end the evening by getting arrested.

So he bought two tickets to some cheesy slasher film. The soundtrack might even help hide what they were doing. Entering during the previews, the darkness was almost total, the safety lights lining the aisles made him glad he'd selected inner seats. The seat selection screen had said there were only fourteen other people, six in a bundle down front, and the rest, singletons scattered throughout. The closest person sat four rows away from them.

Elena had her phone out and Eric watched her turn off the device before storing it in her purse. "You want me to hold yours?" she asked.

"Sure." They settled into seats side-by-side but once Elena had taken his phone, she set the bag in his lap. The maneuver covered the fact that she undid his belt.

Eric chuckled at the screen as if laughing at the theater's dancing logo reminding moviegoers they had to silence their phones, recording was illegal, and snacks were available in the lobby.

His cock was exposed and in Elena's hand by the time the movie's score was playing behind the opening scene. He glanced to the side and caught his wife's smirk, though her gaze was locked on the movie screen while she massaged him from root to tip.

Leaning close to her, he whispered, "I don't have any napkins."

"I don't intend to make a mess," Elena said. With her free hand, she lifted her dress and discreetly pushed down her underwear. He thought for a moment she would jerk him off into it, which would certainly be fine, even great, feeling the soft fabric wrapped around his cock. But she bent forward and instead lifted herself from her seat onto his lap in just a few breaths. He closed his eyes as her tight wet heat quickly enveloped his cock. She straightened, kissed him over her shoulder and said, "Got it."

To anyone looking, Elena barely moved, but her inner muscles rhythmically squeezed Eric, often matching the tempo of the movie's screams and soundtrack. Eric wrapped his arms around Elena, one across her waist, but the other hidden under the length of her dress, fingertips just reaching her clit.

Resting his chin on her shoulder, he let the feeling of both holding his wife and being held by her so intimately permeate his whole body. He could ride this slow ebb and flow for close to an hour if she didn't change tempo on him. She grew more and more slippery against his fingers.

"Enjoying this?" he asked. If anyone overheard they might simply think the two were discussing the movie.

Her pussy squeezed his cock abruptly. He massaged her labia, easing off attention to her clit. "Mm hmm," she murmured, biting her lip.

They stayed like that for almost half the 98-minute film. Her pussy rhythmically squeezed and edged him close to orgasm, then his massaging fingers eased her, and himself, back from the precipice.

The climax of the movie, when it arrived, was underwhelming. Eric's climax on the other hand was strong and Elena's orgasm rippled her inner muscles over him repeatedly and caused smaller ejaculations. He squared his jaw and stiffened his posture to prevent his hips shoving up erratically as he wanted and giving away what they were doing.

"So god damn good," he murmured, kissing her jaw while his fingertips found her clit again and her body shuddered against his.

Her pussy's grip on him remained firm. When she settled back onto her seat as the lights started to come up, his grip on his cock to tuck it into his pants revealed he was almost completely clean.

She stood with her purse and handed him his phone. "I'm

going to the bathroom."

Eric knew she was going to clean up and he almost wished he could join her, wanting nothing more in that moment than putting his mouth on her pussy and sucking out all his own cum.

He watched her walk down the aisle, head up. When she turned to take the exit ramp, she smiled at him.

A few minutes later, just as he was reaching the lobby from making his own adjustments in the bathroom, his phone buzzed with a text message: "*Wish you were here (heart)*." Elena had attached a close up of her fingertips spreading her labia and a bit of his cream leaking from her pussy.

He licked his lips and typed back, "*Same (heart)*."

A half hour later, laying in the middle of their bed, her dress bunched to her waist, Elena held Eric's head and urged him on as he licked her clean. She felt like queen of the world listening to his hums of enjoyment and feeling the nuzzles of his nose in her pubic hair.

When he finally stood to go into the bathroom, she pushed him against the wall, dropped to her knees, and sucked his cock, enjoying the feel of his hands cradling her head and stroking through her hair. Her name was the moan on his lips when he came.

CHAPTER TWENTY-THREE

"THIS IS wonderful." Elena inhaled over her coffee cup and the platter Jess had just placed on the poolside table in front of her. The aromas of tomatoes, cheese and eggs added to the air of coffee, easily overwhelming the slight chlorine scent from the newly cleaned pool.

"Happy day after Valentine's Day. This is so much warmer than the mountains in February."

"I bet." Elena took a bite of her omelet. She hummed her appreciation, delighting in the blush her sounds brought to Jess's paler cheeks. "You were in the mountains a year ago?"

"In Georgia. Had no plan, just putting one foot in front of the other." Jess lifted her coffee mug toward Elena.

"What did you do, last year for the day?"

"Well, I wasn't seeing anyone. I bought myself a dollar soda and a bag of message hearts, and read them to myself while sitting by a pond."

"That's depressing."

Jess gave a self-deprecating laugh. "Buzzed on sugar for nearly the whole next day." She shook it off. "You and Eric have made me feel like I can look toward more than just the next day."

Elena lifted her mug and clicked the edge to Jess's cup. Her skeptical expression made Jess insist.

"You have. I know I got scared, but you didn't tell me I couldn't feel that way. Just waited for me to figure it out." Jess shook her head as Elena layered their hands together on the table. "I've really never had unconditional support like this. It makes me realize just how alone I was growing up."

"Surely not all your foster families were awful."

"Maybe not, but it's...I feel more a part of a family here, with you. You're teaching me a lot."

"I hope you think of yourself as a partner. I know I was opinionated, even pushy, about you living with us, but...I don't want to be your parent."

"I definitely don't need or want you to be parents," Jess said. "You still might make amazing parents someday. Have you thought about it?"

Elena shook her head. She and Eric had been flying every which way from the start of their marriage. A child, an infant, would need so much attention and care that Elena wasn't certain she could give enough. She hadn't liked her own mother as a role model and didn't think she'd be very good at it. Even now, though she'd told Eric she wanted to help Jess if the young woman came up pregnant, she was very glad that the situation had worked out.

Jess was smiling so beautifully, however, Elena said lightly, "The only constant in life is change, right?"

"Right." Jess leaned across the table and gave Elena a kiss that made her feel like the matter was safely closed.

At the sound of a door opening, Jess turned from the hall mirror. She'd been smoothing the collar of her polo over the collar of her jacket. At the sight of Elena exiting the master bedroom, she whistled and dusted her nails very dramatically on the front of her shirt. "I have the hottest date."

Elena grabbed the sides of Jess's jacket and pressed her into the wall, languidly delivering a tongue kiss that sped Jess's heart rate and breathing. "I had hoped to hear I am the hottest fucking date you've ever had."

Jess laughed, as always deeply turned on by Elena's well-placed double entendre. "You are certainly that, but I'm trying to behave. The band is supposed to be the center of attention. They probably won't appreciate it if I take you on the table."

"How about under the tables then?" Elena suggested, guiding Jess's hand up and under her dress to reveal that she wore nothing underneath.

Jess moaned at the images entering her mind and the sensation of soft hairs around her fingertips. "You are primed to play tonight," she said. "Maybe we should stay in?"

"No way. Jess Davies, you are taking me out and fucking me tonight or so help me I will..." Her voice trailed off.

Jess pulled up Elena to meet her lips in a kiss, the dress riding up as she lifted the woman with two hands under her bare ass. "You'll what? You know I'd love anything you'd do to 'punish' me."

Elena pouted, pushing out her lower lip. "I know."

Jess laughed. "But if you want, I'll find a way to provide some semi-public pleasure."

Elena pulled Jess's arms close around her. "Let's go." Breathing in Elena's scent, Jess left a kiss on her throat before stepping back and opening the door.

Elena dragged Jess into the bathroom at the Face to Face bar as soon as their cash cover had been paid. Pushing Jess down onto the toilet seat, Elena quickly shut and locked the stall door before straddling Jess's waist and lifting the bottom of her dress.

Lap delightfully full of delectable woman, Jess closed her eyes and enjoyed Elena's kisses. Her hand was guided to Elena's bare center. Needing no more coaxing, Jess stroked and smoothed, then she easily curled two fingers inside; Elena was unbelievably hot and wet.

She sucked on Elena's tongue, prizing the pleased moans breathed into her mouth. When Elena's muscles started pulling at her fingers, Jess rotated the tips a little, bringing them against another part of Elena's center. She pressed her other hand over Elena's mouth then pushed her lover over the edge into orgasm, her gaze locked with wide brown eyes.

They emerged from the bathroom with satisfied smiles on both their faces. Shoulders bumping as they walked close, Jess reached out and twined their fingers when Elena caught her eye. "C'mon, let's get some seats," she said, tugging them toward the left side of the stage.

The crowd was modest but entirely women of every shape, size, color and style. A redhead behind the bar watched them cross the floor and Jess seemed to catch her eye, lifting a hand and giving a brief wave.

"Who's that?"

"That's Monica," Jess said easily. "She owns Face to Face."

"Oh." Elena looked back over her shoulder again at the redhead, who was still watching Jess. She felt a need to show Jess was hers. She recalled how excited she'd been to be seen wearing Jess's shirt the morning after the costume party. Possessiveness was definitely a new feeling.

When they found a small two-seater table empty to the side Jess held out her chair. Elena grasped Jess's hand and put it on her shoulder once she was seated. Jess squeezed lightly and Elena could finally look away from the green eyes. She narrowed her gaze as she searched toward the stage.

The band—the placard by the stage proclaimed them "Persistence"—were shifting into another song. The lead guitarist strummed beats back and forth with the drummer as they cued up their next tune.

"This next one is for all the peace lovers out there. Or just lovers," the lead singer added with a wink that seemed to take in several tables directly in front of the stage. Elena glanced at the patrons there and figured out quickly that one was a girlfriend of the singer, tucked shyly in jeans and a band t-shirt beside a couple of women who had clearly come directly from work, still wearing business-style skirt suits. Almost everyone else was in something a lot less like work clothes and more like date-night clothes, from jeans to dresses, to leather.

Jess's hand slipped over hers on the tabletop. Through the music, her voice was barely audible. "How're you?"

"It's nice music," Elena said. "You wanna dance?"

"Not right now." Jess looked around. There wasn't really 'dance floor', but there was a space between the tables and the band area. The comment was followed by a bit of a nervous squeeze on her fingertips tucked in Jess's hand.

Elena squeezed lightly back. "Later?"

Jess looked around, then scooted her chair closer to Elena. She caressed Elena's fingers in her hand as she brought her mouth close to Elena's ear. "You just want to squeeze my ass in front of all these women."

"Is that's why you wanted me to come to the place you like to hang out? You want me to show them you're mine?" Elena asked.

"I...well, actually, I'm going to start working here next week. Monica had a spot opening up."

Elena glanced over her shoulder again before pressing a kiss to Jess's cheek when she knew Monica was watching. "You're mine." Jess blushed as Elena brushed the lipstick mark with her thumb.

Jess was such a wonderfully complex young woman, by turns sweet, shy and unsure, and other times bold and daring. Elena loved both sides, finding it fulfilling to be here with her like this, listening to music, holding hands, and being a couple together sharing the same experience.

Elena had known she could love women as well as men since her teen years, but she hadn't really thought about the different qualities of that love being equally fulfilling until she met Jess. She honestly believed she loved Jess as deeply and as complexly as she loved Eric, able to be completely herself with both of them. It had been freeing talking to Eric about this the other evening, too. Finding out he'd sensed the emotions before Elena herself had surprised her.

Though part of her whispered, *greedy*, she reminded herself that Eric genuinely supported her. That should be all that mattered. Their entire lifestyle was a buck against society's expectations. She leaned her head against Jess's shoulder as the band's next song selection slowed to romantic. Jess kissed her hair. Elena traced the lines and shape of Jess's fingers in her hand.

"I love you," she said. "Let's dance."

Jess glowed with unmistakable pleasure when Elena wrapped her arm around her waist. She pulled Jess in closer while they walked to the space before the stage that already held a few other couples. Reveling in the feel of Jess's soft curves melting against her own, Elena held Jess's hand on her shoulder, and rested her other hand on the curve of Jess's ass just above indecent. She nosed into Jess's throat, kissed her jaw, smiled at the hum vibrating through her lover's throat, and closed her eyes.

She whispered, "This enough of a claim?" Sliding her thigh between Jess's legs, she tucked her fingertips inside Jess's back pockets as they shifted steps in their dancing.

Jess's voice told her all she needed to know. In a breathless, awed whisper, she responded simply, "Um. Yeah...I...mmmm."

Resisting a chuckle, Elena eased her head back. Jess's chin lifted and their gazes met. She claimed a hard, dominating kiss from parted soft thin lips. Continuing the kiss, she moved her hands onto Jess's shoulders and threaded her fingers through the bits of blonde hair curling against the woman's neck. Finally she securely wrapped her arm around Jess's back. *Mine.*

CHAPTER TWENTY-FOUR

AFTER DANCING together through the remaining songs by the band, Jess and Elena both decided they wanted to continue a more intimate dance between the sheets. Back at the table collecting their bags, kisses turned to nibbles and they agreed it was time to head home.

Just barely in the doorway to the house, Elena asked, "Where?" Her hands were already removing Jess's clothing, her jacket already hanging off her right arm.

Jess unzipped Elena's dress before Elena silently sank to her knees on the hallway floor, kissing the tops of Jess's thighs. Then she stepped out of the pants being pushed to her ankles. Elena stood and parted Jess's top, button after button, kissing the skin of her chest as it became revealed.

"Where do you want?"

"Your bed," Elena said.

"It's kinda small."

"Jess Davies, you took me out. *You* are taking me home." It was just as much a statement of Jess having claim on Elena as Elena's bold grasping of Jess's mouth and body in public had claimed her. And she loved it.

Tugging on Elena's shoulders, Jess encouraged her to stand

again. When Elena met Jess's lips, their tongues and lips slipped and tangled together. Elena's breathing hitched, a sure sign she was aroused and almost painfully needy. Jess asked, "Do you want to get anything from your room?"

"I have all I need right here." Elena's fingertips danced down Jess's muscled arms and up the side of her ribs, skimming the underside of her breasts. Jess's nipples were already stiff when Elena's fingertips reached the peaks. Taking Elena's hands from her breasts, Jess led Elena to the small second bedroom.

The walls were still mostly bare, except for shadow boxes of keepsakes that Elena had hung from her and Eric's travels. Pulling out a stool that had been tucked under a small table, Jess nudged Elena down to sit with kisses and gentle pressure on her shoulders. As she eased her back, Jess moved aside papers where she'd been doodling numbers, addresses, or job descriptions from job leads.

"Sheets," Jess said suddenly, realizing the futon was still folded up. Elena patiently waited to the side while she quickly pulled out the sheets from the closet.

When the sheets were on, Elena moved from the stool to the bed and tugged Jess down next to her. "Make love to me."

"Yeah," Jess breathed.

Elena turned her body into Jess's, cupping her cheek. Gradually, Jess moved on from her mouth to her throat and laid Elena back. She laid down herself and coaxed Elena to roll on top of her, their legs settling around each other. Elena crossed her arms over Jess's breastbone, holding her head up as they leisurely continued tasting one another, bodies entwined.

Jess's heart thumped strongly in her chest under Elena's arms, and her hands massaged up and down Elena's body, from between her shoulders, then down her back and, finally, lingering over her ass. Elena hummed happily into her mouth when Jess traced the dimples at the crest of her hips.

Elena gave in to the urge to grind into Jess's firmly muscled figure. She parted her legs and rolled her center over Jess's hard thigh. The slow pace seemed to be suiting them both. Jess slightly bent her leg and readjusted her arm so that the fingertips of one hand dipped between Elena's legs from behind and stroked at the inside. Then, ever so gradually, Jess's fingers probed Elena's center.

"Jesssss..." Elena's voice trailed away and she rolled her hips, circling her center on Jess's thigh again, which increased the pressure against her swollen clit.

Jess cupped one hand behind Elena's head and continued to stroke Elena's folds. While nipping and plundering Elena's mouth, she stroked Elena's clit. Soon Elena rolled her hips uncontrollably and she gasped in Jess's mouth as often as she was making half-sounds in her throat and squeezing her eyes shut. She felt the edge approaching.

Jess's voice encouraged her. "There, that's—just a little—more—mmm—hmmm—yeah, Elena, go ahead...come on." Warm lips moved against Elena's ear. "Oh, you are so, so wet. Yeah, just a little—like that...mmm—"

Starting low in her belly and rolling outward, Elena's orgasm washed through her. Her head throbbed, her heart pounded, her arms shook, and her fingertips tingled. She grasped Jess's arms while Jess continued to massage her center with broader movements now, over the hood, into her folds. Elena swallowed, trying to wet her mouth at the same time as she was panting hard.

Jess murmured into her shoulder, "I love being able to give you pleasure." Rolling Elena into her side, Jess lifted her hand to her lips and slowly sucked Elena's essence from her fingers. Her green gaze reached deep into Elena's chest.

She swallowed and murmured, "Being with you gives me pleasure, Jess. I had a really good time tonight." Tucking her leg in more tightly over Jess's own, Elena caressed Jess's soft stomach. Skin damp with sweat, Jess's muscles quivered. When Jess tenderly moved aside locks of her hair moistly stuck to her face, Elena lowered her head and kissed the side of Jess's closest breast. Trailing her fingers and drawing nonsensical patterns on Jess's soft skin, Elena gradually circled lower, entering her core. She watched her lover's hips roll into the pleasure created by Elena's fingers.

Jess panted, half-coherent, murmuring, "please," and "more, Elena," and "oh god." Elena sucked the near nipple between her teeth and chewed. She turned her finger, curved it and brushed against throbbing inner walls. Jess's back arched entirely off the bedding and her mouth opened in a surprised 'O', her hands clutching tightly at Elena as she came.

Sliding down between strong thighs as Jess quieted, Elena bent shaking legs at the knees and pushed them wider with her shoulders. Languidly she sucked and licked the woman through several more orgasms.

CHAPTER TWENTY-FIVE

ERIC LINGERED within sight of the Panther Arena's ladies room. They had yet to go find their seats and when she had seen it, Jess said she worried she'd not know when was a good time to take a break and quickly kissed his cheek before stepping away.

He walked past the snack lines to a vendor hawking the sports team's logo wear. Food, drinks, even private bathrooms were available in the club seating though Jess didn't yet know that. He used the few minutes to buy jerseys. For Jess he chose one with a number 10 on it. He already owned, and was currently wearing, a certified jersey from the team's leading scorer.

Jess emerged from the bathroom and he crossed to meet her in the middle of the concourse. "No snacks?" she asked.

"Where we're going we don't need snacks," he said, trying an imitation of Doc Brown.

She laughed and wrapped her hands around his arm. "OK. So where are we seated?"

"You'll need this," he said, handing her the jersey.

"You got me a team jersey?" Jess gaped. Her fingers clutched the fabric as she studied the number and the lettering. "Why?"

"Because I love seeing a girl in uniform," he teased.

She laughed again and pulled the jersey on over her collared button-up blouse. She wore a dark blue pair of tight jeans, too. This was hockey after all, not a night at the theater.

"You are definitely a ten." He stepped forward and helped free her collar from beneath the jersey, smoothing it down and then sliding his hands down her shoulders.

"I love it," she said. "Thank you."

Her green eyes met his, warm with her feelings, so he followed his desire, cupping her cheeks and pressing his lips to hers. She melted into his body as their lips continued to soothe across each other. He heard her moan, felt her hands grip at his shirt, and moved his mouth away. "It may be a week late, but this is our Valentine's Day, right?"

She nodded, rolling her cheek into his still cupped palm.

He kissed her forehead and then turned her so they were shoulder to shoulder. He wrapped his arm around her back. "Come on. Our seats are this way."

As they walked, he pulled out the tickets from his pocket. The Club Corona logo was easily visible. There were perks to winning a corporate drawing. They walked up to an entrance where an events volunteer asked, "Tickets?"

He held them up.

Nodding them past, the volunteer said, "Enjoy the game."

Jess gripped his hand at her waist as she took in the wide padded seats, the Corona logo tables, the bar along the side wall, and the view of the ice. A number of other people were already settled, eating, drinking, and talking. She leaned close to his shoulder. "What do tickets for this go for?"

"No idea. Nice perk of piloting," he replied. "Come on. Let's get a table." They found an unclaimed table and he held out her chair. "You want something?"

She looked at the menu visible over the bar then significantly looked up at him. "Surprise me."

Eric grinned, dropping a quick kiss on her lips. "All right."

Looking around the club room, Jess noticed only one other woman. Wearing a snugly fitting little black dress, she had a cocktail of some sort in one hand, looking out the window to the ice, as two men in suits chatted away next to her. The woman was clearly some executive or executive's wife, there more for the business connections than the hockey.

"Here," Eric said, drawing her attention as he set down a nacho plate—an actual plate, not one of those cardboard boats—in the middle of the table, then passed her a tall glass. "Diet Coke and lime," he said. "I'll have them add alcohol to the next round if you want."

He sat down next to her, taking a sip from his own glass. She cupped her hand over his on the table between them. "Thank you."

Leaning toward her, he said, "The bathroom is over there." He pointed. "So you don't have to search later when you need it."

She chuckled. "You knew there'd be one here. Why didn't you say something?"

"Gave me time to get the jersey for you," he replied with a shrug.

"I know you said you thought this wasn't a traditional Valentine's Day," she said. "But this is perfect for me, really."

"You like hockey?"

"I like sports in general," she said. "Don't know much about hockey, but I really enjoy getting to spend quality time with you. As much as you work and I work, it seems sometimes we only see each other in bed."

Eric looked down for a moment then smiled when he looked up and squeezed her hand. "I hope you know I care for you more than just sleeping with you."

"I'm beginning to understand that," Jess replied.

"Yeah, I know we all started this as something just for fun, but I'm pretty sure that Elena and I feel the same way about you."

"She says she loves me," Jess said.

"Yeah. Do you love her?"

"I think so."

"And me?"

Jess met his blue gaze holding her so tenderly. "I haven't wanted to," she said quietly.

"Mm hmm." His fingers slid around her hand.

"But I, yeah, I do."

"I know that makes you feel vulnerable, particularly with me, a guy, but..." He leaned forward, keeping her hand trapped under his, and captured her lips with a strong kiss that made Jess's belly start to throb. "Maybe this will help. I'm in love with you, too," he said.

Jess and Eric shared drinks and food before the puck dropped. Then she enjoyed his arms wrapped around her shoulders and his chest against her back as she straddled his lap, looking out the window at the ice throughout the game. Eric's steady breathing against her ear and occasional kisses to her cheek made her feel the most secure in her life. For once, she didn't question it, simply went with the feeling, not thinking beyond right now or wondering what it meant or what she was supposed to do.

When they got back to the car after the game, Eric reached across the center console and took her hand as he drove. "Did you have a good time?"

"This was wonderful," she said. "Too bad the team couldn't manage a win." She plucked at her jersey, Eric's gift. "It was exciting seeing this guy make a goal though."

"You like seeing a guy score, huh?" Eric's voice was teasing.

"You can score with me anytime," Jess replied, flirting back.

"What do you want to do? It's only nine. We don't have to go home yet."

Home. She heard the word and smiled at the notion that she had such a thing. Not just a place where she slept, but where there were people who cared for her, who wanted her in their lives. "What do you want to do?"

"Would you like to walk on the beach?" he asked.

"Sure." She sat back as he turned the car at the next intersection.

As they exited the car, Eric watched Jess take in the sight of the thin stretch of sand. "This is just the bay not the ocean," he said. "But we can walk here."

She took his hand when he held it out to her then shifted into hugging his side when he put his arm around her back. They walked along in comfortable silence, listening to the waves and the occasional boat horns sounding out on the water. He remembered saying she really needed to get her own car, if only to go to the beach.

"What do you like most about Miami?" she asked. "What makes you say this city is home even with all your traveling?"

"It's definitely warmer than the Midwest where I grew up," Eric said. "And it's got nightlife and doesn't get hung up about a lot of shit."

"That's right. You didn't grow up here."

"Nope. After the military, I settled in Chicago to start my commercial flying."

"Right. When did you get transferred to Miami?"

"About eleven years ago now. It wasn't love at first sight, but it's definitely grown on me. It helps that El and I started hanging out. Even though she isn't native either, she arrived right out of high school and knows Miami better than I do."

He walked them over to a half-eroded bench of wooden slats screwed to coquina stone. When he sat down, he was not terribly surprised when she moved to settle on his lap instead of next to him. He wrapped his arms around her back, studied her windblown hair and face for a moment then kissed her.

"Just hanging out?" Jess asked. "You were at layover parties together."

"Yeah, but just like we've been with you, we were not all about the sex."

"That has been something to get used to," Jess said. "One night stands were my thing."

"We're way past one night here. It's been more than six months."

"Well, if I hadn't been stupid and run in December."

"Forget it." He brushed his fingers through the hair falling forward over her cheeks and tucked strands behind her ears, cupping her cheeks. "I just...I'm glad you're here now."

Jess leaned forward and pressed her lips to his, moving them softly from corner to corner before pulling back. She cupped his face. "So am I."

As they continued to kiss, Jess rocked her hips, which put pressure on his groin. Along with the heat of her he felt even through both their jeans, Eric's cock started to swell. Her reaction when she felt the growing bulge in his pants was to rock more. He groaned into the skin of her shoulder, nosing aside the jersey neckline and finding her satin skin where he pressed kisses. "Uh. God."

She wrapped her arms around the back of his head and chuckled into his ear, making him groan again, and his cock became even harder. "So, how's your photography coming along?" she asked.

"Mmm." Eric wrenched his attention away from his cock and the desire to sink into Jess's body. "Um. Hmm. It-it's good. Thinking of posing some more?"

Jess's slow shifting renewed the pressure on his cock and, once again, he felt his brain short-circuit. "You do have that auto-snap feature, and"—she trailed off as Eric grazed the pulse in her throat with his teeth—"uh, video."

He slid his hands down Jess's back until he was pulling on her ass, helping her rock herself against his cock. He ordered himself not to come, but that didn't mean that he was going to leave Jess with dry underwear. "You're so hot and wet just thinking about us on camera, aren't you?"

She may not be the same level of exhibitionist as Elena, turned on by just anyone watching her have sex or be naked, but he'd learned enough that he knew it turned Jess on to be the reason someone else was turned on. Namely him or Elena.

"Because I'm hard enough to pound you for hours just thinking about it, too."

Jess groaned and buried her face in his neck. He continued to rock her bottom to keep up the pressure for her. The heat pouring from the center of her jeans was intoxicating. "Oh, god," she groaned and he could see her biting her lip.

"Go ahead and come," he murmured. "I'll clean you up when we get home."

That apparently did it for her. The mention of home. That he'd take care of her. "Er-ic, god, Eric!" She gasped when he pressed one hand down the front of her pants, the button bursting behind the pressure of his knuckles. He pushed past her clit and felt her body's spasms, her juices coating his fingers and then soaking her underwear.

Slowly he withdrew his hand and she blinked. She focused on his eyes then his fingers as he put them in his mouth and tasted her. He hummed; her skin flushed. He smiled and continued moving his tongue over his fingers until they were clean. "Mm hmm," he said. "Time to get a woman home and clean her up."

Jess still felt her knees wobbling as Eric held her against him on their walk from the car to the front door. Inside the foyer she noted the time on the wall clock as Eric locked the door and threw the deadbolt behind them. She didn't hear anything beyond the ticking of the clock; it was after eleven now. They'd walked for a long time on the beach after the movie and even the humping they'd done on the beach had been slow and sensuous.

Eric walked her down the hall to her bedroom. She opened the door and waved him in to join her.

"You still want to clean up?" Eric asked.

"You don't have to," Jess said, toeing off her boots.

"I want to," he replied and his blue eyes were so soft and warm.

She pulled up and off the sports jersey. "All right. Help me?"

"With pleasure." He slid to the floor on his knees and unbuttoned her jeans before grasping the waistband and tugging down.

Tossing her jersey to the floor, she was removing her shirt when Eric pressed kisses above the waistline of her underwear. His lips and his mustache brushed softly on her sensitive belly and she hummed. When her jeans and underwear were gathered at her feet, Eric held down the pants as she lifted out first one foot then the other. He grasped her ass and she looked down to catch his hungry expression just before he pressed his face into her pussy and started to suck and lick. She gasped. "Oh, god. Eric, fuck." And grabbed his head to steady herself.

But his hands on her back steadied her instead, guiding her back on the futon bed. He hooked her legs over his shoulders and he used his fingers to press open her center. Then he pushed his tongue and face completely into her pussy. The happy sounds he made and the feel of his tongue pushing into her so thoroughly made Jess feel incredible. He seemed determined not only to clean her up, as he had offered, but to make her come again.

This definitely was his goal, she realized, when he shifted his thumb to stroking her clit and darted his tongue up and down, in and out, all around her pussy. She felt her inner muscles start to throb, her need growing to squeeze down on something. Her pussy flooded. She slid her fingers through his hair. He paused only a moment to ask, "Fingers?"

"S-some-thing," she stuttered. "Now."

He lifted up on his knees, coming above her and kissing her. A finger curled inside her, pressing deeply. "That's it," he encouraged.

Jess felt his finger seeking and then, when it found her G spot, her body wanted to curl into a ball and explode at the same time. "Oh, god," she panted. "God, god, gooood." She exhaled and fell into euphoric release.

Blinking, she felt him withdraw his fingers, again putting them in his mouth as he leaned over her. He smiled; she hugged him. He kissed her and she tasted a little of herself on his lips. He'd been very thorough cleaning her. "I loved everything about today," she said. "Thank you."

"Anytime. Good night, Jess."

"Good night, Eric."

He tucked her naked under her sheet then kissed her temple before he went to the door and let himself out.

Chapter Twenty-Six

"WHO'RE YOU texting?" Val bumped his shoulder.

Eric looked up from thumbing through HR's app on his phone. "Just putting in for a week off next month." He and Val boarded the shuttle to the nearby hotel in New York where they'd crash tonight before piloting the last leg of their circuit back to Miami.

"You're taking time off?"

"Yeah, I put in a lot of replacement hours, so I've got comp time coming."

"Did you want to do something together?" she asked.

He shook his head. "I've got plans."

"What plans?"

"I'm going to take Jess to Chicago."

"Jess? Oh, the blonde from the party last year." She settled on the bench seat next to him. "Didn't know she was still around."

"She's living with us now," he said.

"That's new." Eric couldn't decide what that flat tone of Val's actually meant she was feeling, but he got the idea it wasn't positive.

"She needed a place to stay."

"But you're taking her to Chicago."

"Decided to show her some fun places where I hung out as a

newbie."

"And you're telling me this because..?" Her voice trailed away and he knew then she was upset.

"Because I thought you should know that Leo agreed to pick up my flights."

Leo Barnes had been one of Val's partners when Eric first met her. They were not cozy.

"I don't need you handling me. I'll deal with Leo just fine," Val replied. She frowned, shook her head and then sighed. "Look, you know I'm cool with casual, and I like your wife. But that's sort of our quirk."

"You know I date other people."

"We haven't spent any time together outside the hotel rooms in a while." Val fidgeted with the shoulder strap of her bag. "Are you still interested in me? If you're sleeping with her, *and* me, *and* Elena, don't you think you're spread too thin?"

"But I haven't missed any of our time together."

"I got you at work and Elena had you at home. That's the way it worked. But now you have this Jess and Elena both at home."

"I took you to the house party."

"I *came* to your house party," she corrected. "I actually thought that meant something was changing with us."

Eric frowned. "We needed people we all knew well for our first try at hosting."

"None of us had met Jess before that night."

"She was dating Elena at the time."

"From the sounds of it, now she's dating Elena," Val replied, "and you."

"I want to spend more time with her. There's nothing wrong with that."

"I think I'll bunk with Kai tonight." She stood as the shuttle came to a stop.

Kai was another flight attendant. "Why?" Eric said.

"I don't want to just keep getting a smaller and smaller piece of you, Eric."

"I told you."

"I know what you said, but just...OK, look...spend the time with Jess you want. I liked being with you," she said. "But your head's not here with us much anymore. It's back in Miami."

Eric strode off the shuttle and watched Val hurry forward, catching up to Kai.

She broke up with me. Hmm. He thought it should hurt. He wondered why it didn't.

Jess had time with Elena when he wasn't in Miami. He wasn't jealous though. He hadn't felt that Elena was less in love with him even as he watched her falling more and more in love with Jess.

He also liked the relationship he was building with Jess. All the times he and Jess spent together, with or without Elena, made his heart warm. He thought about her insistence that he continue his photography, and her interest in helping him out. He thought about what he'd done, reporting the Caliente. He thought about Elena's remark so long ago about romancing Jess. Was he doing that? She and he connected on some level different from what he shared with Elena.

He was gripped by a need to reach out to Elena and Jess in Miami. *Guess Val was right about that.* He pulled his phone out of his pocket again. With a smile at the thought that she'd be pleasantly surprised to see a message from him, he sent Jess his memoji, blowing her a kiss.

Jess felt the bed dip and opened her eyes in the darkened room. Elena slept serenely, her back tucked against Jess's front. Her own fingers flexed lightly against the woman's bare skin. Just when she had finished registering their positions were the same as when they had fallen asleep, she felt a big warm arm slide over her hip and a hair-covered muscled chest press to her naked back. She turned her head blindly. "Hey," she murmured in the darkness, seeing Eric's silhouette.

"How are my girls tonight?" Eric asked, his voice rumbling soft against her neck as he kept his voice barely audible.

Jess lifted his hand and moved it to join hers on Elena. "Glad to have you home," she whispered back.

Eric tucked his head into the curve of her shoulder and neck, then fitted his hips against hers. He still wore underwear, she realized, when his cotton-covered bulge mushed softly against her bare ass.

Elena's voice rumbled into the darkness. "Hmm? Eric?"

"I'm home, babe," Eric said. Jess felt his arm move again, this time brushing Elena's shoulder.

Jess kissed Elena's cheek when the woman half-turned her head. "Hmm?" The drift in the Latina's hum suggested she hadn't really awakened.

His smile evident against Jess's shoulder, Eric's lips soothed over her skin. "Go back to sleep," he whispered.

Letting her eyes drift closed again, Jess fell back into dreamland.

Eric listened as Elena and Jess talked about their progress. Elena felt she was closing in on her goal. She had secured sponsor agreements from an adult party planning company and the site managers of a swingers online bulletin board. She already had an ad running on the bulletin board site that had generated several reservations.

Jess was finally signed up for her first job training classes, covering office skills like answering phones, typing, and filling. He had chuckled at that, then asked if she started right away.

"No, the training starts in two weeks. It's a 'class' of fifty."

"Wow." He hugged and kissed her and then suggested they find some dessert.

The consensus was doughnuts and coffee.

When they sat together at the outdoor table, Eric fished the cruller from the bag and handed it to Elena, who was cupping her coffee. Eric asked, "My sophisticated entrepreneur." She smiled and took a bite. "I love you," he said. "And I am so proud of you."

He leaned in to kiss her, but paused when he saw Jess on the other side. Catching Jess's eye, he nodded. Together, they pressed kisses to both of Elena's cheeks. Jess left behind a dark lip print from her chocolate frosted doughnut.

"I'm a little nervous," Jess said. "I haven't been in a classroom in ten years."

"You have your GED right?"

"Yeah, but this is...it just feels like it will be different."

Eric chuckled and joked, "Maybe we should get you ready for the classroom again."

"Like roleplay?" Jess asked.

"Something like that," Elena said. "It might be fun."

"You up for it?"

"With you?" Jess asked. "I'm up for anything."

CHAPTER TWENTY-SEVEN

LIGHTLY TAPPING at the master bedroom door, Jess saw on the wall clock in the hallway that it was just past ten a.m. When there was no answer and thinking she could slip into bed with them still sleeping, Jess gingerly turned the knob and leaned in. The king-size bed was not only empty, but neatly made and the Tanners were nowhere in the space.

She searched for signs of the couple who were becoming closer to her than any family she had ever had. Walking through the house, she found no sign or sound of Eric or Elena in the living room, kitchen, or out on the back deck lounging since everyone had the day off. She found the couple's convertible parked in its usual place. She put her hand on the hood as she pondered where to look next.

A door closed somewhere inside the house. Rushing back inside, she checked the front door, opened and closed it to be sure that the couple hadn't gone into the front yard. Maybe Elena was gardening. But when she didn't see anything, she began checking all the doors in the house again. She closed the door to the playroom after seeing and hearing nothing down in the dark depths.

The only place which remained unchecked was her bedroom. She approached the hallway once again and saw her door was closed; she had not shut it that morning when she exited.

Smiling, thinking she would find Eric and Elena rolling around on her futon ready to invite her to play with them, Jess pushed the door inward and entered her room.

"Getting started witho-?" Jess cut herself off. The futon had been folded back into its couch position; a stack of freshly washed clothes sat in the middle of the cushion. She thought at first it was her laundry, but when she inspected the items closer, she realized the colors didn't match anything she owned. And there was a note on top. Picking it up, she smiled at the words:

"Time for a new uniform, Miss Davies," the note declared. "School starts at ten-thirty in the basement of Tanner Hall. Do not be late. Your safe word: drop out."

So they had been in the basement, Jess realized, impressed that they had managed to be so silent in the dark space when she looked down the stairs. She pictured Elena clamping her hand over her mouth when the light appeared at the doorway. Elena was not known for being able to hide much of anything when she was excited.

From the bedside clock Jess realized her search for the Tanners had taken a lot of time. She had less than three minutes to dress and report for "school." Dropping the note, she picked up the clothes, all the requisite parts of a private school girls' uniform: white oxford shirt and a red and black plaid skirt which barely reached her knees. She slipped on the baby-doll lace cradle cup bra which made her nipples push even more at the fabric of the tight shirt. Knee high socks and patten leather shoes completed the ensemble.

Dressed quickly she fretted about her hair ~ braiding would take way too long. A pair of long pig tails would have to do. She tied them off with elastic bands. Then she gathered up one of the textbooks she had already purchased for her classes, and a notebook and blue pen.

As she stumbled a little in the tight shoes toward the basement playroom, Jess felt her body heat rising. She wanted to find out what "lessons" her two teachers had in mind for her today. A rush of warm love and lust filled her as she pulled open the basement door.

She started to flip on the light at the top of the stairs, surprised she hadn't thought of it earlier, when the area below illuminated suddenly. Eric stood next to the bottom of the stairs, now as lookout.

As she came down the steps, she took in his attire. He had dressed in a conservative gray business suit—Jess was surprised he owned such a thing—Eric checked his watch. When she was only a few steps away, he slapped at the railings and blocked her way. Surprised at the sudden move, Jess jumped and met his gaze.

"Miss Davies, you are late. Again. You cannot expect to get a quality education when you are constantly late to school."

Jess blinked. His tone was perfect, reminiscent of the principal at her last high school in the hinterlands of Kentucky, when she'd been sixteen. Apparently though, she had waited too long to respond because his voice boomed once more. "Nothing to say for yourself?"

"I'm sorry." She considered a meek tone was most appropriate for the scenario. "Mr. Tanner. I won't be late again."

He corrected her. "*Principal* Tanner. You say that every time, Miss Davies, and it is clearly untrue. You know the punishment for lying." He pointed toward a table where a small wooden paddle lay.

Jess swallowed. "Oh please don't." She finished stepping off the stairs, still hugging her school supplies. Still in character.

"I know you are one of our scholarship students, Miss Davies, but you cannot be allowed to continue with this lackadaisical attitude. You must learn your lessons to better yourself." He went to the table, lifted the paddle, lightly tapping it between his hands. They'd talked about discipline as a sexual activity and used spanking before. In discussing this roleplay, she had agreed to try it. Jess found herself growing wet now.

"I can do better," she replied. "I swear—"

He shook his head. "We are a catholic institution, Miss Davies. There will be no swearing here." He grasped her arm. "OK?" he asked.

She said, "yes."

He tugged her forward. "Shall we start with ten?"

She had only taken his bare hand before this, the occasional swat when he was thrusting into her. Including the paddle, the goal was to push her limits, to remind her she had perseverance. He tapped her hands with the flat of the paddle, both a reminder he was waiting for a response and so she could become familiar with the paddle's weight and texture. "Bend over the table and drop your panties."

"Yes, sir," she said. She lifted her skirt; Eric's palm warmed her back as she slowly revealed the globes of her ass to his view. "Like this, sir?"

His palm moved warmly over all of her ass and Jess felt her body softening to his touch. She laid her cheek against the tabletop and sighed. A light swat to the fleshiest part of her ass with his palm accompanied the instruction, "Pay attention to the lesson, Miss Davies."

"Yes, sir." She lifted up on her hands and glanced over her shoulder.

Eric gave her ass a single swat with his open palm. It barely stung so she didn't react. She watched and waited.

Taking a moment to position the paddle carefully in his hand, Eric paused before pulling back and, with careful aim, he smacked it against the same ass cheek. That had marginally more sting than his hand. "Are you certain?" He checked in with her again.

She nodded. "Yes, sir."

"Now. Count."

Because he was determined to be so careful, Eric's swats with the paddle were not rapid. But the paddle was quite a bit harder than having just his hand. Jess's breathing became harsher as she controlled her response. She counted obediently until the last stroke.

Eric's final use of the paddle was far harder and faster than she'd expected, so she yelped, "Ten!" He rested the paddle against Jess's skin and the tingle which had been building slowly from his measured swatting became a throb. Jess was dripping and ready for fucking.

Eric's fingers swiped through the moisture but then instead of pulling up her panties, he fully removed them from around her one ankle. When he had pushed Jess back from the table and down onto the chair, she watched him licking his fingers and inhaling her scent from the cotton.

"Good, sir?"

"You are very good, Miss Davies." He winked at her. "But I wonder if you have learned your lesson yet?"

He perched on the desk, lifting his leg and placing his shoe between her thighs. She stared up at him as he brushed a few tears from her cheeks.

She nodded. "I don't want to quit, sir. I know that education is the only way I'll make something of myself."

He cupped her chin, lifting her eyes. "You will have lunch detention here, with me, every day."

"Every day?" she clarified. "What will I do?"

"You will learn skills every young woman needs to succeed in the world."

She squirmed. "What sort of skills?"

"Have you taken the business skills class, dear?" This was, in fact, one of the classes she'd signed up for. "Can you do typing? Filing?"

She remembered the laugh they'd shared as she read through the skills the course would teach. She looked around and then leaned forward. "And *dictation*, sir?" she asked conspiratorially. "I can help you with that."

Eric smiled at her. "That's what I like to hear."

He grasped her hands and pulled her to her feet. Assisting her with straightening her clothing, his hands cupped her breasts through her shirt and then cupped her center through the skirt as he kissed her.

She pulled back from him coquettishly. "Oh, no, sir. I'm a good girl."

"That's why you will start your lunch detention today. Now." He pushed her down again into the chair. He removed his belt. She started to her feet. He pushed her back down. "Do I need to restrain you?"

Jess gripped the sides of the chair under her. He wrapped one end of the belt around her wrist and tugged her forward between his thighs. "No, I...tell me what to do?"

"First you will take some simple dictation." He removed the belt from her wrist and then lowered his pants, revealing his hardening cock as it wobbled in midair between them.

She glanced up, showing what she hoped was a questioning look despite the eagerness in her belly to suck on this wonderful man's cock. He laughed; obviously her desire was easy for him to see. She grasped the head of it with one hand, testing the sponginess and smirked. She promised herself that she would make him want to explode.

Mindful that the slower she went the harder he would become and the longer he would last, she rolled the head between her fingers, then gripped firmly thumb to fingers and slid her fist down the shaft only an inch or so before she dragged it back up, outlining the veins starting to appear in relief. She stopped under the mushroom head and began again. Up and down, squeezing and releasing, she worked him. She reveled in his every groan and the occasional shudders. She elongated her strokes until she was massaging the entire length of him, from root to tip and back again. Eric bent forward and captured her lips.

"You are very good, Miss Davies," he praised against her mouth.

"I told you, sir." Jess smirked and it came out in her voice.

"Lippy. That should get you another detention."

"What will I do about my classes, sir?"

"Oh, I intend to let your teacher have a crack at you," he said. "But I intend to start." He pushed her head down. "Put those lips to better use."

She smiled, letting him push her head down until she had her mouth around the top of his cock. She lapped at the pre-cum seeping from his slit and lushly moved her mouth around the head, finding the sensitive spot just underneath and licking it. His cock jerked in her mouth and she smiled. He pushed her head harder, tugging on her pigtails.

She worked him into her mouth inch by inch. He wasn't so hard yet that his cock made her gag, but she had her mouth full by the time her nose buried in the hair at his groin, and the head filled the back of her throat. She worked her tongue around his shaft and as it twitched, now fully engorged, she backed up slowly, finally releasing the tip with a noisy pop.

His hands were clenching in fists; a sign he was nearing a point of no return. She wanted him to fuck her now.

Jess spoke with an over the top suggestive tone. "I think I'm ready for an extended *dic*tation, sir." She wriggled her ass and left a shiny gleam of her own juices on the smooth wood of the chair. The brief stimulation also took the tiniest edge off her arousal.

"I'll decide that." He helped her up, pulled her against his chest, fondled her breast through the shirt, and kissed her. He grabbed her ass with one hand, and fingered her clit with his other hand. The dual motions, as he had known, made her drip. "You're ready," he agreed.

Again they shared a small laugh. She reached into the pocket of his pants and retrieved a condom, then pushed the pants further down until they dropped past his knees. She unrolled the protection over his shaft with a parting massage. He "thanked" her by pushing a finger inside her and folding it toward her belly, an intimate stroking he knew from experience would bring on even more lubrication.

Sitting down on the chair, Eric adjusted his cock, using her juices on his fingers as lubricant. He lifted her skirt and she watched him rub her juices over her labia and her clit.

Eric's big hands working her with such delicate care never failed to make Jess a little crazy with love for him. When she put a hand on each of his shoulders he lifted her with both hands under her ass. She was filled from the first press of his cockhead just inside. Her pussy lips kissed and sucked on his cock as he slowly penetrated her.

Once she was fully impaled, she rocked, rubbing her clit hard against the base of him and increased her stimulation. He rubbed his fingertips over her ass and then down between, circling softly against her puckered hole.

She started to pull back to ask for a slow fuck, just like this. It wasn't that she wasn't adventurous. "Sir, I—"

His answer was quick and his blue eyes smiled at her while he continued to circle her puckered hole as though he was unaware. "Yes, Miss Davies?"

She asked, "Are you my only teacher today?"

"No, Miss Davies." Eric pushed his fingertip inside as Jess consciously relaxed the muscles. "Your teacher, Mrs. Tanner, still expects to speak with you about your poor attendance. She stated, and I quote, 'I am going to have her ass for missing my class' unquote."

Jess chuckled as Eric continued to slowly soften the tight ring of muscles with his fingertip. Now she knew what to expect when Elena finally showed herself. She kissed him and wrapped her arms around his neck. She murmured in his ear, "But you get to fuck me first."

Eric abandoned her asshole and pulled her down hard onto his cock, pushing his hips upward. The fullness was sudden, and perfect. "What did I say about cursing, Miss Davies?"

Jess gave him a worried look as he lifted her, pulled out, then turned her over across the desk. She smiled then as he laid the warm palm of his hand on her ass and shoved his cock back inside her to the hilt. She clenched when his hand left her back and returned to deliver a sharp slap. "Oh!"

The paddle returned, but Eric only swatted her once with it.

He preferred to finger her asshole while his cock became a piston. He was pulling nearly all the way out before sliding hard and fast to its full depth.

Her pussy clenched his cock as her orgasm sparked. She pushed back into his pelvis and whispered, "Oh. Yes!" He withdrew his finger from her ass and laid that palm on her back as he leaned forward, wrapped his other arm around her hip and fingered her clit until she froze in place. Her pussy milked his cock so he could not hold back any longer. His damp fingers slid up her belly, soothing the spasming muscles there. Softly he tugged at a nipple and set off a secondary wave of pleasure through Jess's body.

He gripped the base of his condom and pulled out. The slow twitching motion continued to feed small aftershocks for Jess and she pressed her heated flesh into the cool wood of the table, focusing on her breathing as she felt the waves gradually undulate to stillness. Sex and sweat permeated the air around her and she inhaled deeply.

Feeling light as a feather on the air currents, she exhaled in contentment. "Same time tomorrow?" she asked, drifting.

Eric chuckled. "I might keep in character a little better if we do this again."

Jess sighed and leaned into his warm palm cupping her cheek. Smiling up at him, she enjoyed the lassitude and connection.

Then it wasn't Eric's voice that broke the ensuing silence. "I see you finally found our truant."

Jess lifted her head to see Elena walking toward them, studying her laying nearly naked on the tabletop. The brown eyes were already sparkling with desires that spoke of both bottomless pleasure and heady taboos. Elena wore a conservative gray skirt suit, walked on four-inch heels that made her hips sway in Jess's direct line of sight, and in her right hand, rhythmically slapping against the palm of her left, she held a short thick pointer. Jess smiled when Elena stopped right beside her. The hem of the skirt was in easy reach. However, the pointer smacked the back of her hand when she tried to peek beneath.

Shaking out the sting, Jess laid her head down on her right cheek and watched as Eric and Elena enacted the brief transitioning of handing "the truant" over for Mrs. Tanner's discipline.

"Now, Miss Davies." Elena's voice had always done funny things to Jess's insides, but the authoritative husk and the formal address made Jess's nipples harden and her clit twitch. Eric had also used this title, but her reaction to Elena was different, as it was in many other ways. She squirmed a little on the seat. She had been put, still without her skirt, back down on the chair, told this was Mrs. Tanner's classroom, and she would be given every one of her missed lessons until her teacher was completely satisfied. "My classroom, my rules. Do you understand, Miss Davies?"

Jess looked at Elena, still absorbing the stunning appearance of the other woman. She wanted to say the conservative look was hot enough to make any liberal want to switch teams. She opened her mouth. The pointer slapped down on the desk. Jess flinched.

"Answer me. Miss Davies, do you understand?"

"Uh, yeah." Another slap of the pointer, this one breaking the air next to Jess's knuckles enough to raise the hair on her arms. "Yes, ma'am," she self-corrected.

"Good."

Elena placed a book open on the table but at some distance so that Jess would have to lean over the table in order to read it. "You will take in every lesson I give you, until I am satisfied with your performance." Jess wondered if there was more spanking involved in this scene. She'd certainly be positioned for it.

"Yes, ma'am."

"You will not skip a single day."

"No, ma'am." Jess's throat heated as Elena lifted her chin with a surprisingly uncharacteristic grip to the touch.

"An education is the key to success, Miss Davies," Elena said. "Your mind must be nimble and ready to be filled up. If you have any hesitation, this is perhaps not for you, and I will inform Principal Tanner you wish to drop out."

Recognizing her cue, Jess nodded. "I want to stay. You only want what's best for me," she said meekly.

"I do," Elena replied, cupping Jess's shoulder. She pulled Jess's shirt entirely off and told her to bend over the table. "Read." Naked flesh pressing again into the smooth cool wood of the table, Jess bent forward, leaving her feet on the floor. She rested her chin on her crossed hands and scanned the open page. "You will read aloud until I tell you to stop."

Her palm soothed over Jess's still slightly reddened ass. Jess hissed a little as the tingle caught her off guard. "Still tender from the principal's punishment," Elena said.

It wasn't toned as a question, but Jess answered it anyway. "Not much."

A drawer under the table opened. Jess started to turn around. "Start reading," came the instruction.

So she started to read as Elena's hands, slick with warmed cream, moved over her ass cheeks. It really didn't hurt much, but the tender attention was typical of both Tanners. Gradually the lotioning became a massage, from Jess's lower back down through the thick muscles of her glutes and into the big muscles of her thighs.

"*They argued with the men over philosophical, sociological, and artistic matters–*" Jess paused as Elena's palms shifted to the insides of her thighs, spreading her legs. A faint swat brought Jess's attention back to her assigned task, and she continued, "*...they were just as good as the men themselves: only better, because they were women.*"

Jess glanced up at the top of the page, surprised by the feminist thought. "What's this?" She lifted up and checked the cover. "*Lady Chatterley's Lover? D.H. Lawrence?*"

"It's a classic, banned in several countries as pornographic material."

Placing the book back down on the table, Jess settled back in. "Really? When did you first read it?"

"Six years ago. Found it left behind by an international flight passenger. I told you I love books."

Jess nodded. She was thinking about the words in the book when she felt Elena's fingers resuming their motion on her thighs, slipping down and inward. Elena brought her back to the scene. "Read, Miss Davies. I believe you will find it enlightening."

Jess continued to read, the distraction between the words and Elena's motions doing the most amazing things to her body, responding differently to each stimulus. She lifted her hips and opened herself more to Elena's attention.

"*For, of course, being a girl,*" Jess read, "*one's whole dignity and meaning in life consisted in the achievement of an absolute, a perfect, a pure and noble freedom.*"

"That's kind of sarcastic. This guy. When did he write this?" Jess asked.

Elena's hand didn't stop moving. "1928."

"He doesn't sound like he believes it's all good."

"In 1928, it wasn't, not for most women. But Connie has something few women got to do: the chance to control her own life."

"Does it work out?"

"Keep reading."

Jess looked at the page, thought about Elena's words, and

rolled onto her side. "Mrs. Tanner," she started, making sure Elena understood that she was doing this within their scene. "Why did you become a teacher?"

"I wanted to help young women find what they like and develop the confidence to pursue it."

Jess reached out and grasped Elena's hand sliding over her hip. "I like you, and I'd like you to get to know me better."

"Inside and out?" Elena asked, breathing into Jess's mouth before Jess closed the gap and sealed the deal with a kiss.

"Oh yeah. Teach me, teacher."

Chuckling, Elena filtered the loose hairs from Jess's pigtails through her fingers and possessively covered Jess's lips with her own. As Jess laid back on the table, Elena palmed her breasts, pinching and twisting the nipples. Jess writhed and cupped Elena's hands on her, keeping them in contact.

Leaving Jess's breasts, Elena slid her hands down Jess's belly. Her tongue and teeth swirled on the nipples instead. Cupping Elena's head, Jess arched her body seeking contact with Elena's. The woman's hands skimmed down to Jess's thighs and back up, cradling her hips and then down, parting her thighs and squeezing the muscles there. Jess's center throbbed at the promise of more to come.

A fingertip dragged through her labia and circled her clit. Jess slammed her hips back against the table and arched again quickly. Elena chuckled in the valley between her breasts.

"You are eager to learn, Miss Davies."

"Yes, ma'am." Jess breathed out as Elena's fingers eased inside her. Three fit easily because she was so ready. Elena positioned Jess's legs over her shoulders, continuing to twist and thrust her fingers. The drawer opened again. Jess then felt cool cream on Elena's fingers circling and massaging her asshole.

"Let's get some of those lessons *inside* you," Elena said as she kissed down Jess's chest to her belly, where the muscles twitched in arousal growing warmer and warmer as fingers circled and swirled, making her body feel like a flower opening. She arched her back and grasped the table, pushing herself onto Elena's hands. She was stretching and full, and eager to be fuller, yet so relaxed she could have happily let Elena do this for hours.

"On your stomach, Miss Davies." Jess was bereft as Elena completely withdrew and stood aside. "Back to your reading." She flipped the book that had been next to Jess's head to another bookmarked spot.

Jess rolled upward onto her elbows and stared at Elena. "Are you serious?"

"This is my lesson," Elena said.

"Um, right." Jess rolled onto her stomach.

Elena adjusted her legs. "Stand beside the table." She nudged her foot between Jess's legs which opened her stance wider.

"Yes, ma'am."

Her asshole opening steadily under Elena's attentions, Jess read aloud a scene where Constance, also known as Connie, engages in public anal sex in a competition to win a surfboard. She chuckled as the crowd reacted. She was full to the hilt with Elena's handheld glass dildo as she gasped in outrage at the result, "She didn't win? Robbed, I tell you."

Elena laughed and pumped the dildo steadily as she worked fingers underneath and back into Jess's pussy. "You would win the prize, for sure," she said. "Watching you with Eric earlier—"

"Where were you?" Jess asked, gripping the table and panting a little as the stimulation continued to rise.

"Behind the harem curtain," Elena said. Her thumb brushed Jess's clit and Jess's body convulsed hard. "Yeah, that's what happened to me when you climbed onto his cock. I was masturbating."

Jess groaned at the mental image of Elena trying to be silent and masturbating as she watched Eric and Jess in the earlier scene. Her mouth watered. "Please." Sure this wasn't meant to be part of the scene, but envisioning Elena in her head and on edge, she suddenly, desperately wanted Elena in her mouth.

Elena continued pumping the dildo and twisting her fingers in Jess's channel. "What do you want?" she asked.

"You, in my mouth," Jess panted. "Your taste. You—" Jess was rewarded for her desire by Elena once again sliding her thumb along her clit. "Oh, Go...ddd." She panted.

Elena eased out slowly. Jess twitched at feeling empty. Elena directed her, "Roll over."

With sloppy quick movements, Jess banged her elbows as she obeyed.

Her reward was perfection. Elena slowly parted the blouse buttons and unzipped the skirt, standing in only a lacy black small cup bra and garters without underwear. The hairs covering her center were damp and slicked in places, evidence of her earlier claim to masturbating. Before Jess could whistle appreciatively Elena reclaimed the dildo, clambered onto the table, straddled Jess's head, and draped herself down Jess's belly, groin in Jess's face and hands and mouth returning to Jess's center.

Wasting no time, Jess wrapped her arms around Elena's hips, pulling her quickly to her mouth. Elena's own efforts to return to Jess's center were interrupted by a gasp when Jess's nose bumped her clit. Jess chuckled and then repositioned quickly and sucked the nerve bundle.

"Oh, God," Elena murmured, and her hips ground down onto Jess's face.

Gradually Elena worked the dildo back into Jess's ass, using more lubricant, while she sucked on Jess's folds. Jess interrupted her tonguing of Elena's slit to moan again in pleasure.

"You are so good," Elena murmured into Jess's flesh as Jess swirled her tongue around Elena's labia and then sucked one side between her lips.

The dildo pushed inside further, and Jess rocked her hips upward, shifting the angle so it would slide deeper still. Elena's tongue flicked almost daintily at Jess's clit, but the sensation was so sharp, so sudden, Jess couldn't stop her orgasm from washing through her in a rush.

She buried her cry in Elena's flesh and the other woman's orgasm wet Jess's face from lips to chin. She lapped at all of it while Elena's cry was muffled in her own flesh.

Panting, Jess felt Elena trying to move. She held her tighter. "Hey."

"I'm not leaving," Elena said, her voice awash with breath. "Just readjusting." Her hand planted on the table beside Jess's hip, lifting her chest up a bit from Jess's belly.

Jess looked down their bodies and saw Eric, pants dropped, presenting Elena with his renewed cock cupped in his left fist. Elena guided it into her mouth. Jess watched, enjoying the sight of his cock disappearing between Elena's lips. Eric reached below his wife with his right hand. Jess thought he was going to fondle Elena's breasts, except she felt the dildo still in her own ass shift and start moving inward once again.

"Don't let my arrival interrupt your studies, Miss Davies," Eric said.

Jess moaned and sighed happily. "Yes, sir." She returned to eagerly licking Elena's folds. "Education is so important, you're right,

Mrs. Tanner. And quite"—she paused and blew a slow stream of breath against Elena's clit—"filling." She smiled when Elena's hips twitched exactly as she knew they would. "Uh, I mean, fulfilling."

Elena laughed around Eric's cock and he chuckled, his shaking shoulders making the dildo inside Jess also move. "I'm so glad, Miss Davies."

"Oh yeah," she murmured, feeling another slow rolling orgasm ripple through her gut.

Elena and Jess walked out of the master bedroom. Eric had left for work several hours earlier and left them both sleeping. Jess was wrapping her wet hair in a rolled up bandanna before moving to the kitchen. "Egg muffins?" she asked.

Collecting her laptop from the living room, Elena answered, "Sounds good." She returned to the dining table to set out breakfast items and found colorfully wrapped packages and envelopes at her and Jess's places. She frowned, but then lifting the card she remembered a conversation with Eric about a spring trip. *He must've been able to swing it*, she realized. "Jess, come out here for a sec."

"What's up?" Jess appeared at the space between the dining table and kitchen entry. "Presents?"

"Presents. You've got a card." Elena pointed.

"What for?"

Elena had already opened her envelope with a card. "It says 'All That Jazz'." She caught a piece of paper that fell from the card. "Oh. I think–oh!" She quickly pointed to Jess's place setting. "Open yours."

Jess walked to her package and envelope, going for the package first. Elena could feel her own excitement building as she anticipated Jess's reaction to Eric's gift. Out of the clown-wrapped paper, Jess removed a green and gray sweatshirt.

"When am I going to be able to wear a sweatshirt in Miami?" Jess asked. She turned it around studying the sweatshirt with a big Shamrock between the words "Too cute to pinch."

"The card," Elena said, finally unable to hide her impatient excitement. "Read Eric's card."

Jess lifted the flap out of the unsealed envelope and removed the card. "All That Jazz," she read aloud then flipped open the front cover. Elena held her breath. "A plane ticket?"

Elena held up her own. "To Chicago!"

"What's in Chicago?"

"You know Eric started there."

"Yes, we've talked about it." Jess read the ticket information. "March 16. March 18. Three days?"

"Right over St. Patrick's Day," Elena explained pointing at Jess's sweatshirt then her own, now unpacked and also in green which read: *Not Irish. Just Drunk*. "Eric and I have gone a few times. Now you'll get to experience it, too. They dye the river green and everything is just..." She stumbled to explain. "You'll love it," she finished.

Jess slowly smiled and lifted her gaze from the ticket, meeting Elena's.. The light in her green eyes was brightly sparkling. "I've ...wow. They put dye in the river? How? I've never...this is....a ticket." She sank to the chair still holding the ticket and shirt.

Elena knew speechless meant Jess was overwhelmed. She now wished Eric could have been here to see the reception his gift received. She only wondered how he had gotten the ticket; Jess wasn't legally family.

Knowing the younger woman had traveled a lot, Elena was surprised that Jess hadn't been to Chicago or known of the city's quirky St. Patrick's Day festivities. However, Elena mentally patted Eric on the back. Somehow he must have learned or guessed it would be a new experience for her. The way Jess was smiling and looking a bit shocked, he had found the perfect gift.

Jess sank to the seat of her chair. "Wow."

Walking around the table, Elena smoothed her hands over Jess's blonde hair and kissed the top of her head. "I think you'll enjoy Chicago."

Jess nodded, then kept her head down, gripping the ticket and sweatshirt between her hands.

Chapter Twenty-Eight

"I TOLD you there's a reason it's called the cockpit," Elena teased Jess. Elena sat on Eric's lap with her halter dress bunched at her waist. His pants were open and his cock poked through his underwear. Lifting his hips, he was thrusting up into his wife. The two had gotten permission to take Jess on a tour into the cockpit of a 717 being serviced as they came through the cargo area to the international airport.

Jess leaned back against the console as Eric fingered her, his hand up one leg of her cotton shorts. Looking sideways out of the plane's windshield, she had a view of several gantries inside the service hangar, but the hangar, like the rest of the airport at three in the morning, was empty. Jess, Eric and Elena had seats on a five a.m. flight to Chicago, courtesy of Eric's employment perks.

I love this perk, Jess thought when Elena's hand joined her husband's. Both husband and wife fingered Jess while Elena nibbled on Jess's lips. Elena bouncing on Eric's cock and rubbing up against Jess at the same time with both his and her fingers curling together inside and trying to reach her G spot had Jess nearly out of her mind.

She braced her hands behind her on the console, thrusting her hips forward over and over again. Knobs shifted under her fingers.

Repositioning quickly, she finally found a relatively dial-free space and used the leverage to rock up and down on her lovers' hands.

Elena threw her head back and bared her throat. The cockpit lighting shined on her damp skin and Jess felt her arousal ratchet even higher. Leaning forward, she sucked on Elena's pulse point, tasting salt and skin and feeling deliriously happy.

She groaned when the tingling started in her belly. "Oh, fuck," Continuing to rock, Jess fought to keep her eyes open and focused on Elena. Brown eyes crinkled and lips, parting around tiny gasps, curved up in a delighted smile.

"More?" Elena asked.

Unable to articulate her need beyond a moan, Jess nodded. Their single fingers became two each. The muscles of her pussy spasmed, loosened, and pulled them deeper.

Eric groaned abruptly. His fingers left Jess and she whined, missing the fullness. Elena's fingers inside her multiplied, replacing the loss. Jess opened her eyes at Elena's hitched squeal.

Eric had grabbed Elena's hips, pulling his wife more firmly down onto his upward thrusts.

"Oh, god, yeah," he growled; Elena's gasps became delighted moans. Her four fingers in Jess rotated and curled at the same time she braced her other hand on the console, leaning forward as Eric stood from the chair.

"Kiss me," Elena breathed, her brown wild-eyed gaze sucking in Jess instantly.

Jess shifted her weight onto her right hand on the console and cupped the back of Elena's head with her now free left hand. Pulling their faces together she claimed the woman's mouth in a soul-sucking kiss.

Elena gave Jess every sensation back through her fingers and mouth. They cried out together. Then Jess couldn't hold back any longer. Her groin convulsed. She froze when Elena's thumb massaged her clit. "Oh, god," she groaned long and slow as the orgasm rumbled through her like a freight train.

Eric's rapid breathing hitched and then he groaned, long and low, signaling the arrival of his orgasm.

As her tremors ebbed, Jess trailed her kisses away from Elena's mouth, onto the warm, sweat-damp skin of the other woman's throat. Elena dropped her head to Jess's shoulder, chest heaving, lips panting, recovering in the aftermath of her own orgasm.

They stroked their fingers tenderly through each other's hair, both needing the grounding touch. Eric leaned across Elena's shoulder. Jess met his smiling blue eyes then kissed his lips, quivering when his mustache brushing her lips shot tingles into her.

They arrived at the Airbnb condo located on the fourth floor of a building on Chicago's northeast side around noon, tired and worn from the flight. Elena opened the key box with the combo from the confirmation email. Jess leaned tiredly on the wall next to the door. She exchanged a look with Eric who hugged Jess to him.

With the door open, they each picked up their bags and Eric stepped in first, looking around. "Two bedrooms."

"Three people," Elena said. "The algorithm wouldn't let me go lower than two beds."

"Gotta keep up with the times," Eric said. "So you and Jess take one room? I'll take the other?"

"I can take the one room," Jess said. "You two—"

Eric cut off Jess's words with a kiss. "Three," he said.

"Pfft," Elena scoffed. "We'll save one for naps." She led the way to the furthest bedroom.

Though not as large and spacious as the master bedroom at the Tanner home, it was still nice, Jess thought. A queen bed with polished oak headboard and side tables dominated the room. A large mirror set atop a short two-by-three drawer chest against the opposite wall. Setting down her bag, Elena lay back on the white duvet, dark hair and features outlined by white sheets and white pillows.

Jess turned away and pulled off her jacket, looking for and finding a hook on the back of the door to put it up. Dark brown eyes drank her in as she approached the bed. "You see something you want?" Elena asked.

From the closet door, Eric asked, "You wanna christen the bed? We don't have any place to be."

Despite herself, Jess yawned. "Nap it is," Elena said, opening her arms. "Come here."

"I'll take the other bedroom," Eric said.

"No, sweetheart, this bed's big enough." Elena patted the surface next to her as Jess crawled in against her left side. Jess looked like she needed some snuggling time.

The three of them stripped to their underwear. Returning to the bed, Elena felt Jess's muscles melt when she wrapped her arms around her, kissing her as she coaxed Eric's body to mold to Jess's back. He kissed Jess's neck and shoulders, while Elena shifted to kissing Jess's collarbones.

"I'm sorry I'm out of it," Jess said.

Elena wasn't going to say that she and Eric were seasoned travelers. In her own way, Jess was too, and that would reveal exactly where this exhaustion was truly coming from: Jess feeling like she had to act a certain way because of where she was. "We have three days."

She saw Jess tug Eric's hand against her belly. Cupping Jess's head, Elena held it to her chest over her heart. Her heart beat steadily under Jess's ear, no doubt soothing the younger woman. Meeting Eric's eyes, Elena smiled.

"Sleep well, Jess," she murmured into the golden hair, planting a kiss. Though she was not particularly tired, Elena found the peace and quiet relaxing and was soon asleep, too.

Jess suspiciously eyed the green beer Eric passed her from the beefy man tending the bar's taps. "You sure about this?"

"It's tradition," he replied, sipping from his own iced mug.

"Does it have mint?" The green made her think of mint jelly. Jess curled her lip; she wasn't a fan.

"God, no! Dive bars do that, adding creme de menthe. This is just food coloring."

Lifting the mug to her lips still wary, Jess sniffed. No scent of mint. She took a cautious sip. Definitely still beer. She nodded when she had lowered the mug. "All right."

"Now, drink up. It's mandatory to get drunk today."

"I thought it was a saint's holiday. Weren't those guys teetotalers or something?"

"Who the hell cares," Eric said. "Bonsai!"

"That's Japanese." Jess laughed. She heard a nearby pair toast and click their mugs. She echoed them. "Slan-cha," she said in a close approximation.

Eric smiled at her and clinked his mug against hers.

Jess laughed, but then she drank.

The three of them had come here to start what Eric had called the St. Patrick's Day "revelry." It wouldn't be the holiday until tomorrow, but this place clearly started the night before.

The jukebox at this bar, Shinnick's Pub, was rolling out Irish tunes. Patrons in every corner belted out drinking songs and ballads. Eric wasn't any more Irish than Jess, who knew nothing of her parents or family heritage. But a holiday with beer, singing, and laughing? She could get behind that.

The two of them leaned side by side against the bar, sipping their green beers, and watched a group of college-aged guys play beer pong. Eric's shoulder shifted against hers. Elena had gone to the bathroom after consuming their pub grub dinner.

Jess looked up. Eric leaned in as they watched a redhead freckle-faced college student chug his beer to his buddies' triumphant yells and cheers. "Happy anniversary."

"Anniversary?" Jess's face drained of heat.

"Yeah, *our* anniversary." His fingers rubbed hers. "You've been part of our lives for almost eight months."

Has it really been that long? Jess was shocked. *What was that saying? Time flies when you're having fun?* She looked up and found his blue eyes smiling at her.

Eric's arms came around her when she crashed into his chest, overwhelmed by the gesture, by his smile, by... everything. Hot tears slid down her cheeks. "Fuck," she breathed around sobs. "Fuck, fuck, fuck."

He kissed her head and moved his hands soothingly on her back, murmuring around gentle chuckles. "We can do lots of that on this trip, too."

Jess pressed a weak fist into his stomach and then flattened her other hand against his chest, trying to get a grip on herself. Choking back on a half-sob, half-laugh, she forced out barely a whisper. "Thank you."

Against her head, in a gentle and understanding tone, Eric said, "You're welcome."

She let him hug her tighter.

Elena emerged from the bathroom to find Jess still being hugged by Eric. "You told her how long it's been, didn't you?"

"I can't believe it," Jess said.

"Believe it." Elena brushed the tear stains from Jess's cheeks before kissing her lightly on the other cheek. "Love you," she murmured against the woman's ear.

Jess's fingers tangled with hers and squeezed lightly.

"For luck?" Elena asked as Jess used edible fingerpaints to sketch a four-leaf clover over Elena's belly as the woman lay on a towel on the lakefront beach. She wore a bathing suit, though her shoulders were still covered in a wrap. It was officially St. Patrick's Day and they had awakened early to see the city's river flowed with varying shades of green, the dye spreading through the current.

Eric had then taken them to shop along the shore of Lake Michigan where they ate and laughed. Jess had purchased the novelty paints when Elena had seen Jess's interest in the display and commented she had some back in Miami, a Christmas gift from Eric.

"I'm very lucky," Jess replied, continuing to paint, her fingers diligently filling in the outline. The sensations were starting to make Elena's belly quiver.

"Mm hmm." She decided to simply lay back. If she soaked her panties, so be it.

"Anyone interested in a naughty leprechaun and his platter of gold?"

Opening her eyes, Elena saw Eric returning carrying a tray. "Lunch?" At the mention of food, Jess put down the paints and wiped her fingers on the corner of another towel.

Eric crouched to the ground, putting the cardboard tray down next to them before settling to its other side. "Classic Chicago dogs." Several of the fat sausages in puffy white buns, with their neon green relish and bright yellow mustard, sat in crenelated white cardboard alongside three plastic bottles of soda.

Resettling into crossed legs, Jess grabbed up one of the dogs and bit into it quickly. "Mmm," she hummed as she chewed.

As she sat up, Elena chuckled then rubbed the woman's knee. "Slow down."

"There's six here," Eric said. "And I can get more."

"What's so naughty about you, Mr. Leprechaun?" Elena asked as she picked up one of the dogs, intending to eat much more slowly, even as she eyed Jess finishing with her first and reaching for another.

"I packed a little blue magic. I can serve both of you all night. However you like."

Elena leaned forward and kissed him, then used her thumb to remove the mustard that had transferred from her lips to his. "So we've captured the leprechaun, hmm? Jess, what do you think we should do with him?"

Looking over her shoulder, Elena caught Jess's green eyes crinkled at the corners, her grin evident. Jess chewed, swallowed, then said, "I can think of a few things I want. Typically there are three wishes."

"Oh, I think three *each*," Elena said with a chuckle. "Don't you?"

Eric hadn't needed any help getting hard. Though he took the pill to be sure, he had been semi-turgid ever since delivering the offer of himself. When the three of them returned to the condo, he ordered another classic—a Chicago deep dish pizza. Already taking charge, Elena had ordered him into his Speedo bathing suit by the time the delivery man arrived.

Elena and Jess were sharing the large tub, cleaning up and laughing and splashing loud enough for the delivery kid, probably barely in his 20s, to look around curiously.

"Thanks," Eric said. "Here's a tip: when a woman tells you something, listen." He then pressed a ten in the kid's hand and sent him away.

Turning away after closing the door, he put the pizza and sodas on the dining table before going to the bedroom door. "Pizza's here."

A splash told him they were still in the tub. He stepped up to the closed door in time to hear "Coming!" from Jess. Then Elena laughed and Jess uttered a throaty, "Fuuuck."

He opened the door to see Elena crouched between Jess's thighs as the young woman leaned on the side and rested back against the tile wall. Her hands were cupped on his wife's dark head. Both were naked and wet and, as Elena pulled away from her undoubtedly delicious feasting, he saw that she had been fucking Jess with a fat pink flesh-colored silicone cock. Elena pulled the massive dong free and he saw Jess's spread, flushed, glistening and gaping pussy. His balls pulled tight to his body, ready to burst, and his cockhead pushed past the waistband of his Speedo.

Elena stood and turned, water sluicing off her body. Eric drank in the hardened peaks of her nipples, the lush curve of her hips and the trimmed wet hairs covering her center. He licked his lips, then raised his gaze to meet her brown eyes. "Hi."

His eyes moved over Jess while Elena held her hand, helping her stand and step out of the tub. When Jess's gaze met his, her pupils were wide, the green bright. Elena had painted a four-leaf clover on each of Jess's cheeks, and red hearts had been drawn around each nipple. A blue line led down to the patch of blonde hair between her thighs.

"She was going to shave me and paint a pot of gold," Jess said.

"Ah, sorry to have interrupted."

"You can do it," Jess replied. "Later."

"I take it that means my offer of food is more intriguing?"

Elena and Jess remained nude, only taking towels with them to the dining table. Eric enjoyed watching the rapture on Jess's face as her stomach filled with the pizza.

He welcomed their slow building tease, starting while they were still nibbling pizza and sipping soda, telling him to lick various drips of pizza sauce off their bodies. Then, when the food was finished, they stood up from the table and told him to clear the things into the kitchen. When he came back, he found them sitting on top of the oval tabletop, legs spread. Elena had her fingers between Jess's legs rubbing her clit and Jess rubbed Elena's. Both of them were glistening wet once again.

Breaking off from kissing Elena, Jess said, "Time for dessert. Her cream, then my cream, and finally, we get your cream."

Eric asked, "This is your wish?"

Elena pointed down. "One more thing. On your knees."

Jess nodded. "Leprechauns are only waist high."

Eric knelt, now looking up at both women. "Come here," Jess patted Elena's center and his wife closed her eyes at the undoubtedly pleasant feeling. He reached for Elena's legs. "No hands."

Ah, he thought. *Got it.* He shouldered himself between Elena's knees and clasped his hands together behind his back. Her belly button was directly in front of him, so he kissed that first. Her scent made his mouth water. He knew her taste would be savory, particularly after the oregano in the pizza sauce. Elena's hand moved to his head as he trailed his kisses from her belly button to her center. Flattening his tongue, the tip found her clit first and she grasped his hair tightly.

He rubbed his nose against the bundle of nerves while his lips and tongue pulled at her folds. Gorging as devotedly on Elena's pussy as Jess had been when eating her pizza earlier, he listened for Elena's reactions, moving his attention on or off her clit as she gasped or squealed. She threw her legs over his shoulders and the angle allowed him to push his tongue fully inside her. He heard the table creak and moved his attention to her opening, sucking at the cream dripping there.

Jess slid off the table after kissing Elena. Elena's brown eyes rolled back in her head, clearly thrilled by Eric's talented tongue. Under the table Jess saw Eric's cock had sprung fully free of the Speedo. Only his balls were hidden and the veined shaft stood out stiff and proud.

Finding her bag in the bathroom, she withdrew condoms and hurried back to the show. Eyes clenched shut, Elena was gasping for breath. Her nipples were stiff atop her breasts, chest arched and heaving as Eric's tongue lashed her closer and closer to climax. "Er-Eric! Dios mio, por favor! Oh, si, si...ah, me folle."

Chuckling, Jess caught Eric's eye as she ducked under the table. "You heard her," she said. With deft fingers she unrolled a condom down his shaft. "Go for it."

Eric stood and was balls deep inside Elena between one breath and the next. Her legs locked behind his hips and he rocked on his heels. He groaned at what was probably the pleasure of Elena's muscles squeezing him tightly.

Jess watched his length withdraw then disappear again inside his wife. She grasped Elena's nipples tightly and murmured in her ear. "I love seeing your face when he's satisfying you."

Eric groaned; his eyes opened, finding hers first then searching lower. She glanced down to see Elena looking up. She backed up and watched them pull at each other until Elena was up and wrapped in his arms; Eric thrusting and Elena bouncing.

Swallowing at her own dry mouth from witnessing their passion, Jess drank in the sight and sounds as they came apart...together.

Settling on the nearby couch, Elena leaned back with a glass of water as Eric gave Jess the tongue-lashing Elena said she deserved for letting him orgasm before both of them were done. The dining table was still their "sexual buffet" spot, with Jess splayed across the wood. Elena had given Eric permission to use his hands. His hands stroked her sides, pulled a little at her nipples, and his mouth moved between her legs.

Jess was flushed, her pale body a rosy pink all over as she writhed under Eric. Her hands cradled Eric's head and Elena was able to see his tongue swirling around her clit and his face crush to her pussy each time his tongue dove deep. Jess was not as vocal as Elena in the throes of sex, but Eric adjusted his touches to meet her needs. It probably helped, too, that Elena had already made Jess orgasm at the hands of her thick toy.

"Is she spicy or sweet today, Eric?" Elena asked.

"Savory sweet," Eric replied, lifting momentarily from his attentions, briefly replacing his mouth with his fingers. Elena watched Jess jump.

"Eric," Jess murmured, "yes."

"Do you want Mr. Naughty Leprechaun's fingers or his cock?" Elena asked. Eric brushed his thumb across Jess's clit again making the woman squirm. Elena bit her lip to stop a laugh from escaping. "He's here to grant your wishes. So if you'd like both, all you have to do is say so."

Eric's thumb swirled directly. Jess gasped. "Oh, god, yes. I want your cock."

"There you go." Elena leaned forward, sucking on Jess's nearest nipple at the same time Eric pushed his thumb inside Jess's channel and stood. She replaced his fingers on Jess's soft hot center, keeping up the stimulation while Eric tore open a condom and rolled it down his still-hard cock.

Elena stepped back when Eric grasped Jess's side. "I've got you, Jess," he said. Jess's gaze sought his as he slid his arms behind her back, slowly lifting her off the table. The shift in position smoothly moved her onto his shaft. Elena watched him cradle Jess as he thrust up, bouncing her on his cock, and her legs wrapped around his hips.

Jess wrapped her arms around Eric's shoulders and head and they kissed. "Mmm," she hummed, obviously tasting herself on Eric's lips and mustache. Then Eric rested his face against her breast, continuing to bounce her.

"Hold tight," he said. "Yeah, that's it." He grunted then laid Jess back on the table, bending over her. He lifted Jess's knees and pushed into them with his shoulders. Elena could see his cock moving in and out of Jess and he brought his thumb against her clit again, triggering Jess's orgasm.

Eric groaned, pulling out and pushing his cock back in. Jess cried out in pleasure at the return of his hard shaft. Elena licked her lips and exhaled, her own groin pulsing as she watched them kiss tenderly. Eric cupped Jess's cheek and she turned her lips into his palm. "Hey," he said.

"Hey," Jess replied. She sat up, propping herself with her left elbow.

Seeing Eric's brows crease, Elena moved around Jess's leg and kissed him. She looked down at his cock to see his fingers on the condom. It was askew and coated with his and Jess's cream. "Condom came off," Eric said.

Feeling Jess's thigh tense under her hand, Elena said, "Foam spermicide's in the sex bag."

"Can't be much." Jess looked down at her crotch. "Besides I started the pill."

"Still...I'll help. Make it a little fun," Eric said.

Jess put a clean applicator on the spermicide tube. While Eric cleaned up in the bathtub, Jess sat on the edge of the bathroom counter. Elena licked all over Jess's pussy and then used a washcloth. Stepping back, she watched Jess insert the applicator and squeeze the tube. "Probably should use the foam for a while in addition to condoms," Jess said.

"And Mr. Naughty Leprechaun doesn't come out to play again until we're sure," Eric said, retreating to his bags and retrieving underwear and a shirt.

CHAPTER TWENTY-NINE

IN THE weeks after Chicago. Jess threw herself into working. She had started the paid customer service phone bank training and would continue it for another two weeks. The day classes left her time to work part time for Monica at Face to Face. Both jobs paid very little, and she took buses everywhere, but she gave nearly everything left to Elena–without telling the woman that–so she could feel like she was contributing.

She relished Sundays before Eric flew out. They all woke up together then spent the day in and out of bed, watching movies, talking, laughing. Since Chicago though, Eric hadn't once penetrated her with anything other than his fingers. She'd watch him fucking Elena and feel her groin clench at the memory of how it felt when he filled her.

Working in Miami was difficult. She felt like an outsider not knowing Spanish, surrounded by so many who spoke the language easily. She asked Elena for some help, which Elena did, teaching her in the evening between dinner and sleep.

Her reward for mastering a dialogue about colors and numbers had been Elena filling her with ben-wa balls, her counting each one–in Spanish of course. The different size words had been another lesson, Elena filling her with increasingly bigger vibrators, dildos, and rubber cocks.

But it wasn't the same. Jess sighed. She knew her period finally showing up might be the answer, but it was already a couple days late. She sighed.

Across the room, Monica called, "Table 6, order's up."

Jess finished filling the water glasses at table 4, smiling at the two women before walking over to the bar.

"How's it going?"

"Fine."

"Are you sure you don't want to be full-time?" she asked.

"I need the job training they're offering."

"You go there before coming here, right?"

"Yeah." Jess picked up the food tray.

"What about working later? Through dinner rush?"

"I gotta get home."

"Home?"

"Yeah, I live over in the Shores."

"How do you live there and need to work here?"

"It's not my place. I've got a room."

"Kitchen privileges?"

"Yeah." She grinned, thinking about Elena and Eric. "There are a few other perks, too." Jess then asked, "What's with the questions?"

"I was just thinking you might...increase your time with..." The bar owner faltered. "Here. But it sounds like you've got a good arrangement going."

"Mm hmm," Jess hummed. "I should get these over to Table 6."

"Bathroom break," Jess said, placing down her empty tray and walking past Monica at the bar. "Be right back."

The woman nodded. Pauline and Dena had arrived for the evening shift so it wasn't like the place would be short-handed.

Stepping into the stall, Jess sat and relieved her bladder. Cleaning up she noticed the spotting on her underwear. Relief swept through her. Finally. She texted Elena: *Cardinal finally arrived.*

The reply was quick. *You sure? We were kind of vigorous last night.*

Yeah, she typed back, *definitely my period.*

I'll draw a bath for you when you get home, Elena replied. *Anything in particular you want to eat?*

Jess queried her stomach. *Milk and cookies.*

Chocolate? We might still have a frozen box of Thin Mints.

Sounds perfect, Jess replied. Tidying herself up, she stood from the toilet and texted, *I'll be home in an hour or so.*

I'll be waiting.

Elena exhaled as she set aside the phone. Jess had gotten her period. She felt the sudden release of strain in her shoulders and back. Looking at her business papers, she realized she had thrown herself into more business planning as a way to distract herself. While they'd cleaned up following the incident in Chicago, Eric had insisted he wouldn't touch Jess again until her period showed up. And he hadn't. The last few weeks had felt...stilted.

She forwarded Jess's text to Eric. No immediate response suggested he was in the air. Though she wanted to know his thoughts, she would have to wait.

Despite knowing there was no pregnancy this time, Elena walked through the house in a daze. For the first time she really considered it with the mindset of a *family* home. When they were shopping for a place, she and Eric thought the largely open floor plan perfect for entertaining their airline friends and then later, their swinging partners. But there had always only been two bedrooms. The master and the one they'd made the house accounts office, which was now Jess's bedroom. Until Jess they'd never really considered anyone else living with them.

Not just anyone, Elena thought, *a baby*. If Jess had been pregnant, what would they have done?

She tried to remember back to the beginning, when they'd done the careful questioning of partners, and she'd used the spermicide sponges. Over time though they had become more concerned with STDs than pregnancy, and regular testing had satisfied them they were safe. Her own periods were regular as clockwork and she couldn't recall the last time she had been late, even by a day.

Elena felt shame that she hadn't been more attentive. She should have put more thought into safe sex with Jess. For tonight though, she intended to care for her, relieved the bigger question was, once again, able to be put off.

Eric let go of his flight bag handle and extracted his phone from a zippered pocket. Turning on the power, he was surprised to see a text message alert flash on the screen. He noted it was from Elena as he thumbed it open.

Cardinal finally arrived. The message puzzled him. He'd never known Elena to talk about birds. Then he noticed that it was actually a forwarded message from Jess. Cardinal?

He texted her. *Where'd you see a cardinal?*

Jess's reply was quick. *Not a bird. My period.*

Oh. He typed again. *You don't usually mention it. You OK?*

It means I'm not pregnant.

Eric sat down on a chair in the airport, ignoring the flow of people around him. While he hadn't forgotten, he was suddenly struck by a wave of relief that told him he'd been very tense about the whole thing since Chicago. Quickly he texted the only response that seemed appropriate. *Are you OK?*

On my way home to a warm bath.

That wasn't really an answer, Eric thought. He thumbed over to his favorite contacts and tapped her name, opening a call.

"Hey," she answered. Her tone sounded like she was smiling.

"You're not driving right?" he asked.

"I'm on the bus," Jess said. "What's up?"

"Just want to make sure you're OK."

"I'm fine. Really. Pregnancy wasn't something I wanted either."

"All right," he said. "You'd tell me if it was?"

"I would, Eric. Take care."

"Enjoy your bath."

"Thanks."

Eric closed the call and texted Elena back. *We should all talk.*

I agree, she replied.

Elena hugged Jess in the tub, soaping her solicitously. "I'm sorry," she said.

"I didn't want to talk about it either," Jess said. "You and Eric were always telling me to communicate. I thought I didn't need to say anything if you weren't."

"I forgot what it was like when we started out," Elena said. "You just slipped in so easily."

"So, what will we do going forward?"

Elena kissed her cheek, rubbing her breasts with the sponge. "If you do become pregnant, or I do, for that matter, what would you want to do?"

"It would be Eric's, too."

"He doesn't want to be a father."

"Elena, I already gave up one child. I don't think I could do it again."

"You..." She had a moment of clarity. "The boyfriend who left you?"

"Yeah. I had a...a boy, at a halfway house after jail. Put him up for adoption."

"Oh my god, Jess." Elena hugged her closer, wrapping her up in arms and legs, and kissed her shoulder as they sat together until the water got cold.

"So, how do we make sure no one gets pregnant?" Jess asked.

Eric, Elena and Jess fell silent. Sitting at the table after dinner, they'd finally broached the topic on their minds since Jess's message.

"I can get a vasectomy," Eric said. Preventing pregnancy was everyone's responsibility. He'd set aside the pamphlets after the January scare. A vasectomy would be his best contribution to their collective peace of mind.

"It's surgery," Elena said. "We might as well tie my tubes and Jess's. That would do the same thing."

"This is minor compared to that," he said. "Outpatient, snip, snip. Done."

"Why would you do that?" Jess asked.

He reached to grasp her hand across the dining table where they all sat. "I've been playing with loaded dice all this time. I realized I've been the most reckless despite our pledge for safer sex."

Her eyes were hazel green. "Still, surgery's a big step."

"I don't want any of us to have to worry like we have been." A deep conviction settled on Eric as he spoke. He would do this to be the man he professed to be: compassionate, responsible, and respectful.

Chapter Thirty

Elena went with him to the appointments. The doctor had told them to talk about children. In the waiting room they both still agreed they did not want to be parents and Jess's situation mattered. They didn't want her to be anxious like that again.

When the outpatient surgery occurred, it was surprisingly straightforward. He was sore for a week, actually taking time off work, and Elena and Jess took care of him.

When he was asked for the fourth time if he wanted a compress, he replied that he just wanted to snuggle. They sandwiched him gently. Jess made him laugh with her attempts to put her hand "some place that won't hurt." He grabbed her hand, kissed it, then her, and placed her palm on his stomach. Elena kissed his shoulder and he managed a short nap.

After his second post-op check confirmed his 'swimmers' were all gone, Eric felt enormous relief.

After four months of standby living with the Tanners, by April Jess accepted that her relationship with them was deeper than friends-with-benefits. Eric's decision to get a vasectomy had been startling, a commitment she'd never expected.

He was expected home from his latest flight assignment tonight and he'd promised them both he was ready to play again.

"I can't wait to see him slide inside you," Elena said. "I know how much you enjoy it."

"You too," Jess said.

Legs intertwining on the couch where they'd settled to listen to music, they kissed. Jess laid back again and Elena slid on top of her, the heat of her center through the thin dress rocked into Jess's belly.

***

Eric stepped into the house, shaking himself out of his uniform shirt. He could hear John Denver crooning and expected to find Jess and Elena snuggled in front of the TV. He knew Jess had an affinity for the country singer's sentiments, having many nomadic years in the rural areas sang about. No doubt she'd slept out under the stars between jobs, and between towns, many times. And the singer's memories of childhood were the stuff Jess's dreams were made of, things she'd wished to have, but not found.

He hadn't known about her background when he first approached her all those months ago. But he found himself hoping that Jess might be able to say she had found happiness with them.

Leaning into the living room he saw a half-full wine bottle on the coffee table. The master bed was empty. He stepped down the hall and found the door to Jess's bedroom open slightly. Quietly he pushed it in, finally spotting Elena and Jess curled up naked on the futon, Elena's toffee skin complementing Jess's cream.

While looking at them made him horny, there was also a peace in that moment that he didn't want to disturb. They had all the time in the world. He closed the door with a smile and went to the master bedroom where he stripped down and slid under the covers, falling asleep quickly.

Eric awoke to the feeling of hands on his body. Through slitted eyes, as he rolled over, he saw Elena and Jess sitting on the bed to either side of him.

"Good morning," Elena said, her hands sliding over his right pectoral muscle.

"We thought you'd wake us up last night," Jess said, her exploration starting at his left knee.

"Decided not to disturb you," he replied. Hearing his own voice filled with the roughness of sleep, he cleared his throat.

Jess's hand halted just scant inches from his crotch. "Before we ravish you," she said, "are you hungry?"

"Not for food," he replied.

"That's all we wanted to know," Elena said. She bent over and teased his nipple, while Jess raked her nails lightly over his thighs and calf muscles. Both moving in circles, stimulating his arousal.

He reached out, putting one hand behind Elena's head, sifting his fingers through her hair as she sucked on his nipple. With the other hand he caressed Jess's hair as she trailed kisses closer and closer to his thickening cock.

He arched into their attention and requested, "I would like someone to eat out now."

Green and brown eyes lifted and met across his body. "Elena first," Jess said.

Elena straddled his head, bending forward so she could still tweak his nipples while Eric held her steady with one hand. While Eric stroked Jess's hair, Elena took his cock in her mouth. He angled his neck on the pillow and kissed Elena's folds once before slicking his tongue from front to back. She hummed and sighed. He briefly tongued her clit and was rewarded with a moan and juices streaming out onto his tongue.

Jess's attention to his cock was warm and soft, her tongue circling over his head and along the underside. He wanted her to suck it. And he wanted the sheath of her body. Soon. She tongued his balls. Eyes rolling back in his head, he decided he would keep them hairless if this was the attention they received.

He held Elena's hips firmly and pushed his tongue inside her center, seeking more of the wetness, more of her taste, and welcoming her flavor on every surface of his tongue.

Jess returned her attention to swallowing his cock's length, and the heat and warmth made him moan. The vibrations of sound against her pussy made Elena gasp. Jess rubbed between her own legs, clearly turned on by how much she was turning them on.

Elena moved aside and Eric placed both hands on Jess's head as she continued sucking him off. She took a condom from Elena's hand. "I want you to fuck me," she said simply, tearing open the foil packet and unrolling the latex down his length. She tongued his balls again and his hips jumped of their own volition.

He sat up. "What if I want to eat you first?"

"Yeah?"

He stood. "Come here." He coaxed her down onto her back on the bed and massaged her clit while kissing her. She wrapped her legs around his hips when he moved between her thighs.

"You're already hard. I don't want to wait."

Eric asked, "Are you sure?" He brushed his lips and mustache down her chest and belly, closer and closer to her center.

She gripped his shoulders. "I'm sure."

Holding the base of the condom in place, he guided his cock up and down the length of her opening. The pressure against her clit made Jess arch and moan.

They all watched his cock head disappear. Jess gasped and sighed. Her folds parted around his girth and her clit stiffened, coming completely out of its hood. Eric put Elena's hand on Jess's breasts. "Play with them," he told her. "Make her throb and come all over my cock."

Bending forward, he kissed Jess again then Elena as he straightened. Grasping Jess's hips, he moved his cock in an inch at a time, relishing the tight feel of her surrounding him. Meeting her gaze, he watched her smile, roll her eyes back and felt the moment she tilted her hips, taking him deeper. Elena replaced her fingers with her mouth, sucking on the hard points of Jess's nipples.

Eric moved his hips in longer strokes, pulling nearly all the way out before plunging back in, causing the bed to shift and straining the wood joints of the frame.

Jess reached toward him. Catching the underside of her thighs instead, she pulled her knees up. The move changed his angle again and he felt his cock rub that spongier spot inside her.

"Eric..." She gasped. He felt her channel quiver along its entire length and then clamp tightly. "God!"

"Good. F-ungh." He managed to keep moving despite the grip she had on him and that felt like being squeezed in a velvet blanket. Head down, he gripped her hips and pulled her toward him even as he thrust forward.

Elena's hand on his waist made him look down. His wife's brown gaze was fixed on watching his cock sliding in and out of Jess. Gradually she curled up against Jess, skin to skin, stroking down the woman's belly and sliding through her folds to touch where he and Jess met. A moment later she stroked up to Jess's breasts, palming the left. Slowly she covered Jess's mouth with her own, lingering. Tenderly she shared her breaths before sealing their lips for a searing kiss. Eric drank in the sight of his wife's dark curls and Jess's to life. Not only had their friend and teacher been restored to them, but now they understood who He truly is. They clasped the feet of their Savior and worshiped their Lord.

It's touching how Jesus called the disciples his "brothers." A few days before, He had called them "friends" (John 15:15). These words tell us of Jesus' love for his followers and how He invites us to share in his ministry. We like thinking of ourselves as Jesus' friends, but we should never forget that He is also our Lord, the Son of God, the King of Kings, the Alpha and the Omega. Like the women who met him that beautiful morning, our hearts should fall down and worship him. Jesus is risen and deserves our praise forever and ever.

Jesus, I love You and praise Your name. Thank You for dying for me and for rising again. You are my Savior and my Lord, and I will worship You forever. Help me to share the news of Your resurrection with others so they can worship You too. Amen.

Matthew 28:16-20

Then the eleven disciples went to Galilee, to the mountain where Jesus had told them to go. When they saw him, they worshiped him; but some doubted. Then Jesus came to them and said, "All authority in heaven and on earth has been given to me. Therefore go and make disciples of all nations, baptizing them in the name of the Father and of the Son and of the Holy Spirit, and teaching them to obey everything I have commanded you. And surely I am with you always, to the very end of the age."

Jesus left his disciples, including us, with a truth, a mission and a promise. These final verses of Matthew's Gospel record some of Jesus' last words before He ascended into heaven. They are also some of his most important. The truth Jesus declared has to do with his Lordship over our lives and over the whole world. He said that all authority has been given to him. Given, of course, by God, meaning that Jesus, who died and rose again as our Savior, must also be our Lord, honored and obeyed above all other rulers or powers in this world. In fact, Jesus' authority extends beyond this world to heaven, where He sits at God's right hand exercising authority over all. When we acknowledge Jesus' authority, we are confessing that all He says is true and meaningful in our lives. His is the first and best voice that we listen to. His teaching, as recorded in scripture and brought to understanding in our hearts by his Spirit, supersedes and surpasses all earthly knowledge and wisdom. All authority belongs to Jesus, and we submit ourselves fully and joyfully to him.

Jesus also gave us a mission. This passage is often referred to as the Great Commission, the church's marching orders for ministry and evangelism. We are to make disciples everywhere we go, in all nations, from all parts of this world, of all people. This is the wonderful truth of salvation, that Jesus offers new life to everyone who will submit themselves in faith to him. Jesus asks us, despite our weaknesses, to carry on the work He

DEVOTIONS WITH JESUS

started. Each of us, gifted and empowered by the Holy Spirit, has a role to play in inviting others to receive God's grace through Jesus our Savior.

Finally, Jesus spoke a word of promise over us. He assured us that He will be with us always and forever. For his first disciples, these words must have been comforting and yet a bit confusing. Soon after Jesus said this, He was lifted from the earth into heaven before their very eyes. They must have wondered how He could still be with them as He disappeared into the clouds. Soon they understood, as the Holy Spirit descended upon them, filling each believer with the living, powerful presence of God. The Risen Savior is with us still – today, right now, where you are and where I am. Praise be to God!

Father, You are mighty and merciful. Thank You for sending Jesus to be my Savior, and thank You for the promise that Your Spirit lives in me today. Help me to submit myself to Jesus' teaching, to share His message with others, and to trust in His wonderful promises. Amen.

194

ABOUT THE AUTHOR

Mike Mirakian has served as Pastor of Broadway Covenant Church in Rockford, Illinois since 2013. After completing a Master of Divinity at Gordon-Conwell Theological Seminary, Mike was ordained in the Evangelical Covenant Church in 2002. Mike and his wife Laura have been blessed with two wonderful children, David and Noelle.

Made in United States
Troutdale, OR
10/27/2024